Knife
The Murder Mile

Christine Pattle

Copyright

Copyright © Christine Pattle, 2024

Christine Pattle has asserted her right to be identified as the author of this work in accordance with the Copyright, Designs and Patents Act 1988.

All rights reserved. No part of this book may be reproduced, stored in any retrieval system, or transmitted, in any form or by any means, electronic, mechanical, photocopying, recording or otherwise, without the prior written permission of the author.

This book is a work of fiction. Names, characters, businesses, organisations, places and events other than those clearly in the public domain, are either the product of the author's imagination or are used fictitiously. Any resemblance to actual persons, living or dead, events or locales is entirely coincidental.

Chapter 1

Helen Trenton knocked cautiously on the headteacher's office door, unwilling to put this off any longer. If she failed to report the issue now, it might be too late. Hopefully, Bill Gizzard, the headteacher, would take her seriously.

"Helen, what can I do for you?" Gizzard seemed surprised to see her.

Helen sat down without being asked. "I'm worried about a pupil."

"Nothing new there." Gizzard let out an exasperated sigh. "You worry about all of them. If you maintained a higher standard of discipline, they wouldn't give you any trouble in the first place."

"It's got nothing to do with discipline." Helen resented Gizzard's implied criticism. If he'd been allowed to, she imagined Bill Gizzard keeping a cane behind his desk to dish out six of the best to any misbehaving pupils instead of wasting everybody's time keeping them after school in detention. Thank God corporal punishment became illegal years ago. Fortunately for the children, Gizzard didn't do much actual teaching these days. The less contact he had with the pupils, the better, in her opinion.

Gizzard snorted. "Which one is it this time?"

Helen hesitated, suddenly unsure if she was doing the right thing. Gizzard was a dinosaur, more into old-fashioned teaching, involving discipline and children keeping their opinions to themselves. Luckily, he would be retiring at the end of the school year. Otherwise, Helen would be first in the queue to suggest forcing him out to make room for a more progressive style of running the school. She pulled herself together quickly. "It's Bethany King."

Gizzard stared at her quizzically as if trying to remember which particular child Bethany King might be. "I'm not familiar with her," he admitted.

That simply proved her point. He really was a class A dinosaur. Taylor Park was a big school, Helen conceded. Even so, she doubted Gizzard would be able to name more than a handful of its pupils. She wondered what chance she'd stand if she applied for the head's job when they advertised it, or whether the position would automatically be given to the deputy head. Helen gave a quick description of Bethany for Gizzard's benefit. "She's in year eight, long dark hair." Helen stopped herself from mentioning Bethany's recent nose piercing, mindful that Gizzard's outdated reaction to the piece of jewellery would detract from the main purpose of the conversation.

Gizzard nodded as if he might actually have the faintest idea of Bethany's identity.

Helen continued, giving him no chance to interrupt. She needed to report this, to set the wheels in motion, for everyone's sakes. "I'm worried about her. She's become withdrawn in class, hardly interacting with other pupils or the teachers. Her schoolwork is suffering, too. Maybe there's something going on at home. We should get her some counselling before she does something stupid. She's really not her normal self."

"Yes, probably something at home. It's usually the parents' fault, and they expect us to pick up the pieces for them."

Helen cringed inwardly at yet another of Gizzard's shortcomings. He blamed the parents for everything as if parenting was easy and everyone should be able to navigate through the child's first eighteen years perfectly. Children didn't come with an instruction manual. And if they did, it would require an extremely heavy tome to deal with even half of the complexities that made up the average teenager.

"I'll add Bethany to the list for Monday's meeting," Helen said. The staff attending the regular weekly meeting to discuss problem pupils would no doubt have something to say about Bethany King next week. "But I wanted to flag up the issue as soon as possible. I'll suggest to some of her teachers that they keep an eye on her in the meantime."

"Good idea." Gizzard stared at her as if she were nuts. "The list for Monday is already pretty long. We may not even get around to discussing Bethany until the following week."

Helen hoped that wouldn't be the case, but she was powerless to change anything. Perhaps she should apply for the head's job. Her vision might make a real difference, as would having a school head who really cared about the children. "Thank you." She made a mental note to flag up Bethany's behaviour with some of her colleagues during morning break.

Bethany hurried along the corridor. The bell would ring soon for the end of lunch and she needed to get her phone from her locker to call Mum and check what time she planned to collect her later. They were taking the Eurostar to Paris for the weekend to visit Euro Disney, then do a day of sightseeing. Bethany couldn't wait. Was the Eiffel Tower really as tall as it looked in the pictures? She'd been practising her French, although probably no one would be able to understand her. At least if she tried to speak the language, Dad would be pleased. He'd only agreed to take them to help get her French conversation skills up to scratch. What a shame that now he wouldn't be coming. As usual, he spent more time working than with his family. Mum said he was stuck in America for a few more days doing something really important for work.

The pounding of footsteps behind her made Bethany whip around fearfully. Ava Browning thundered towards her with all the grace of a galloping hippo, which took some doing with her petite figure. Bethany shrank back against the wall, willing Ava to go straight past her and leave her alone.

No such luck. Ava skidded to a halt directly in front of her. As Ava paused to catch her breath, Bethany considered trying to run, but fleeing would be pointless. Ava would only catch up with her later. Despite

Ava's dainty size, Bethany knew from experience that she could punch like a heavyweight. If she was going to take a beating, best to get it over with.

"Mr Wyvern's looking for you." Ava's laboured breaths blasted the stale odours of her lunch straight into Bethany's face.

Bethany tried to step back, afraid of what might come next, but Ava already had her pinned against the wall.

Bethany didn't want to see Mr Wyvern. She'd almost prefer a slap or a sharp kick in the ankle from Ava. She didn't like the teacher. It creeped her out the way he leaned in a bit too close when he spoke to her. He'd never actually touched her or anything, but some of the other girls reckoned he'd tried it with them, although they were mostly troublemakers who probably made up the stories to get attention.

"What does he want?" Bethany glanced at the big clock hanging high on the wall at the end of the corridor. The bell for afternoon lessons would ring in a couple of minutes. She barely had time to get her phone out of her locker and call Mum.

"How should I know?" She shrugged. "Perhaps he's going to chuck you off the cricket team." Ava gave a particularly evil smile. "He says it's really urgent. He's in the gym equipment store."

That made sense, seeing as Mr Wyvern taught PE. Bethany had tried out for the year eight girls' cricket team at the beginning of term, only just scraping in thanks to Madison Pearce kicking her in the leg during the trial, making it so painful to run, it was a miracle she'd been selected at all. Cricket was a new sport for the girls at Taylor Park, but thanks to the success of the England women's team, it was now firmly on the curriculum for both sexes, although only year eight had enough enthusiastic girls to form an official team. Bethany loved sports and fervently wanted to make the team until she found out that not only was Wyvern coaching, but Ava Browning, one of the biggest bullies in year eight, would be team captain. When Bethany learned that, she'd actually been pleased to only make reserve. If Wyvern wanted to put her on the team proper now, she might say no. "I'll find him later," she said, wriggling out from Ava's grip.

Ava grabbed her hand, preventing her escape. "No, he said it's really urgent." She propelled Bethany gently in the direction of the gym, releasing her hand but standing in the corridor with her arms folded, blocking her exit in a rather intimidating way for someone of such a small size.

Bethany knew better than to argue. The last time she'd disagreed with Ava, she'd got a dead leg for her trouble. It wasn't only Ava. Her friends, Madison and Shaz, were almost as bad. Some days, the trio left her alone, but other days, they were relentless: stealing her homework to copy for themselves, sticking embarrassing photos on the locker, or tripping her up on her way into class. Then they'd pretend to be friendly, like the time Shaz held out her hand to shake and apologise, and like an idiot, Bethany fell for the ploy, making it easy for Shaz to grab her wrist and give her a Chinese burn. Against the three of them, Bethany never seemed to stand a chance. They all backed up one another with sweet, innocent smiles that fooled the teachers into believing them and blaming Bethany. Between them, the three girls made her life hell. And now Ava, the ringleader, demanded that Bethany find her least favourite teacher when she really needed to phone her mum. She didn't dare disobey Ava.

In all probability, there would be a sting in the tail, with Ava setting up some nasty prank at Bethany's expense. She shouldn't let them treat her like that. It made her so angry. Briefly, she contemplated ignoring Ava and heading in the opposite direction. Or better still, marching back to Ava and punching her hard on the jaw. But she lacked the gumption to take either action. From bitter experience, she knew she'd pay the price for defying one of the hallowed triumvirate.

Bethany took a deep breath, which did nothing to cool the blood boiling inside her. As she meekly headed towards the gym, she imagined her blood exploding out through the top of her head like molten lava, showering Ava's pretty face and melting her china-doll features into an ugly, scarred mess. Bethany hated Ava. She hated Madison and Shaz, too. Right now, she hated everybody.

She kept walking. The last thing she wanted was to be alone with Mr Wyvern in the gym equipment store. She might double back a different way, avoiding Ava. And, if she ran flat out, she'd still have time to get her phone and call Mum before the bell rang for the end of lunch break. If she pretended she never received the message, it would be her word against Ava's. No one could prove any different. Except Ava would give her hell if she got into trouble for not passing on the instruction. She'd likely take it out on Bethany for the rest of the summer term.

An air of silence hung over the deserted gym, and the door to the equipment store was firmly shut. Bethany hesitated. What if the rumours were true about Mr Wyvern being a dirty old pervert? She didn't want to be alone with him. Reluctantly, she reached for the door handle, knowing that whatever Mr Wyvern may or may not do to her, nothing would be as bad as several weeks of relentless bullying from Ava Browning. If Mr Wyvern tried anything, Bethany would knee him in the groin or kick his shins and scream. He'd get a shock if he tried to take advantage of her.

Chapter 2

"How are you feeling, Alfie?" Rose Marsden perched on the end of the hospital bed while Alfie fidgeted to get comfortable with his shoulder strapped up.

"Great, for someone who's been shot." Alfie grimaced. "At least I can go home as soon as someone from the pharmacy shows up with my painkillers."

"I can't believe they're letting you out so soon." Billie Cooper sat on the solitary chair next to her father and took hold of his hand.

Rose smiled, happy to see Alfie and Billie getting on so well after being estranged for twenty years until recently. "I'm sure the doctors wouldn't let him out if they were worried about him. Besides, he's got you to take care of him for a while." Luckily, Billie managed to extend her stay in the UK before heading back to her home in New Zealand.

"I'm really glad the police caught those men," Billie said. The gang of people traffickers who abducted her and Alfie was safely locked up, probably looking at long prison sentences.

"So am I." Alfie smiled at Billie. "Mostly because you'll need to visit again to give evidence against them when the case goes to trial, and..." He trailed off and looked past Rose, his lips curling into a huge grin. "What a nice surprise."

"Alfie Cooper. What are you doing here?"

Rose turned around to see Irina King, a cleaner at Brackford General Hospital, standing behind her, with a mop in her hand. Irina was a regular customer of Hale Hill Stores, the shop that Rose and Alfie managed between them.

"I'm going home soon," Alfie said. "Just waiting for some painkillers. Don't worry, I'll be back at work in no time."

"You will not." Rose and Billie spoke almost simultaneously. Rose was about to launch into a lecture to Alfie about taking it easy and giving himself time to recover properly, but a nurse who ran up to Irina interrupted them.

"Have you heard the news?" The young nurse struggled to get the words out in her excitement.

Irina turned to face her. "What news?"

"About Taylor Park School. Your Bethany goes there, doesn't she?"

"What about Taylor Park?" Irina looked concerned.

"It's all over social media," the nurse blurted out. "Someone's been stabbed."

"Stabbed?" Irina froze. The mop clattered to the floor.

"What happened?" Rose asked. "Who's been stabbed?" Her first thought was no doubt exactly the same as Irina's, worried that the victim might be Bethany.

"It didn't say."

"They'll bring them here, won't they?" Rose imagined they'd find out the victim's identity soon enough.

"They're not bringing anyone here," the nurse announced. "They'll be going straight to the morgue."

Rose shuddered. She rushed to Irina's side to reassure her. In a school as big as Taylor Park, what were the chances of the victim being Bethany? Almost nil.

"I need to get to the school," Irina said nervously.

"Let's not jump to conclusions." Rose tried to usher Irina towards a chair, but she refused to move. "Why don't you try phoning Bethany first?"

Irina found her phone, her hands trembling as she pulled up her daughter's number. "She's not answering." The panic showed in her voice.

"She's probably in class, and I'm sure they're not allowed to use their phones in the classroom." Rose silently berated herself for suggesting Irina should phone her daughter. "It will either be switched off or in her locker." In all probability, Bethany would be safely in class, blissfully ignorant of the tragic event.

"I need to find her," Irina insisted, jerking away from Rose.

"Irina, wait." Rose ran after her. "You can't drive in this state. Let me drive you."

Irina nodded and handed Rose her car keys. Rose fished out the keys to Alfie's car from her handbag and gave them to Billie. "Look after your dad. I'll drop in later."

Rose pulled out of the hospital car park, realising she'd forgotten to adjust the seat to accommodate her longer legs when she got into Irina's car. She glanced over at Irina. Her ashen face confirmed Rose made the right decision not to let her drive.

"I'm sure Bethany will be ok," Rose said. "There must be well over a thousand pupils at Taylor Park school. Bethany's sensible enough to stay out of trouble." Was Bethany sensible? She'd grown up fast recently. Thirteen-year-old Bethany's recent attempts at flirting with Jack, Rose's son, who was six years Bethany's senior, did nothing to reassure Rose. Bethany might actually enjoy diving headlong into trouble. But this was different.

"But someone's been stabbed." Irina clasped her hands together to stop them from shaking. "What if it is Bethany? I've got a bad feeling about this. A mother knows these things."

Rose concentrated on the one-way system through the middle of Brackford, trying to remember the shortest route to Taylor Park school. "Why don't you phone her again?" It might put Irina's mind at rest if she spoke to Bethany. A one in a thousand chance. Hardly likely. The victim would more likely be a boy, some little toe-rag dragged into a fight that got out of hand.

Irina held the phone to her ear. "She's not answering."

"She's probably still in class," Rose said. A school that size wouldn't grind to a halt because of one incident. Once the offender was apprehended, there would be no reason for most of the pupils to even find out about the incident until they watched the evening news on TV. They'd carry on with double geography or whatever class they were in, in blissful ignorance, at least until the police sirens sent everyone rushing to the windows to find out what was going on.

"You'll have to park on the road," Irina said. "The car park's only for teachers."

Rose found a parking space a short distance from the school. A row of enormous flowering cherry trees lined Cherry Tree Road, where Taylor Park school was situated. Most of the petals lay on the path beneath like confetti at a wedding. The pretty pink carpet of petals almost made her forget why they'd come.

"We should find the school administrator," Irina said, jerking Rose's mind back to reality. "She'll be able to tell us what's going on."

"Good idea." Rose's friend, Maggie Mahoney, recently started as the school administrator at Taylor Park. Even if she wasn't supposed to tell them anything, Maggie wouldn't be able to resist divulging the full story to her. It would be the quickest way to learn what was going on.

As they hurried towards the school, Rose wondered again what might have happened. Most likely a teenage fight getting out of control. Too many of the lads around here carried knives. Sooner or later, one of them was bound to get hurt or killed. A cold shiver passed through her, despite the intense sunshine almost melting the tarmac. She prayed the victim wasn't Bethany. Irina would never cope with that. She tried to reassure herself with the same logic she used earlier on Irina: one thousand pupils. What were the chances?

Several police cars filled the small car park in front of the school, all of them haphazardly abandoned as their occupants raced to enter the building.

"You can't come any further." A man wearing a green fluorescent jacket pivoted towards them as they approached.

Rose recognised him instantly. Detective Constable Kevin Farrier. They'd had several dealings in the past. She nodded at him, adding a glimmer of a smile in the hope that he might treat her as an old friend despite being only on mild acquaintance terms.

"What's going on?" she asked. "Is anyone hurt?"

DC Farrier showed no signs of regarding Rose as a special case. "I can't tell you anything." He glared at Rose as if she were toxic.

Rose took a step forward. "Irina is worried about her daughter. She needs to be sure she hasn't been hurt."

"No, she hasn't," Farrier snapped. "Now, will you please leave the premises?"

"But you haven't even asked her daughter's name."

Farrier's statement virtually confirmed the stabbing victim must be a boy. A huge wave of relief swept through Rose. Even so, it would pay to make sure. And they should find Bethany and take her home.

"We need to see the school administrator," Rose said. "Mrs Mahoney." Maggie would tell her what happened and help them locate Bethany.

Farrier turned to Irina. "Trust me, your daughter's fine. Either you leave immediately, or I'll arrest you both for obstructing police business."

"Perhaps we should go," Rose whispered to Irina. Maggie Mahoney only lived a few minutes' walk from Rose's flat. She'd get the full story from her this evening.

Irina shook her head. "I arranged to pick Bethany up soon, anyway. We're off to Euro Disney for the weekend. May as well save a second journey. And I'll feel better knowing for sure that she's safe."

The front door of the school opened. Immediately, Irina made a bolt towards it. Rose and DC Farrier chased after her, Rose's size five feet making neater work of the fiddly stone steps than Farrier's size twelves. As Irina ducked inside the entrance, Rose caught up with her, slipping through the doorway just before the door slammed shut.

Irina faced the well-dressed woman in front of her. "Miss Trenton, I need to find Bethany." She gazed at the woman pleadingly.

Miss Trenton took a step back. "Mrs King, you really can't be here. Please leave." Miss Trenton's bloodshot eyes suggested she'd been crying heavily.

Rose assumed Miss Trenton must be one of the teachers at Taylor Park. She gently took Irina's arm as the door creaked open behind her. "It's probably best if we leave." They shouldn't stay here and intrude on someone else's grief. Somewhere, two parents may have lost their son. She thought of Jack, her own son, and her heart broke, thankful it wasn't her facing that situation.

"Mrs King, please." Miss Trenton trembled visibly.

"Mrs King?" DC Farrier looked over at Miss Trenton.

Miss Trenton nodded almost imperceptibly. She stepped back against the wall, seeming to need its support to hold herself upright. "She's Bethany King's mother."

Rose's whole body tensed. Had Farrier been lying? Was it a girl who died, after all? Was it Bethany?

DC Farrier took Irina's arm, less gently than Rose had done, propelling her quickly back towards the entrance. "We need to talk to you," he said.

Rose feared the worst. "What's going on? Is Bethany all right?"

"Please," Irina begged. "Tell me the truth."

"We can discuss it at the station, Mrs King." DC Farrier turned to Rose. "Go home, Mrs Marsden. There's nothing to see here."

Rose followed them down the steps. "Where are you taking Irina?" She ran past the pair and stood in front of them, blocking their way. "Can't you see she's upset? You need to tell her what's happening."

Farrier opened his mouth to answer, but a sudden commotion behind them drowned out his words. Two female police officers were trying to push a girl into a police car. She screamed, a piercing shriek that cut right through Rose.

Immediately, Irina turned towards them. "Bethany?" she shouted, jerking herself away from DC Farrier and running towards them.

"Mum." The anguished scream was muted as the police officers finally managed to shove her into the car and slam the door shut.

Farrier ran to catch up with Irina and grabbed her roughly.

"That's my daughter. I need to see my daughter. Where are you taking her?" Irina screamed.

Farrier retained his grip on Irina's arm as she stared at the police car driving across the car park and disappearing onto the road. "They're going to the police station."

Irina stared at him, speechless.

"Why?" Rose asked. At least Bethany was still alive. She didn't appear to be hurt, either.

Farrier ignored Rose and turned to Irina. "Mrs King, your daughter stabbed someone. She killed a teacher."

"No." Irina shook her head in disbelief. "No. What are you saying? You're wrong. Bethany would never do that. Never."

"I'll take you to the police station. As Bethany's only thirteen, you can be present when we interview her."

"But she didn't do anything."

Rose put her arm around Irina. "You should go with the officer. Bethany needs you. I'll follow in the car."

"Go home, Rose," DC Farrier spoke sharply.

"I've got Irina's car. I drove her here. I'll have to come to the station so I can drive her home afterwards," Rose said firmly.

Farrier scowled at her but didn't argue.

"I need to phone Richard," Irina said. "My husband."

"You can phone him from the station. We need to get going." Farrier ushered her towards his car.

"Try not to worry, Irina." Rose hoped the police had made a dreadful mistake. In the meantime, nothing she could say would stop Irina from worrying. The poor woman trembled from the shock. She needed a cup of tea and a hug, not DC Farrier treating her like a criminal.

Chapter 3

As soon as DC Farrier left the school with Irina, Rose snuck back inside, hoping to discover more about what happened because Farrier hadn't been at all forthcoming with the facts.

"Can I help you?" A middle-aged man wearing a cheap suit approached her. Rose presumed he was a teacher.

"I'm looking for Mrs Mahoney, the school administrator." Rose tried to give the impression of being here on legitimate business.

"She's busy," the man said curtly.

Rose thought quickly. "In that case, can I see Miss Trenton, please?" She would use the pretence of being worried about Irina.

"Most of the teachers are in class."

Rose glanced at her watch. "It's lunchtime."

"No, it's not. Our lunch hour is early. Besides, we're keeping the children in the classrooms, in view of the tragic event."

"Of course. What a dreadful thing to happen. A teacher, the police said. What a terrible loss for the school."

The man shook his head sadly. "I don't understand it. The children all liked Mr Wyvern. I can't believe this happened to him, of all people."

"No, me neither," Rose said. "Did he argue with the girl?" She wondered what subject Mr Wyvern taught.

"I don't know about that. Mrs Knight found them. She's the other PE teacher. Apparently, the girl was standing over the body, holding a knife." He shook his head in disbelief.

Rose shuddered. That was damning evidence indeed. "Where can I find Miss Trenton?"

"You should come back another day, when she's calmed down," the teacher said.

Rose wondered if Helen Trenton and Mr Wyvern were close. She remembered how shaky she'd appeared when she'd met her with Irina. Or was that simply because of Irina being Bethany's mother? Maybe

Miss Trenton knew something. Something must have happened to make Bethany do this, but what? Irina might get some answers out of her, except that Irina was in no fit state to think straight and ask sensible questions. Of course, the police should do that, but since someone caught Bethany red-handed, Rose lacked conviction that the police would dig too deeply.

"Perhaps you can point me in the direction of Mrs Mahoney's office. I can wait until she's free." Rose wondered how long that would be. She ought to go to the police station. Someone needed to support Irina, and Rose still had Irina's car.

"I'll take you to her office."

Rose wished he'd give her directions instead, then she'd be able to nose around on the way. She also worried that, sooner or later, the teacher might start asking her difficult questions, like *who are you, and what are you doing here?*

The teacher knocked on Maggie Mahoney's office door, pushing it open without waiting for an answer. "Someone to see you, Margaret."

"Come in," Maggie said as soon as she caught sight of Rose. Rose shut the door behind her, leaving the teacher in the corridor.

"What's going on? What happened with Bethany King?" Rose immediately began firing questions at Maggie.

"I'm not supposed to say anything." Maggie sat behind her desk, fiddling nervously with some pieces of paper.

"Oh, for goodness' sake, Maggie. It will be all over the Internet in a couple of hours. I came here with Irina. We saw the police taking Bethany away. Someone said she stabbed a teacher."

"That about sums it up," Maggie said.

Rose sat opposite Maggie, thumping her hands on the desk in frustration. "Come on, do you really believe Bethany would do that?"

"She was caught holding the knife."

"Even so, there must be a good reason why she did it. What do you know about this teacher, the one she killed?"

Maggie sighed. "You should stay out of this, Rose. She stabbed him. It's an open and shut case. Let the police deal with it."

Rose shook her head. "I've just watched Irina witness the police dragging her daughter away screaming. How can I stay out of it? Someone has to help them."

"There's nothing you can do." Maggie dropped the piece of paper she'd been fiddling with into the bin. "How is Irina?"

"How do you think she is? She's in pieces."

"Seriously, Rose, don't get involved. A thirteen-year-old killer? The whole case will be toxic. Irina will be ok. She's got her husband to support her. He's a lawyer, isn't he?"

Rose doubted if Irina would ever be ok again. "He's an accountant, and he'll probably be in the same state as Irina as soon as he finds out. I would be if Jack did anything like that." Thank God her son had never been screwed up enough to murder anyone. "I have to help them."

"You're not a lawyer, either."

"No, but I have a friend who is," Rose said, remembering Billie Cooper. Billie didn't do criminal law, and she qualified in a different country, but she might still offer some useful advice. Rose resolved to talk to her later. "Now, are you going to tell me about that teacher?"

Maggie let out a long sigh. "Grant Wyvern. He's a PE teacher."

"So how come Bethany has anything to do with him? Wouldn't he only teach boys?"

Maggie drummed her fingers on the desk nervously. "No. PE teachers can teach both boys and girls. Lots of our sports are mixed classes now, and the girls are playing football and cricket. The only thing he can't do is go into the girls' changing room."

"How long has he been at the school?" Rose asked.

"Let me look it up." Maggie tapped at her computer keyboard. "He only joined us last September, from a school in Basildon, Clayborne Grammar."

Why would Grant Wyvern leave a nice grammar school to teach at a rough comprehensive like Taylor Park? "What else do you know about him? Does he have a family?"

Maggie scrolled down the page on her computer. "Says his next of kin is his brother, Daniel Wyvern. No mention of a wife."

At least that was something, Rose thought, although there might still be an equally distraught partner. And his brother, and other family and friends, as well as many of the teachers at the school, would no doubt be distressed by the tragic news. So many lives affected. So many consequences. What had Bethany done?

Chapter 4

Helen Trenton was so wrapped up in her thoughts that when a whirlwind of blond hair shot around the corner towards her, it nearly knocked her off balance.

"Madison! Walk."

"Sorry, Helen." Madison skidded to a halt on the shiny floor.

Helen couldn't help admiring Madison's fitness. The girl was barely out of breath despite running at a fair speed. "Madison, we're at school." It was important for discipline for Madison to address her properly at school, regardless of Jenny, Madison's mother, being Helen's best friend.

"Sorry, Miss Trenton." Madison looked contrite, making Helen melt instantly.

"Where have you been?"

"Nowhere." Madison screwed her face up.

If Helen didn't know her better, she'd swear the girl was about to cry. She softened her voice slightly, taking the sting out of her words. "Madison Pearce, don't lie to me. You've got dirt on your shoes." Her hair looked slightly damp as well. She definitely hadn't been nowhere. Helen let Madison get away with a lot. She and Jenny had been friends for over ten years, since they used to be neighbours. Outside of school, Helen regarded Madison almost like a daughter or at least a favourite niece. But at school, she made a big effort to treat her like any other pupil. In her experience, if she lost the children's respect, they'd all take advantage of her and make her life hell.

"Sorry, Miss Trenton. I went shopping in Brackford. I needed to get something. It was really important. Please don't tell on me. I don't want to get into trouble."

Madison's usual cocky confidence had disappeared. She appeared so flustered and vulnerable that Helen longed to give her a hug.

"There's been an incident." Helen noticed her voice waver as an image of Grant flashed into her head. Perhaps it was she who needed the hug.

"Incident?" Madison looked worried. She put a hand out and held on to the desk as if to stabilise herself.

Helen noticed a red mark on her wrist and wondered if Sharon Fletcher had been dishing out Chinese burns again. She couldn't deal with a problem like that now. She needed to say something to Madison about what happened but was still unsure how much to tell her. Best to keep it to the bare minimum. She'd find out soon enough from her friends. "There's been a stabbing. One of the teachers." She couldn't bring herself to say his name. If she said it, that would make it real, then she'd never manage to hold herself together for the rest of the day.

"It would be best," she continued, "if you said you were with me. The police may want to talk to everyone. If they ask where you were, tell them you were in my classroom, handing in your homework."

Madison nodded. Helen couldn't tell if she was relieved or shocked.

"Run along now. Go to your class. You're late." Tears began to mist up her eyes. She needed to find a quiet corner to calm down before facing her next class. If only she could go home, but the police insisted that no one left until after they were interviewed, which might take hours. How would she manage for that long without breaking down? God knows why the police wanted to waste everyone's time when the identity of Grant's killer was painfully obvious.

"Thanks, miss." Madison set off at a run towards the science block, seeming as keen to get away from Helen as Helen was for her to go.

Helen watched her for a few seconds, hoping it wouldn't come as too much of a shock to Madison when she found out the full story of what happened and who was involved. Wasn't she friends with the King girl, so it would undoubtedly be a big shock when she learned what Bethany had done? Helen wished she'd found the courage to break the bad news herself. Perhaps, if she felt up to it, she'd call in on Jenny tonight to check on Madison. Or perhaps she'd open a bottle of wine at home and drink until she fell asleep.

Chapter 5

Rose found Irina sitting in the waiting room just inside the police station. As soon as she saw Rose, Irina rushed over and hugged her.

"What's happening?" Rose gently extricated herself from Irina's grip.

"They won't let me see Bethany." A fresh flood of tears flowed down Irina's already reddened cheeks.

Rose was pretty sure that the police were legally obliged to give Bethany's mother access to her daughter. "Have you got a solicitor?"

"No. The police are finding one for Bethany, but it's taking so long."

"Did you phone Richard?" Rose asked. Irina's husband really should be here to support her. He might be a lot more use to Bethany than Irina was proving to be, assuming he didn't fall to pieces as soon as he heard the bad news.

Irina shook her head.

"Do you want me to phone him for you?" The news might be better coming from someone calmer. Irina would most likely send him into a total panic.

"He's in San Francisco, on a business trip."

Rose did a quick mental calculation. It would be very early morning there. A phone call now would probably wake him up, but at least it might prove easier to speak to him now. Later, he'd likely be in some high-powered, important meeting, then it might prove impossible to get hold of him. "Give me your phone."

Irina unlocked her phone, her hand shaking so much as she passed it to Rose that she nearly dropped it.

Rose found Richard's number. It diverted to voicemail after a few rings, so he might still be in bed. She hung up and tried again. The bad news couldn't be explained in a voicemail, and she didn't want to wait for several hours until Richard found time to call back.

"When is he due home?"

Irina didn't answer, too busy staring into space.

"When is Richard coming home?" Rose asked again.

Irina jerked back into the present. "He's staying a few more days. It's really important for him to be there. He won't be happy if we interrupt him."

"This is really important," Rose said. Whatever vital business meeting Richard needed to attend, Bethany's arrest trumped it in the importance stakes.

"Irina? It's five forty-five in the morning. What the hell do you want?"

Rose pulled the phone away from her ear, considering herself lucky Richard hadn't deafened her with his outburst. "Richard? It's not Irina. This is Rose Marsden. I'm a friend of Irina's." She had never met Richard King. If he was always this rude, she hoped she never would.

"Where's Irina? What's happened?"

Rose upgraded her opinion of Richard as he sounded genuinely worried now and, to be fair, she had woken him rather early. She took a deep breath. As soon as she explained the morning's events, Richard King's worry level would explode off the scale.

"Irina's all right." She wasn't all right. Rose glanced at Irina. She'd gone into a catatonic daze from the shock. "Something happened this morning," Rose said quickly before Richard got a chance to interrupt. "Irina needs you here. You must come home."

"That's impossible," Richard said immediately. He didn't even consider the option. "We're in merger negotiations. I'm a key member of this team and there's no way they can manage without me. Anyway, you said Irina's all right."

Rose wished she'd thought things through before she made the phone call. There was no easy way to break this news. "It's Bethany."

"Bethany? Has she had an accident?" He paused for a second. "Is she..."

"She's been arrested," Rose blurted out.

Richard snorted down the phone. "What for? Shoplifting? Or is it one of those antisocial behaviour things? I'll phone our solicitor, but I'm not coming home for that."

"I'm afraid it's a bit more serious than that," Rose said.

"Really. What then?"

Richard King's lack of concern for his only daughter made Rose warm to him less and less. She stopped trying to dress up the truth to spare his feelings. What difference would it make, anyway? She'd simply tell it like it was. "She's been arrested for murder."

Silence.

"Richard? Are you still there?" He'd better not have hung up on her.

"Murder?" The word came out as a whisper as if all the air had been knocked out of him, collapsing his lungs into nothing. He found his voice after a few seconds. "That's not possible. It must be a mistake."

"I'm sorry." Rose began to sympathise with the man. "Apparently, Bethany was caught standing over one of her teachers, holding the murder weapon." Rose waited for him to protest that his daughter wouldn't do that. No protest came. "Bethany will need that solicitor. And both her and Irina need your support. You really do need to come home."

"I'll make some calls," Richard said. "I'll get back to you later." He hung up before Rose got any chance to argue.

Rose wasn't sure if that meant he intended to come home, or if he simply planned to organise a solicitor. She noted that he never asked to speak to Irina. Perhaps that was a good thing. In his current state of mind, he'd only pile on extra stress. Time enough for that when, or if, he showed up in person.

She was about to discuss it with Irina when they were interrupted.

"Mrs King, you can see your daughter now." Detective Constable Wendy McKay approached them in the waiting room. "Would you follow me, please?"

Irina and Rose both stood up.

"Sorry, we can only allow the girl's mother to see her." Wendy gave no acknowledgement that she'd met Rose before. Perhaps she had genuinely forgotten.

"Her name's Bethany," Irina said.

"Yes, well, like I said, we can only allow you to see her." Wendy turned to Rose. "You can wait out here."

Rose sat down again, wondering how long this would take. Irina had shrunk inside herself as if trying to hide within her own skin by making herself as tiny as possible. If Irina was supposed to be taking care of Bethany, who would look after Irina?

The interview room was a much rougher version of Irina's living room at home. Bethany sat on a worn beige sofa next to a female police constable. The moment Irina saw her, she pushed past DC McKay and ran towards her daughter, then threw her arms around her. Immediately, Bethany began to sob.

"It's going to be ok, sweetheart." Irina tried to sound positive, but her words didn't ring true. She had no idea how to get Bethany out of this situation, short of grabbing her and running as fast as possible until they got far, far away from here. But, outside of her fantasy, she knew they wouldn't even make it out of the room. She hugged Bethany tighter, never wanting to let her go, drinking in the smell of her hair and the warmth of her skin. Irina had never felt so useless. She wished Richard were here. He'd fix everything for them. That was what her husband did. He fixed things.

"Mrs King."

Irina felt a gentle tug on her arm.

"Mrs King, can we sit down, please?" DC McKay tugged at her again, more firmly this time, prising Irina away from Bethany.

Reluctantly, Irina sat opposite her daughter. She noticed now that Bethany wore a cheap pale grey tracksuit, a dark patch on her right shoulder betraying Irina's flurry of tears, which she thought she'd hidden so well. Of course Bethany's own clothes would have been taken for evidence. That was a good thing, Irina tried to convince herself. It would prove that their accusations were rubbish, then they could go home and put this dreadful experience behind them.

"Bethany, do you understand why you're here?" DC McKay asked.

"I want to go home." Bethany began to cry.

"Leave her alone," Irina shouted. "Let me take her home." She rose to her feet.

"Mrs King. Please sit down. You're not helping."

Bethany's tears turned into a long, heart-wrenching wail. Irina lurched towards her daughter, but DC McKay stood between them.

"Sit down."

"I can't." Irina's tears returned. "I need to take her home. Can't you see she's upset?"

"Mrs King, I don't think you understand the seriousness of the situation. I'm afraid Bethany won't be going home today."

Irina stepped back. "But she didn't do this. Why can't you understand that?" In front of her, Bethany dropped her head between her knees and rocked from side to side. Irina didn't know how to help her.

The detective inspector, whose name Irina forgot, came over to her. "Mrs King, I think you should go home. You're not helping." He turned to DC McKay. "Wendy, can you arrange for the doctor to see Bethany, please?"

DI Waterford escorted Irina back to the reception area.

Rose got up. "Irina, what's happened?"

"Rose." DI Waterford acknowledged her with a nod. "Mrs King needs to go home. She's upset."

"What about Bethany?" Rose asked.

"We'll look after her."

Chapter 6

The Kings lived in an upmarket, modern house at the opposite end of Hale Hill to Rose. As Rose pulled into the driveway, she nearly knocked over an estate agent's For Sale sign, which leant over at a jaunty angle as if it had already taken a battering.

"I didn't realise you were moving house." No doubt, with Richard's apparently high-powered career, the Kings could afford to live in a much nicer area than Hale Hill.

"We're not. We've been trying to sell since Christmas, but every time people find out where it is, they lose interest. It's on the edge of the Murder Mile. I wish people had never started calling it that. Richard says that puts people off. Anyone who can afford the price is frightened to live here. The only offer we've had was so far under the asking price that we would have ended up owing the bank money on the mortgage. We're imprisoned with negative equity, Richard says."

Rose considered poor Bethany. There were worse places to be imprisoned than this rather nice house. One look at Irina's face, suddenly screwing up with tears, told her that Irina was struggling with the same thought.

Irina stopped on the doorstep, turning to Rose.

"You shouldn't be on your own," Rose said before Irina got a chance to speak. "Shall I come in for a while? We can phone Richard again and find out when he's coming home." Perhaps she could fix them both a meal at the same time. Her stomach rumbled noisily, reminding Rose that neither of them had eaten all day. She'd lost track of how much time they'd spent waiting at the police station and the lateness of the hour shocked her. Then there was the issue of how to get home. She guessed she'd be expected to find her own way. It would take twenty minutes to walk, but that would mean taking a shortcut through the Briar Road estate, notorious for being unsafe at this time of night, and darkness was setting in fast. She'd prefer to wait for a taxi inside.

Irina hesitated. Rose took advantage of the pause, gently pushing past her through the open door. She couldn't leave Irina alone, not now, not when she was on the verge of falling to pieces. At the very least, Rose needed to call someone to come and stay with Irina.

"Let me make you a cup of tea and fix something to eat," Rose suggested. Her empty stomach complained again, loudly agreeing with her.

Irina didn't protest, so Rose took that as a yes. She filled the kettle before Irina changed her mind and opened the fridge to see if it contained anything that would transform into a quick meal.

The well-stocked refrigerator yielded up some eggs, along with a yellow pepper, some spring onions, and half a packet of smoked salmon. Rose decided to whip up an omelette as that would be really fast.

The kettle clicked off as Rose poured the beaten eggs into the pan. Quickly, she found some tea bags and produced two cups of tea before the omelette finished cooking.

"You'll feel better when you've eaten." Rose cut the omelette in half, sliding each half onto a plate. It would take much more than an omelette to make Irina feel better. Rose was a mother too. It would destroy her if her Jack ever got arrested for murder. She shuddered at the notion.

"What did Bethany say in the interview?" It must surely be a stupid mistake. Irina was adamant that Bethany could never murder anyone, and Rose wanted to agree with her. But if it was a mistake, wouldn't the police have released her by now?

Irina cut off a tiny piece of omelette, leaving the fork hovering near her mouth as she spoke. "She didn't say much. She wouldn't stop crying." The fork dropped back onto the plate, clattering in protest as the floodgates opened again on Irina's bottomless supply of tears.

"Has your husband phoned back yet?" Rose asked. It had been hours since she'd spoken to Richard. If Bethany were *her* child, she'd be phoning every five minutes for a progress report, but perhaps he was already on a plane across the Atlantic.

Irina shook her head.

"You should phone him. It will be early afternoon by now in San Francisco." Rose wolfed down a few mouthfuls of her omelette. The smoked salmon made a lovely treat. Irina's omelette remained virtually untouched. Rose wondered if it would appear rude to eat Irina's leftovers. She hated to waste good food.

Irina shook her head again, more adamantly this time. "Can you phone him for me, please? I can't talk to him like this."

Rose guessed that Richard King wouldn't want to speak to her again. "Yes, of course I can." Much as she didn't want any more contact with Richard King, she would have to get on with it.

Rose wondered how to help Bethany. Would Irina allow her to search Bethany's room? It surprised her that the police hadn't done so yet. It was a bad sign, implying they already had enough evidence for a conviction. It must be worth a try. She might find something in Bethany's room that would reveal a good reason for her actions. Rose would get the phone call to Richard over and done with, then broach the subject of Bethany's room with Irina.

"Did the police mention searching Bethany's room?" Rose asked after a failed attempt to get through to Richard. Irina slouched on the sofa, staring into space, forcing Rose to repeat the question.

"I don't think so. I don't remember."

Rose wasn't surprised at that. Irina had been in a dreadful state earlier, too upset to take in anything. "Did they take your house keys?" Perhaps someone came to search the house while they were at the police station.

"No." Irina shook her head.

Rose's concern increased. Perhaps she was right about the case against Bethany being so strong that the police wouldn't bother to search for further evidence? She sat next to Irina. "May I search

Bethany's room, please? It might help her if I can find proof that it's not her fault." She couldn't imagine what, but she needed to do something positive instead of simply sitting here futilely attempting to comfort Irina. Besides, if the police did make a mistake, forgetting to search Bethany's room, it gave her the perfect opportunity to get in first. If she found anything remotely useful, she'd be sure to tell Bethany's solicitor before the police got to hear about it.

"I suppose it might help," Irina said. "Her bedroom's at the top of the stairs."

Rose found Bethany's bedroom easily. Luckily, Irina didn't follow her upstairs. It would be much easier to sift through Bethany's personal things without her mother watching.

The room was exactly what she expected for a thirteen-year-old girl. Posters of the controversial rock singer, Luke Stone, completely covered two of the walls. A small amount of makeup spewed out of a brightly coloured bag, spilling some of the contents onto the dressing table. Next to the dressing table, a large teddy bear, wearing a pink dress, with a bright pink bow adorning its head, occupied a white wooden chair: a reminder that, despite the raging hormones and the attempt at being a grown-up, Bethany remained very much a child.

Rose rummaged through the dressing table drawers. She needed to be quick, in case the police realised their error and showed up to do a search, or in case Irina changed her mind and resented Rose poking through Bethany's personal things. She tried to remember where she used to hide her private stuff at the age of thirteen. Not much stuck in her head from over thirty years ago. Rose didn't recall being a particularly secretive child. As an only child, she'd had no need to hide anything from inquisitive siblings, and she never did anything shocking that she might need to hide from her parents.

More recently, she'd hidden a few things from Philip, her soon-to-be ex-husband. Not that he was particularly thorough at searching for anything, frequently failing to find his own stuff, even when it sat right in front of his nose. She had generally buried anything important in her underwear drawer. He'd long since stopped taking an interest in its contents.

Reluctantly, she pulled out Bethany's underwear but found nothing hidden among it.

If only she knew what she was looking for. A diary would be great, depending, of course, on what Bethany had written in it. That sort of thing might work for or against her. She lifted the mattress, running her hands underneath it for any signs of a hidden journal. Nothing. Did teenage girls even write journals these days? Everything was on smartphones or computers now.

Rose moved over to the wardrobe, which comprised mostly of hanging space, leaving few options for hiding anything. She checked the pockets in Bethany's clothes, but they were all empty.

After twenty minutes, Rose was ready to give up. If anything useful was hidden in Bethany's bedroom, she didn't know where to find it.

Despondent, she trudged down the stairs. Irina hadn't moved.

"Does Bethany own a laptop?" Again, Rose needed to repeat the question. Irina remained in a world of her own, and judging by the expression on her face, it wasn't a good world.

Irina pointed towards the cupboard in the corner of the room. The laptop sitting on top of it appeared nearly new.

Rose picked up the laptop. "Is this Bethany's?"

"Yes."

"Do you know the password?"

"No."

Rose wondered if Irina would get beyond one-syllable answers in what was left of the evening. She sat in an armchair opposite her, placed the laptop on her knees, and opened it up. She plugged for the obvious guess, typing in *LukeStone*.

It didn't work. She tried again. *LukeStone1*.

The computer sprang to life. As soon as it booted up, Rose opened up Bethany's email, breathing a sigh of relief when it didn't demand another password. Bethany must have saved the email password to her laptop. Hopefully, she would have done that with everything she accessed. It would certainly make Rose's task much easier. She focused on the task, concentrating hard, eager to complete the job as quickly as possible.

Irina had vacated her armchair and was manically cleaning the kitchen when Rose finished her fruitless search of Bethany's laptop.

"Richard says he can't get a flight home until tomorrow evening."

Rose doubted the truth in that but didn't want to upset Irina further by saying so. How many flights must run every day from San Francisco to London? Of course Richard would be able to book himself on a flight first thing in the morning, or probably even tonight, if he wanted to. Did he dread having to face this disastrous mess? Or did his job mean more to him than his daughter? If Irina weren't so distressed, Rose would have picked up the phone right then and given Richard King her opinion on how he should start reassessing his priorities.

"I can't cope with this on my own," Irina wailed.

Rose put her arm around Irina's shoulder. "You're not on your own." It had been a long day, and she really wanted to go home. "I'll stay as long as you need me." A small part of her hoped that Irina would beg her to leave and give her some space. It didn't happen.

"You can stay in the guest bedroom if you want," Irina suggested.

"Of course." Rose's head suddenly filled with a long list of things she desperately needed to do at home. She tried to blank out the list. No way could she leave Irina alone, not with her in this state. "Let me make you another cup of tea, and you can tell me everything the police said. That may throw some ideas up on how we can help Bethany." Rose reviewed in her head the sparse facts she'd gleaned so far. Bethany had been found standing over the PE teacher, Grant Wyvern, with a bloodied knife in her hand. However she looked at the evidence, she couldn't see any possible way of helping the girl. This wouldn't end well, not for Bethany, and not for Irina. If Rose possessed any sense at all, she'd walk out the door right now and run like hell.

The kettle boiled. Rose poured two cups of tea, mashing the tea bag around in Irina's mug to make the brew as strong as possible. A strong cup of tea probably wouldn't make any difference to Irina's state of shock. Rose wondered if she'd find any gin in the cupboards but decided that plying Irina with alcohol wouldn't do anything to make the problem disappear and would simply give her a hangover.

She placed Irina's mug of tea on the table in front of her. "Did Bethany tell you why she did it?"

Irina went berserk, jumping up out of her chair, grabbing the mug of steaming hot tea, and smashing it against the wall in front of her. "She didn't do it," Irina screamed. "My daughter is not a murderer. How can you even think she might be? She would never do that."

Rose backed away. "I'm sorry." She tried to remain calm. "I didn't mean... Of course she wouldn't do that." As far as she knew, Bethany had offered no defence to the accusation and was caught red-handed. It was admirable that Irina believed in her daughter and supported her, but sooner or later, she'd be forced to face up to reality. The best she could hope for would be if the teacher had attacked Bethany, forcing her to act in self-defence. She wondered how she might set about proving that scenario.

Irina stared at Rose as if she were some sort of monster.

"Perhaps I should go home," Rose suggested.

"No. Please don't leave me," Irina begged. "I'm sorry. I've spent all afternoon with the police telling me my daughter's a..." She couldn't bring herself to say the word *murderer*. "You do believe me, don't you? I need your help. The police won't even consider that somebody else must have done it. Bethany needs your help."

"I do understand what you're going through." If having a volatile temper ran in the family, then Bethany might be guilty after all. Rose shook the thought from her head, forcing herself to remain open-minded. "Of course I'll try to help. It's getting late. Perhaps we both need some sleep." She doubted that Irina would get any sleep tonight, although Rose was exhausted and certainly intended to get some shut-eye herself. With any luck, things might improve by the morning. If her subconscious got the chance to process the day's events, it might throw up a brilliant idea that hadn't yet occurred to her.

Chapter 7

DI Paul Waterford sat in his office at the end of a long day. He should go home to his wife. Clarke had phoned him earlier, asking what time he'd finish work. Yet again, he'd disappointed her as he'd arrive home very much later than promised. Clarke knew what she'd signed up for when she married him. He'd been in the middle of a difficult case, then. It had even managed to ruin their wedding day in spectacular fashion. But he still hated the disappointment that showed on her face every time he let her down because of the demands of the job. And the more understanding she was about it, the more the guilt ate into him.

He couldn't get the image of Bethany King out of his head. Thirteen. How did she get to this point? What had happened in her short life to drive her to murder?

They still hadn't been able to interview Bethany properly. At first, she'd been hysterical, so the doctor gave her a sedative, which left her practically catatonic. According to the doctor, she wasn't fit to interview yet, and he'd arranged a psychiatric assessment for tomorrow morning. Meanwhile, with every second that ticked on, she'd forget vital details or invent some fantastical story to cover her actions. They had no choice but to follow the doctor's guidance, especially with Bethany being a minor. They had to play everything by the book.

Paul put his head in his hands. When he'd first become a detective, his DI used to keep a bottle of whisky in his desk for times like this. He could really use a large glass of whisky now. But times had changed. In the last few years, he'd seen a big crackdown on police standards, especially in this station. No one tolerated that kind of behaviour anymore. Probably just as well because in his current mood, Paul would glug down the whole bottle.

He forced himself to get up from his chair, noting the time with surprise. Nearly eleven o'clock. Even later than he'd realised. At least

Clarke might be in bed by the time he got home, then he wouldn't have to face her disappointment.

As Paul pulled into his driveway and parked, he noticed the light in the living room.

Clarke came into the hallway to meet him.

"Sorry," Paul said, kicking off his shoes. He seemed to say that word a lot. "We've got a difficult case on."

"Is it the one at the school?" Clarke gave him a hug. "I heard a teacher got stabbed."

"Yes." Paul willingly returned the hug. Holding his wife helped calm him and take him to another place after the harrowing events of this afternoon.

"Have you eaten?"

Paul shook his head. He'd had nothing since his sandwich at lunchtime. He didn't really feel like eating now, but with the inevitable early start tomorrow, he needed to be fit to do his job. Reluctantly, he followed Clarke into the kitchen. The delicious smell that wafted out as soon as Clarke opened the door woke up his appetite.

"I cooked roast beef." A slight edge tinged Clarke's voice.

"Sorry," he said again, not knowing what else to say. "It smells wonderful."

Clarke opened the oven door and removed a plate of food. The smell of roast beef made Paul salivate with longing. He was much hungrier than he realised. Then Paul noticed the dining table, laid with the best tablecloth. Two candles in cast iron holders sat on the table amid a small vase containing a single red rose. Immediately, a feeling of intense guilt threatened to overwhelm him. Had he forgotten their anniversary or Clarke's birthday? No. Neither of them was this month. But Clarke had obviously gone to some effort to cook him his favourite meal and make everything nice, and he'd gone and ruined it by arriving home so late.

"This looks lovely." He was never going to guess what they were meant to be celebrating. "What's the occasion?"

"It will wait until another day," Clarke said. "Let's eat before it's completely spoiled."

Paul wasn't sure if she was referring to the occasion or the food. He dug into the meal of roast beef, crispy roast potatoes, and his favourite vegetables. The meat and potatoes had dried up slightly, no doubt from sitting in the oven waiting for him for the last three hours, but drowning the plate in a rich, beefy gravy quickly rectified that. "This is delicious." He meant it, thoroughly enjoying the food, even as the guilt carved its way into his heart. How lucky he was to be married to Clarke. Unlike some police wives, she never complained when his job got in the way, which happened far more frequently than she deserved.

He wiped his plate clean with a piece of bread, soaking up every last bit of the scrumptious gravy. "You'd better tell me. What special occasion did I forget?" he said when he finished his last mouthful. He'd racked his brain while he'd been eating. Birthdays. Anniversaries. He usually remembered anything important, but nothing came to mind for today's date.

Clarke took his hand across the table. "You worry too much," she said. "It's good news. I'm pregnant. You're going to be a dad."

Paul stared at her blankly, his mouth slowly opening into a big O.

"Well, say something."

Paul pulled himself together. "That's great news." He got up and went round the table quickly to give Clarke a hug, hoping she wouldn't see how forced his smile was. The news had taken him by surprise. It *was* great news. Really. Except all he could think about was Bethany and Irina King. Mrs King, destroyed by her daughter's actions, and Bethany, with her life totally wrecked. Paul shuddered slightly. What if his son or daughter did something like that? Mrs King seemed like a good mother, but she hadn't been able to prevent today's tragic occurrence. What if he couldn't stop his child from doing something similar? He didn't even spend much time at home, not with the long hours he worked. How could he possibly be a good father? Being a parent was a massive responsibility, and right now, it absolutely terrified him.

Clarke pulled away from him. "You're not happy." It wasn't a question.

"Of course I'm happy." Seeing the hurt in her eyes broke his heart. She'd given him the best news ever, and he was ruining the moment for her. "It's just that I can't stop thinking about the case, the murder at Taylor Park school. It's a really traumatic one."

"You don't usually get emotionally involved with cases," she accused. "Is it someone you know?"

"No, of course not. They wouldn't let me investigate if it were."

"Then what?" Clarke looked even more worried.

"I'm not allowed to discuss the case." He took the easy way out. Now wasn't the time to tell her about a little girl who turned bad, who'd screwed up her life and that of her parents, and currently lay in a police cell in a state of extreme shock. "We should go to bed. You need your sleep now that you've got our baby to think about." He wanted to apologise for being a crap husband, but at this hour, they both needed sleep. One thing was certain. Paul had a lot of making up to do tomorrow.

Chapter 8

Richard King waited for his luggage to appear on the carousel at Heathrow terminal two, trying to blend into the crowd. He spent the whole flight dreading what might await him on his arrival back in the UK, half expecting to be snapped by paparazzi, since his daughter's notoriety made it onto all the news programs in the States. But, of course, they weren't allowed to mention her name or show any photos, due to her age. Only in his imagination did the whole world know who he was.

He'd worried constantly since he'd received the news, desperately trying to convince himself it must be a terrible mistake, a nightmare that would end as soon as he arrived home to sort things out. But half of him, he was ashamed to admit, doubted Bethany, the half of him that currently boiled over with anger at his daughter for being so stupid. What if it wasn't a mistake? What if her recent metamorphosis into a sullen, bad-tempered teenager went way beyond anything he'd imagined? Perhaps the only person who made a mistake yesterday was Bethany.

He blamed Irina for being far too soft with the girl. His memory glossed over the fact that until a few months ago, he had been the one to spoil Daddy's little girl, far more than Irina ever did. But it couldn't have been his fault. She'd been a sweet girl then. Something in her had changed. He wished he'd cracked down on the problem as soon as he noticed the first signs. He should have sorted it out instantly, then he wouldn't have this much bigger mess to resolve. No doubt, both Irina and Bethany would expect him to fix things, like he always did. He was worried sick that this time, the problem might not be fixable.

His Hugo Boss suitcase swung around the corner of the carousel, nearly tipping off the edge where the luggage handlers had carelessly placed it. Richard pushed through the crowd, aiming to reach the case before it nosedived to the floor and got lost.

This was the worst timing. As if he didn't have enough to stress about already. The company merger his team had flown to San Francisco to discuss this week turned out to be a hostile takeover bid from a massive US corporation. So massive that they'd swallow the smaller company whole before spitting out the bones. His concern over losing his job had escalated to heart-stopping proportions when the US team discovered what his daughter had done. He never should have said anything. If only he'd kept it hidden, but he'd needed to explain why he had to return home suddenly, and he was no longer thinking straight at that point. He cursed himself for the hundredth time for not making up a more socially acceptable excuse, such as a family bereavement or illness.

The realisation had been awful. As soon as it had fully sunk in, he'd been tempted to turn and run, throwing a resignation letter at his colleagues on the way out. Instead, he'd spent an embarrassing twenty minutes apologising and reassuring them that it must be a mistake, and that his daughter would never do such a thing. He'd struggled to muster up the sincerity to make his excuses believable. He should be certain, showing total belief in Bethany's innocence. But he'd never been more uncertain of anything in his life. What sort of father did that make him?

He reached the carousel just as his luggage had already passed, requiring him to stretch out to grab it.

"Do you mind?" The woman he accidentally shoved glared at him as if he'd punched her.

"Sorry." Richard wondered if he should be more apologetic, but he lacked the emotional capacity for that right now. Better for him to get out of here as quickly as possible.

At least he hadn't been stupid enough to resign. Doubtless he'd lose his job. They'd find some way to get him out, and the merger, or takeover, would be the perfect excuse. But they'd be forced to give him a good severance deal. Perhaps enough money for them to survive until he found another position. Unless they spent the next few months haemorrhaging money on lawyers' fees.

He trundled his luggage behind him towards customs, heading towards the *nothing to declare* channel. Did he have nothing to declare? Only that his daughter may or may not be a murderer. That hellish thought made him want to shrink into himself with embarrassment and shame. Was this what his life would be like from now on? He tried to summon up a memory of the sweet girl his daughter used to be. But an angry young teenager covered in blood kept replacing the picture in his mind. If the situation affected him so badly, how was poor Irina faring? She was the sensitive one, the one who always looked to her husband, her rock, to smooth over any difficulties, something that, until now, had proven easy to do with either a hug or a wave of his credit card. It would take more than that to solve this problem. This time, he feared Irina would turn to him and find him lacking. Not a rock, more of a damp sponge. He didn't know how he'd be able to help her through this. Right now, he hated Bethany. This was all her fault.

As Rose washed up in Irina's kitchen from their meal the previous evening, she heard the rattle of a key in the front door and hurried out to the hallway. Irina was still in the living room where Rose left her earlier, drinking a cup of tea.

"Who are you?" A middle-aged man stood in the doorway holding an expensive-looking suitcase. For a moment, Rose was worried, forgetting she'd never met Richard King. Although the suitcase reassured her somewhat, the man seethed with anger and completely blocked her exit.

"You must be Richard. I'm Rose. We spoke on the phone. I've been looking after Irina since..." She trailed off, not quite knowing what to say. She hadn't expected Richard to arrive so soon.

Richard nodded. "You'll want to be getting home."

Rose did indeed want to go home, but she didn't like Richard's curt dismissal or his failure to ask after either his wife or his daughter. This was none of her business. She should leave so that Richard and Irina could discuss things together. "I'll get my things." She headed back into the living room to find her handbag.

Richard followed her in, going straight to his wife, who nearly dropped her hot cup of tea. "What the hell's going on? It's all over the news in the States. Is it true? Is it really Bethany?"

Irina put her tea on the small table next to her. Her hands shook so much, she spilled some of it, leaving the cup sitting in a warm beige puddle. "Of course it's not true." She stood up, almost knocking over the table and the tea.

Rose, who was wondering how to sneak past Richard without saying goodbye to Irina, felt the tension in the room dissipate, then immediately ramp up again.

"So she's not been arrested? You've made me come home for nothing."

"No, I mean yes." Irina sank quickly back into the chair as if her legs had turned to mush.

"Well, what do you mean? Has she or hasn't she?" Richard snapped, sending the tension level rocketing upwards still further.

Rose didn't like the way he hadn't even referred to his daughter by her name yet, but she kept quiet.

"She didn't do it," Irina repeated the words Rose had heard many times over the last few hours.

Richard turned to Rose, who was still trying to find a tactful way to leave. "Maybe I'll get more sense out of you. What's going on with my daughter?"

Rose didn't blame Richard King for being angry under the circumstances, but that didn't stop her from finding his attitude threatening. "Perhaps we should sit down first."

"I don't want to sit down," Richard shouted. "Will someone please tell me what's going on?"

"Bethany is in police custody," Rose said as calmly as possible, trying to manoeuvre herself towards the door without making it obvious. "A teacher at Taylor Park school was fatally stabbed, and I'm afraid the police are convinced Bethany is responsible, but I think we should give her the benefit of the doubt, don't you?"

The evidence against Bethany was overwhelming. Richard would find that out soon enough. In the meantime, she needed to pacify him. Anyway, Irina insisted that Bethany would never have stabbed anyone, although it would probably need a miracle to prove that.

"She'd better not have bloody done it," Richard said.

"She didn't do it," Irina repeated.

Richard wrapped his arms around his wife. "I'm sorry. It's the shock. We'll get her a good lawyer. Everything will be all right now that I'm here."

Rose hoped it would be that simple. She didn't want to be present when the police explained the case against Bethany to Richard. He'd freak out. The police would be able to handle his anger much better than she or Irina could. She turned to Irina, ignoring Richard. "I need to go home." She wanted to call a taxi and wait for it inside, but Richard's arrival made the atmosphere difficult, and Irina didn't need her any longer. Walking a mile back to her flat in the sunshine would give her time to think and the fresh air might clear her head.

Far from clearing her head, the walk home simply made Rose tired. She hadn't slept well last night at Irina's house. Much as she longed to get home, she took a detour to drop in on Maggie, guessing she'd be home at this time on a Saturday.

"Come in. I've just put the kettle on." Maggie Mahoney greeted her at the door, overjoyed to see her. "Can you believe what happened yesterday with Bethany?" she said as soon as she shut the door. "I'm still in shock."

"Have you heard anything more?" Rose asked. She was dying to sit down with a cup of tea but didn't want to stop Maggie from talking. "Irina is certain Bethany didn't do it."

Maggie turned around, her face frozen in horror. "Didn't do it? She was standing over him with the knife in her hand. How much proof do you want? That girl's guilty as hell."

Rose gently pushed past her, making her way into the kitchen in case Maggie forgot her offer of tea. Maggie followed her. "She wouldn't stab him for no reason. There must be something more behind it." Rose sat down gratefully as Maggie dropped a couple of tea bags into some mugs. "And where did she get the knife?"

Maggie pulled the bottle of milk out of the fridge. "I wondered that, too. The school had some trouble last year, so they installed metal detectors at the entrance. It's not the greatest security system. A kid with a brain might find a way round it, but they'd need to put in a bit of effort if they wanted to smuggle in a knife."

"Could the knife have come from the canteen?"

Maggie placed a cup of tea in front of Rose. "Apparently, it was a penknife, one of those Swiss army ones." Maggie found a packet of chocolate biscuits in the cupboard and placed them on the table.

Rose pounced on the biscuits, remembering she hadn't eaten breakfast, thanks to Richard showing up unexpectedly. "Did Bethany have any history with this teacher, Mr Wyvern?" Without a motive, Rose might be more inclined to trust Irina's opinion, that Bethany didn't do it, despite her obvious guilt.

Maggie pulled out a chair and sat down next to her. "Not that I'm aware of, but I only started working at the school a few weeks ago. I'll try to find out, but I'm sure the police will do all that?"

"Perhaps, but they think the same as you do. They're convinced that she did it. What if she didn't?"

"I hope, for her sake and Irina's, that she didn't," Maggie said. "But it's not looking likely." She took a sip of her tea. "Grant Wyvern teaches PE. How sporty is Bethany?"

"I'll ask Irina." Rose wasn't sure when she'd see Irina again. With Richard back home, he'd take charge of things. Her mind started to race with questions. Was Bethany on any school sports teams? Something like that would bring her into regular contact with Mr Wyvern.

"Tell me about Grant Wyvern."

Maggie paused for a few seconds, thinking. "I didn't know him well, but he seemed like a nice man. He was passionate about his teams winning when they played inter-school matches. I got the impression he really loved his job. He didn't deserve this." Maggie wiped a tear from her eye.

Rose patted her on the shoulder to comfort her. "If you hear anything, please will you tell me? The other teachers are bound to talk about him next week." There must be a reason why he was dead, and learning more about the man might throw up something that would help Bethany.

"I'll see what I can find out. If I spend more time in the staff room, I'm sure to hear something."

"Any information might be useful," Rose said, although she wasn't exactly sure how. Perhaps Bethany would start talking soon, then she'd explain exactly what happened and why.

"I suppose I'm expected to go to the police station and sort this out." Richard paced around the room like a caged animal. He needed to do something. There must be some sort of misunderstanding because things like this simply didn't happen to him. It would all turn out to be a dream or a nightmare, and he'd wake up shortly to find the problem had vanished.

He put his arms around Irina. She'd hardly stopped sobbing since he'd arrived home. "It's all right. I'm going to sort it out. Can you cope on your own for a while?" He was loath to leave her in this state, but he didn't have much choice. He wished he hadn't sent Irina's friend, Rose, home, but too late to regret that now. "I'll be back in a couple of hours." Hopefully, with Bethany in tow. He planned to give her a right royal rollicking when he got his hands on her.

Chapter 9

The police station seemed surprisingly busy for a Saturday morning, not that Richard had any experience with such things. "I want to see my daughter," he said quietly to the desk sergeant, not wishing to draw attention to himself. "Her name's Bethany King."

The desk sergeant immediately perked up. "If you'd like to sit over there, please, sir, I'll check if the officer in charge of the case is available."

Richard obediently sat where the sergeant indicated. As he'd never even set foot inside a police station before, actually being here had taken the wind out of his sails. He wasn't qualified to deal with something like this. He needed professional help, but a top-notch solicitor would decimate his savings in no time. Plus, he didn't know how much longer he'd keep his job. He decided to be sensible and listen to what the police said, then assess the situation before he wasted any of his precious cash.

He took some deep breaths. Hopefully, the tightness in his chest would prove to be a harmless panic attack rather than an indication of an impending cardiac arrest. Thirty-eight was surely too young for a heart attack, but he was mindful of the amount of stress heaped on him at work lately, and this situation was adding to his stress levels in spades.

It seemed like hours before someone came out to reception to find him, although, according to the clock on the wall, less than ten minutes had elapsed since he sat down.

"Mr King?"

Richard jerked his head up at hearing his name.

"I'm Detective Inspector Paul Waterford, the senior investigating officer in Bethany's case. Would you like to come with me?"

Richard followed him down the corridor and into a small, starkly furnished room.

"Can you please tell me what's going on?" Richard asked before he even sat down. "I've been in the States on business. I flew in this morning, so I only got what's been covered on the American news networks, that Bethany is being charged with murder, but that can't be right."

DI Waterford pointed at one of the uncomfortable-looking chairs. "Take a seat, sir."

Richard sat opposite Waterford, dreading what he was about to be told.

"I'm afraid Bethany has been arrested for the murder of Grant Wyvern. The evidence against her is compelling."

Richard gasped. The tightness in his chest increased. "But that's impossible." Up until now, he'd been able to pretend that it must be a dreadful mistake, that Irina had got everything wrong, that this nightmare wasn't really happening. Suddenly, everything seemed all too real.

"I'm sorry, sir. Can I get you some water?"

Richard nodded, temporarily unable to speak. A glass of water wouldn't help. Water wasn't going to make Bethany suddenly become innocent.

Waterford got up and filled a plastic cup from a cooler in the corner of the room.

"What happened?" Richard struggled to force the words out. He took a sip of the water.

"A teacher discovered Bethany standing over the body, holding the knife. We've tested the knife for fingerprints. There are only Bethany's prints and the victim's."

Richard shook his head. "No, no, no. That's not possible. You must be mistaken." How had this happened? How could his sweet little girl have come to this? How had he missed the signs? Surely there were warning signs? Had he seen them but turned a blind eye and refused to acknowledge that anything might be wrong? "Who found her? I need to talk to him." They must be lying. Perhaps this other teacher murdered his colleague and blamed it on Bethany.

"That won't be possible, sir. We can't allow you to talk to a witness."

"But he might know something. He might have done it himself."

"We've already interviewed her," Waterford said.

So it was a woman, but women could be murderers too. "She may be lying. What's her name? I'll make her tell me the truth." Richard clenched his fists. He needed to sort this out before it escalated any further.

"Sir, I really must advise you against contacting any witnesses. Let us do our job."

Richard took a deep breath, wondering if he should ask to see a doctor. He'd be no good to Bethany if he had a heart attack. He'd be no use to her either if they carted him off in an ambulance to check him over unnecessarily. "What did Bethany say about what happened?"

"Bethany hasn't said anything yet. She needs to explain what happened and why she did it, but she won't speak. Her mother was too upset yesterday to be of any help. Her presence made Bethany worse, I'm afraid."

Richard took a deep breath. He was upset himself, desperately needing some time to process this. It didn't surprise him about Irina. He imagined she would have been hysterical.

"We'd like you to try." Waterford paused, looking Richard up and down as if appraising his suitability for the job. "How do you get on with your daughter?"

"Good," he replied automatically before asking himself what the detective might be trying to insinuate with that question. His heart thumped against his tight chest, trying to escape and fly out to freedom away from this god-awful mess. "I need some time." What chance did he have of keeping Bethany calm enough to talk when he completely lacked anything resembling calmness himself? "It's been a shock. I need to get my head around this."

"Of course."

"Has Bethany ever mentioned Mr Wyvern to you?"

"Mr Wyvern?" Richard racked his brain. Was he supposed to know this bloke?

"The teacher who died." DI Waterford stared at Richard as if he were an idiot.

Richard hadn't even considered the identity of the victim. His name must have been mentioned in the news reports, but he'd been so completely focused on Bethany and how he could fix this disastrous situation. "No. Not as far as I remember. Irina, my wife, sees more of Bethany than I do. I'm always working. My job is demanding." How much longer would he be employed? Even now, management might be planning how to get rid of him, an embarrassment to the company. "Ask Irina. She'll know."

"We already asked her." Waterford wrote something down on his notepad. "I'm asking you."

Richard strained to try to see what Waterford had written, without it being obvious, but without his reading glasses, the words were an unreadable blur. He waited for Waterford to tell him what Irina had said on the matter, but no information was forthcoming. Never mind, he'd ask Irina himself when he got home.

"I need to get Bethany a solicitor." Richard's hopes of resolving this issue without spending any money died the moment DI Waterford explained what happened.

"We used the duty solicitor yesterday," Waterford told him. "She's a nice woman. She started to connect with Bethany."

"I'll get my own solicitor." Richard wondered how on earth he was supposed to locate a suitably good criminal solicitor on a Saturday and how he'd afford to pay for one if he lost his job, but he had no choice. A *nice* woman simply wouldn't cut it. He needed *great*, not *nice*. He needed a big shark to fight for Bethany because, by the sound of things, she was in deep, deep trouble. The nice woman may be starting to connect with Bethany, but she obviously hadn't connected enough to make his daughter tell them what happened, so what use would she be?

"Shall I give you some time to sort that out? We can reconvene as soon as your solicitor is available, and you can sit in on the interview as the appropriate adult. I expect you want to see Bethany."

Richard stared at the detective, unsure of what he wanted. Whatever was he supposed to say to his daughter? He didn't even know if he'd be capable of making her talk. The touchy-feely stuff was Irina's department. But he needed to be in that interview, if only to find out what they were dealing with. Only then could he begin to make things right.

Irina checked her watch for the twentieth time in the last few minutes. It didn't tell her anything different. Richard had been gone for much longer than the two hours he'd estimated. She was going crazy waiting to hear from him and several times tried to phone him, but he didn't pick up. It shouldn't be taking so long. He'd simply intended to find out what was going on. He wanted to get the whole story directly from the police as if he didn't trust her to remember everything. Of course she remembered everything, despite fervently wishing to forget. He should have come home by now. Did his lateness indicate a problem with Bethany, something he had stayed to sort out?

She went into the kitchen and put the kettle on. Not that she wanted yet another cup of tea, but she needed something to do. Briefly, she considered going to the police station herself, but Richard would get annoyed if she showed up. He'd interpret her action as undermining him or not trusting his competence to deal with the situation alone, and he always hated that. She'd have to bide her time until he decided to come home. But she was being driven completely mad, stuck in the house alone with no one to talk to.

The kettle clicked off. She leaned over it to reach a clean mug, jumping back sharply as the hot steam hit her face.

On an impulse, she swept up her car keys from the kitchen table, where Rose had left them yesterday after driving her home. She remembered Rose would be working today. She'd visit her at the Hale Hill Stores. At least then she'd have some company, someone who understood and was a good deal more sympathetic towards her than Richard. She didn't want to stay here on her own any longer.

It didn't take long to drive the short distance to Hale Hill Stores. She found a parking space at the side of the road nearby and reversed into it expertly, hearing Richard's voice reverberate through her head as she always did when she parallel parked, exactly the way he'd taught her. Stop half a metre alongside the car in front, then reverse into the space at a thirty-degree angle. It worked every time.

The shop appeared more crowded than usual. Irina remembered it was Saturday. She normally only dropped in midweek to pick up a few odds and ends that she'd forgotten to get at the big supermarket in Brackford. She spotted Rose sitting at the checkout and headed towards her, hanging back until Rose finished serving a customer. It hadn't occurred to her that she might not be able to monopolise Rose's attention. Perhaps if she bought something, she'd warrant some of Rose's precious time.

After a few minutes of waiting, Irina started to feel uncomfortable and realised everyone in the shop was staring at her as if she were some sort of freak show. She wanted to stare back, make them feel as embarrassed and ashamed as she did, but her nerves gave out in less than a second and she turned away, pretending to search for something on the shelves. Was this her life now? She hadn't done anything wrong and, she quickly reminded herself, neither had Bethany.

Picking up a packet of chocolate-hazelnut biscuits, Bethany's favourites, Irina queued up at the checkout. She needed to be more confident, for her daughter's sake. She recognised Jenny Pearce standing directly in front of her in the queue. Jenny's daughter, Madison, was friends with Bethany.

Irina tapped Jenny gently on the shoulder. "Hello, Jenny."

Jenny jumped as if she'd received an electric shock, turning to face her and simultaneously backing away so quickly that she nearly fell over. "I didn't expect to meet you here." She couldn't appear more petrified if Irina were to suddenly produce a knife and threaten to stab her. Irina guessed she wanted to run away—anything to avoid having to speak to the freaky murderer's mother—but Jenny seemed frozen to the spot as if unsure how to extricate herself from the awkward social situation.

Rose came to the rescue. "Jenny? Are you ready?" She gestured for her to place her basket on the checkout, smiling as if nothing untoward was happening.

Jenny hurriedly lifted her basket, tipping the contents in a heap in her fervour to speed up her escape.

Irina stared at the back of Jenny's head. Her long, blond ponytail showed off the tendons on her neck, tight and tense like twisted pieces of rope. Tears welled up in Irina's eyes. This was what she had become, a social pariah, someone to be avoided at all costs, in case her predicament rubbed off onto the other mothers and turned their daughters into murderers too. Except that Bethany wasn't a murderer. She wanted to shout it from the rooftops or put up a big neon sign declaring Bethany's innocence, but she'd never draw attention to herself like that. Big gestures weren't her thing. Instead, she preferred to fade into the background and pray for the floor to open up and swallow her whole.

"Are you all right?" Rose asked as soon as Jenny left the shop.

Irina glanced around her, searching through her tear-blurred eyes for the other customers who crowded the shop only a few minutes ago. They had all disappeared. The guilt overcame her, knowing they'd only left because of her. "I should go," she said.

"Jack will be here any minute now," Rose said. "He's working for an hour, so I can take a lunch break. You can come back to my place for lunch."

"No, really. You've been too good to me already." Irina longed for someone sympathetic to talk to, but now she felt dreadful about driving away Rose's customers. How could she accept her hospitality after that?

"I insist." Rose smiled at her.

Irina nodded meekly, lacking the strength to argue.

Jack showed up a couple of minutes later. For a moment, Irina thought he gave her an odd look but quickly convinced herself it must be her imagination.

"I've only got bread and soup," Rose apologised as they left the shop together.

"Really, I don't need anything. I only came because I didn't want to be at home on my own."

"You need to eat," Rose insisted. "Where's Richard? Isn't he at home with you?"

"He went to the police station to find out what's going on," Irina said. "I couldn't bear waiting alone."

"That's understandable." They arrived at Rose's flat. She unlocked the communal door to the block, then ushered Irina inside and up the stairs.

Inside the flat, Rose sat Irina at her kitchen table.

"I keep thinking, Bethany and I should be at Euro Disney today. If only I'd picked her up a couple of hours earlier, this never would have happened." Irina rubbed at her eyes.

"You can't think like that." Rose searched in her food cupboards for some tins of soup. "Is leek and potato ok?"

Irina stared at her, puzzled.

"Soup?"

"Oh, yes, that sounds lovely."

"You can't change history. Let's focus on the present and the future."

"I know, but I still can't help thinking it. I should be with Mickey Mouse. Instead, all I get is Jenny treating me like a piece of rubbish."

"Don't worry about Jenny." Rose opened a tin of soup, pouring it into a saucepan. "She can be a bit of a cow."

"Yes, sometimes," Irina agreed. "I just didn't expect... Bethany, and Jenny's daughter, Madison, are friends." She realised with dismay that the girls were unlikely to be friends any longer.

"So you expected better of her?" Rose placed a bowl of soup in front of Irina.

"This has all been a bit of a shock. I keep thinking, if this is how people react to me, how are they going to react to Bethany? How is she going to cope?"

Rose sat opposite Irina. "Who are Bethany's other friends? If we can talk to them, they might shed some light on events."

Irina sipped at her soup, noticing how Rose neatly sidestepped the question by asking one of her own. She thought for a few moments. "Her best friend is Debbie. Then there's Madison, and Ava and Shaz, although those two seem to be more Madison's friends than Bethany's."

"You should talk to them," Rose said.

Irina laughed nervously. "I don't suppose Jenny will let me talk to Madison now." If the reaction of the other girls' parents turned out to be similar, she wouldn't be allowed near any of them. Social pariah, she reminded herself. She may as well stick a label on herself saying that she ate children for breakfast. It wouldn't make things any worse if she did. "Why don't you talk to them instead?" Rose would be much better at it than she would. Irina wouldn't have a clue what to ask them, even if she managed to avoid getting over-emotional.

"I suppose I could," Rose said, "if you're sure."

"You'd be doing me a massive favour," Irina insisted.

Rose ate her soup, trying to work out how best to engineer a meeting with each of these girls. Hopefully, some ideas would occur to her soon.

Chapter 10

The solicitor took an age to arrive, even allowing for it being the weekend. Judging by her informal attire, Richard guessed she'd been dragged away from some fun family event.

Richard introduced himself. The solicitor, Veronica Roberts, looked young. He'd hoped for someone experienced. Her long hair was braided into a thick plait, and her casual clothes made her appear younger still. Richard had only known her for a matter of seconds and already he was losing confidence in her. He needed a shark, and they'd sent him a goldfish.

Mrs Roberts marched up to the desk sergeant. "Hi, Stan. Can you find me a room where I can talk to Mr King, please, before we see his daughter?"

Stan buzzed the door open. "Room two's empty. You know the way."

Richard followed Veronica into the interview room. He remained standing. "It's Bethany you need to talk to, not me." He didn't see any point in delaying the moment. It wasn't as if he could enlighten her on the case or on what Bethany had done and why. His knowledge of the details remained extremely sketchy, despite his earlier chat with the detective inspector. Besides, Veronica would be charging by the hour. Best to get on with things.

"Mr King, it's important that I find out as much as possible about Bethany before we get into an interview situation. I have vast experience in juvenile cases, so please trust me on this. It's likely that Bethany will clam up in an interview with strangers. She'll be very frightened right now, and there's no telling how that will make her react. Honestly, the most useful thing you can do is to tell me as much as you can about her. It will help me to decide how to approach things for the best."

Richard sat down. The solicitor apparently did possess some shark-like qualities. Richard doubted if anything he could tell Veronica

Roberts would help her deal with his difficult teenage daughter. He decided to cooperate with what she wanted. Mrs Roberts had come highly recommended, and perhaps Bethany would open up more to a young woman.

"What do you want to know?" Part of him hoped this would be brief, and another part of him wanted to put off actually seeing Bethany for as long as possible. He dreaded the moment, more than he would have ever imagined.

Mrs Roberts placed her briefcase on the table. "Tell me about Bethany's academic ability. Would you say she is very intelligent, more average, or not the intellectual type at all?"

The sensible question slightly reassured Richard. Knowledge of Bethany's intellectual capabilities might actually be of use to the solicitor. He wondered what would be the best answer. Was this a test? Would she use the information against Bethany, insinuating she might be something she wasn't? He reminded himself Veronica Roberts was here to defend Bethany. "I suppose she's kind of average," he said. That would be the safest bet. Too intelligent, and they might make her out to be capable of masterminding a murder plot. Too stupid, and they'd assume she was some sort of moron who didn't understand right from wrong. "Sometimes I'm sure she's more interested in sport than schoolwork."

"Interesting," Mrs Roberts muttered under her breath. "I understand the victim was a PE teacher."

Richard's chest tightened. He'd said the wrong thing. He took a deep breath, reminding himself again that he was paying Mrs Roberts to be on Bethany's side and that the police weren't in the room so would have no idea what they spoke about. Solicitors were bound by client confidentiality. Was he the client, or was Bethany? Certainly, he was the one who'd be footing the bill. That must make him the client, surely.

"What sports does Bethany play?"

Richard wasn't sure what relevance that had to anything. He tried to remember. He didn't really take much interest in any of that. By the time he got home from work most days, Bethany had finished any after-school activities and neither of them was that interested in discussing her sporting prowess. He took more of an interest in her academic achievements. He'd been trying to help her choose suitable subjects to study for her GCSEs. "Netball." He was pretty sure she played in the school netball team this year. "And she got into the girl's cricket team, too." He still reeled from the disappointment of going to watch a match and finding out Bethany was only the reserve. "I'm sure she does other sports as well. Her mother would know."

"It's all right. It doesn't matter." Mrs Roberts shot him a vaguely sympathetic look. "How do you get on with Bethany?"

What the hell did she mean by that? Was she implying something? "She's my daughter. We get on just fine." He was aware he sounded defensive. He was defensive. Of course they argued sometimes. What father and teenage daughter didn't? Wasn't that normal?

"Has Bethany exhibited any changes in her behaviour lately? Have you noticed any differences in her attitude?"

"I'm not sure. I don't think so." Had she changed? She'd gone from being a sweet daddy's girl to a belligerent teenager, but he couldn't pinpoint when that change occurred. There were small signs: the shorter hemlines, the dreadful nose piercing, the increased tendency to answer back. It had been so gradual that he hadn't really noticed, until one day, he'd woken up to the fact that his adorable girl had turned into a monster. Wasn't that normal teenage behaviour? She was simply growing up, trying to navigate the stony path towards adulthood—a couple of years too soon, in his opinion. Surely that was normal? Except that now Bethany was allegedly a cold-blooded killer. Not normal. Not normal at all.

Richard fidgeted in his chair. He didn't like this woman grilling him, not even in the interest of helping Bethany. Veronica made him feel like *he* was the guilty party. Perhaps he was. People would say exactly that, wouldn't they? Blame the parents. How could they not notice anything was wrong? How could they have failed to prevent this tragedy?

"When can I talk to Bethany?" Richard suddenly wanted to get the dreaded moment over with. In his head, his lovely daughter had morphed into a devil, with gleaming red eyes and blood dripping from her hands. He shook his head, trying to rid himself of the image. Of course she would have washed her hands since yesterday. There would be no blood. He put his own hands behind his back, pressing them into the chair to stop them from shaking. Fat lot of use he'd be to Bethany. Thank God he'd got her a solicitor. He needed Veronica Roberts to be good, the best.

Richard's first sight of Bethany shocked him. She sat slumped on a tatty beige sofa in the interview room. Two female police officers flanked her. She was in the room, but she wasn't there. What was it psychologists called it? Presenteeism. Her body sat right in front of him, but her mind had gone to another place, leaving nothing but a vacant space in her head. Richard tried to catch her eye, to see if somewhere inside of her was the little girl he loved, but she simply stared blankly ahead like a zombie. Did she even notice him? She gave no sign that she did.

"Bethany, it's Daddy... Dad," he corrected himself quickly. Since Bethany became a teenager, she hated him referring to himself as Daddy. She hadn't called him that for several months.

His daughter didn't respond. She stared past Richard as if he weren't there. He couldn't take his eyes off her, his gaze magnetically drawn by the awful sight, even though it killed him to look at her. Bethany's eyes were red but not in the way he'd imagined earlier. Clearly, she'd been crying. Seeing her, Richard felt like doing the same. The bags under her eyes seemed to take up half of her face—evidence of a total lack of sleep—aging her so much that she might almost have been mistaken for a middle-aged woman instead of a fresh-faced teenager. She hadn't even brushed her hair. Her mop of brown curls resembled an unkempt bird's nest, perching untidily on her head. He half expected a sparrow to fly out of it.

The detective he'd met earlier entered the room and the uniformed female officer left. He sat down opposite Bethany. "I'm Detective Inspector Paul Waterford. My colleague"—he gestured towards the remaining female officer—"is Detective Constable Wendy McKay."

Bethany stared vacantly. It pained Richard to see her like this. Veronica Roberts, the solicitor, spent the last half-hour talking to her alone. He wondered if she'd managed to get any response out of her. Bethany seemed hell-bent on saying nothing at all. He didn't know whether to shake her or hug her. He resisted the temptation to do either. They'd only been in the room for a minute and already he found the whole experience unbearable. Poor Irina must have really struggled to cope. He probably should have appreciated that fact more when he saw her earlier.

"Hi, Bethany. My name's Wendy. How are you feeling today?"

Richard stiffened in his uncomfortable chair. Unlike Bethany, the rest of the room's occupants had to make do with hard plastic furniture. He tried to pay attention and ignore the dark thoughts racing around in his head. The soft lilt of Wendy McKay's voice should be relaxing him, but he simply found it annoying. Doubtless the officer was carefully chosen to try to bond with Bethany. Use a young woman to make her feel more comfortable and get her talking. But the way Bethany stared at Wendy as if she were stupid convinced Richard that his daughter had worked out their tactics as quickly as he had.

Wendy tried another approach. "It's ok, Bethany. We're here to help you. We can talk about whatever you want." Wendy smiled at Bethany, leaning slightly towards her. "What would you like to talk about, Bethany?"

Bethany continued to stare into space—an empty shell in the room with them.

Richard was already losing patience with her. It would be a very long day if she kept up this silent act. "Answer the lady, Bethany." He tried to say it in a kind way, but it came out in his *I must be obeyed* voice that he used when she misbehaved.

Bethany turned her head away from him. Not the reaction he wanted, but at least it proved her awareness of his presence.

"Mr King, please remain silent. You're not helping," DI Waterford said.

Richard groaned inwardly. At least he got a reaction, albeit a negative one, which was more than DC McKay had done. Bethany needed telling. She needed discipline. If Irina had let him use more discipline before her behaviour got out of hand, they wouldn't be in this situation now. He folded his arms angrily. Wasting everybody's time like this wouldn't help her case one bit. Couldn't the solicitor see that? He'd talk to Veronica Roberts as soon as he got the chance.

"Bethany, would you like something to drink?" Wendy asked.

For a moment, Bethany seemed as if she'd keep up the silent treatment. "Apple juice." Her voice came out in a hoarse whisper as if she hadn't spoken for a day, which she probably hadn't if her current performance was anything to go by.

"I'm sure we can find you some apple juice, Bethany." Wendy looked over at DI Waterford. He got up.

Richard snorted. "Surely you're not going to pander to her like this," he said. "She's playing you. She does it all the time at home."

"Mr King," DI Waterford said sternly. "Would you please be quiet? If I need to tell you again, you'll have to leave and I'll get the duty social worker to act as the appropriate adult."

Veronica spoke for the first time. "May I speak with Mr King outside, please?"

Richard glared at her. He wasn't paying her exorbitant rates for her to give him a telling-off. He got up. This would be an ideal opportunity to put her straight on a few things before it became too late.

The three of them left the room together, Richard and Mrs Roberts pausing in the corridor until DI Waterford disappeared from sight.

Richard got in first. "Did Bethany tell you what happened when you met with her earlier?"

"Not yet. She's frightened, so it may take some time to get through to her."

"You need to be firmer with her."

Mrs Roberts stared at him. "Did you not listen to what I just said? She's frightened. I have a great deal of experience with cases like this. She won't tell us the truth if she's forced into it. She'll make something up just so we stop harassing her, and that won't help her one iota." The sound of footsteps echoed from the other end of the corridor, signalling DI Waterford's return. "You need to be more supportive. If you keep interfering, they can make you leave the room. How will that help Bethany, to have yet another stranger to deal with instead of her own family?"

Richard bit back his frustration as DI Waterford caught up with them. He didn't like being told what to do, but if this woman was as expert as she claimed to be, he'd give her a chance to prove herself. Secretly, he thought it would take a minor miracle to make Bethany talk.

DI Waterford placed the small paper cup of apple juice in front of Bethany. "There you go, Bethany, the best apple juice in the police station." He smiled at her. "Enjoy."

Bethany took a cautious sip of the juice as if it might be poisoned. Then, finding it tasted normal, she gulped it down in seconds.

"Wow. You must be thirsty," Wendy said. "Tell you what, if you answer three questions, we'll get you another one."

Bethany glanced up at her, quickly shying away from the eye contact.

"So, tell me, Bethany, do you like school?"

Richard's frustration nearly exploded out of his ears. What did that have to do with anything? The stupid woman had wasted one of her three questions. How was she ever going to get anywhere with Bethany? Why didn't she simply ask her if she did it? That's what he would ask. That was the only question that really mattered. Mrs Roberts glared at him as if she sensed his itch to say something. He bit his tongue, not quite daring to risk being thrown out of the room yet.

"It's ok."

Everyone stared at Bethany as if she were some mighty guru who had spoken two words of great importance. Immediately, Bethany leant forwards and buried her head in her knees.

"That's great, Bethany," Wendy said softly. "That's one question. See how easy it is. Let's try the second question." She paused as if waiting for a reaction from Bethany. None came.

"Do you often go to the gym equipment room at school?" Wendy asked.

Richard looked at his daughter. Her shoulders moved slightly, and he thought he heard a little snuffle. Was she crying? With her face completely buried in her lap like that, he couldn't be sure. He wanted to get up and hug her. Would they let him do that? He was frightened to ask, in case the detective inspector misconstrued it as interference and threw him out. His emotions were all over the place today. Only a minute ago, he'd wanted to smack her.

"Bethany?" Wendy prompted her.

Bethany lifted her head slightly, giving it a little shake.

"So you don't often go to the gym equipment room?"

Why on earth did she go there yesterday? Richard wished they'd leave him to have a proper conversation with his daughter. He needed to find out exactly what happened in that gym yesterday. Half of him longed to side with Irina, who remained steadfastly unwilling to accept that their daughter might be a murderer. And the other half of him, the logical half of him, already realised the situation was hopeless.

Bethany shook her head again.

"That's great, Bethany. That's two questions already. One more question, then we'll get you another apple juice. I might try one too. It smelled delicious."

Richard closed his eyes, trying to imagine he was somewhere else. It pained him to watch his daughter like this whilst being so powerless to help her.

Wendy continued. "Why did you go to the gym equipment room yesterday, Bethany?" Wendy spoke casually as if asking why Bethany went shopping with her best friend last weekend.

The question blasted into Richard's head, despite him trying to shut everything out. At least Wendy had finally asked a question that didn't invite a yes or no answer.

Everyone waited patiently except Richard, who clenched and unclenched his fists behind his back in frustration, forcing himself not to speak.

"Bethany, why...?"

"He... He wanted to see me." Bethany struggled to get the words out.

"That's great, Bethany. How did you know he wanted to see you?"

Bethany looked up. "That's four questions."

Richard almost burst into hysterical laughter. He knew their stupid approach would backfire. How were they going to get her to talk now?

"You're absolutely right, Bethany. I'm sorry."

"Why don't we take a short break?" DI Waterford got up. "Wendy and I will go and fetch some more apple juice." He smiled at Bethany.

The door shut behind them. Their voices echoed in the corridor outside, so Richard guessed they were talking about Bethany. He was sure they wouldn't leave Bethany without a police guard for more than a few seconds. He may not get another chance to talk to his daughter.

He got up and hugged his daughter before Mrs Roberts could stop him. "What happened, Bethany? You need to tell us. We can help you." He so desperately wanted to make this dreadful thing go away, but she needed to give him something to work with. He'd imagined so many possibilities, all of them bad. If only she'd give them a good reason why she stabbed her teacher, this hotshot solicitor might get her off. "Please, Bethany," he begged.

Bethany's body became rigid inside his arms.

"Please, tell us." One of the police officers would be back soon. She was going to miss her chance to tell him.

The door opened and already it was too late as Waterford and McKay quietly stepped into the room behind Bethany.

Bethany appeared not to notice. She stared at the floor in front of her, then her whole body started to shake. Her voice came out in such a quiet whisper that Richard almost imagined he'd heard the words.

"It's my fault," she said. "It's my fault he's dead."

Chapter 11

The room fell silent for several seconds while everybody stared at Bethany.

DI Waterford was the first to speak. "Bethany King, I'm charging you with the murder of Grant Wyvern."

Richard jumped up as DI Waterford read Bethany her rights. "No. You can't do that." He turned to Veronica Roberts. "Tell him he can't do that."

"Mr King, please calm down." Paul moved towards him in case he needed restraining. He certainly gave the impression he might explode at any moment.

"But it's rubbish. She doesn't understand what she's saying. Bethany, tell them it's not true. Tell them you didn't do it."

Bethany didn't react. Paul guessed she'd shut down again, except he could see tears streaming down her face. He nodded at Wendy to deal with her.

"You're really not helping, Mr King. Please sit down and let me handle things." Veronica rummaged in her handbag.

Paul wondered if Veronica was searching for her pepper spray. She was legendary in the police station for once using the spray on a client when he tried to attack her. He didn't want a repeat of that fiasco. Quickly, he put a hand on Richard King's arm. "Let's discuss this outside," he said firmly.

Richard pulled his arm away. "There's nothing to discuss. You're wrong. You need to stop pussyfooting around my daughter and make her tell you the truth. I'm not leaving here until she tells you."

"Mr King, I really have to insist. If you don't come with me now, I'll arrest you for threatening behaviour." It was possibly stretching the imagination a little, but Veronica certainly looked under threat as Mr King raised his voice almost to shouting point. Paul briefly considered leaving him at the mercy of Veronica and her pepper spray but decided that would be unprofessional. He glanced quickly at Bethany. Wendy was escorting her out. Mr King was too busy shouting his mouth off to notice his daughter leaving the room.

"All right, I'm going, but you need to sort this out." Veronica noticed Wendy taking Bethany out. "We'll be applying for bail," she said quietly to Paul.

"The police will oppose bail." Paul wanted to make that clear. Bethany stabbed a man to death, knifing him not once, not twice, but three times. That made her potentially dangerous. They would put up a fight to make sure she remained in custody.

Richard picked up on the conversation. "What's this about bail?" he addressed Veronica. "Isn't that very expensive?"

"Let's discuss it outside." She reached into her handbag again.

Paul was willing to bet that Veronica Roberts would have her hand on her pepper spray throughout the whole of that conversation.

"Where's Bethany?" Richard suddenly noticed her absence.

"DC McKay took her back to her cell," Paul explained. They needed to find her a place in a juvenile detention centre as soon as possible. A police cell was no place to hold a vulnerable thirteen-year-old.

Richard glared at Paul. "I want to see her."

"You can see her tomorrow, when you've calmed down." No way would he allow King anywhere near his daughter while he was wound up like this. He wouldn't put it past him to get physical with Bethany and try to beat some answers out of her. Richard King certainly looked handy with his fists and he'd already shown he possessed a temper. It was no wonder that Bethany turned out like she had. Paul ushered him into the corridor. He really wanted to frogmarch him out of the station right now but remembered that Mr King needed to talk with Bethany's solicitor first.

"You can have your discussion in the corridor," he said to Veronica Roberts. "I'll be just around the corner. If you need me." He wouldn't risk leaving Veronica alone with King. He'd be within earshot if anything happened. Then, as soon as they finished, he'd personally throw Richard King out of the building.

Chapter 12

Rose drove Irina's car to take her home as she had worked herself up into too much of a state to drive safely. Rose didn't want this to become a habit, or Irina would expect it all the time. She wondered if she'd end up walking home this time as well. It annoyed her that the Kings could easily afford to pay for a taxi for her.

"Richard must still be at the police station." Irina dropped her handbag onto a chair. "I should have gone with him, but he said I'd distress Bethany if I got upset."

"Why don't you go tomorrow? That will give you more time to process everything." Rose wasn't sure that Irina would ever calm down enough, even if she waited for another month. This situation was simply too big, too much for her to bear.

"I hope so. Bethany needs her mum."

"Shall I make you a cup of tea?" Rose offered.

"No, I'll do it." Irina grabbed the kettle and started to fill it. "I need to keep busy."

Rose sat down. "Tell me about Bethany's friends." She hadn't gained much information last time she asked.

Irina pulled two mugs out of the cupboard, clanking them together as her hands shook. "Her best friend, Debbie, lives on the next street."

"It would be useful to talk to her," Rose said. "Best friends usually tell each other everything." If anyone understood the state of Bethany's mind lately, it would be Debbie.

Irina poured the tea, overfilling one of the mugs so that streaks of the hot brown liquid dripped down the side of the white china. "You're right about that." She wiped up the mess. "Those two never stopped talking when they were together. But Debbie hardly says a word to me. Quiet as a mouse."

Rose hoped Debbie wouldn't be too overcome with shyness to talk to her. Perhaps if she explained that Bethany needed her help, she'd open up, but she realised it might be difficult, especially if the police got to her first. Being questioned by the police would put the wind up any teenage girl, particularly a shy one. Rose hoped it wouldn't make her clam up completely.

"Have the police interviewed her friends?" Rose asked.

"The police don't tell me much." Irina put the tea in front of Rose and sat opposite her. "I suppose so."

Rose wondered if they may not have spoken to them yet, given that Bethany appeared irrefutably guilty. She knew better than to voice that opinion to Irina. "Tell me about her other friends. I know Madison Pearce." Rose was acquainted with a lot of people locally, thanks to her long hours working in the Hale Hill Stores.

"There's Ava Browning and Shaz Fletcher as well. Bethany used to be friendly with all three girls. They're all in the cricket team with her. She hasn't mentioned them much lately, but she's reached that age where she doesn't talk to her mum as much as she used to."

With a bit of luck, Madison and Shaz would both come into the shop over the weekend. Rose worried about Irina flagging up Bethany being less communicative these days and hoped that wasn't a bad sign.

"Will you talk to them, please? No one wants to speak to me." Irina wiped a stray tear from her cheek. "Part of me wants to hide away until this is all over, but I need to be strong for Bethany. Thank God I've got Richard. He's always been the strong one."

Rose sipped at her tea, looking at Irina over the rim of her mug. Things didn't look good for Bethany. This may never be all over for any of the family.

The front door slammed, causing Irina to spill her tea.

"Irina?" A shout came from the hall.

Irina cheered up instantly. "Richard's home. Maybe he has good news. Do you think Bethany is with him?" She jumped up out of her chair.

Rose very much doubted that Richard's powers extended to springing Bethany out of police custody. It would need something monumental to happen for her to be released so quickly.

Richard entered the large kitchen before Irina reached the door. Irina flung her arms around his neck and hugged him.

"Where is she? Where's Bethany? Did you bring her home?" Irina spoke excitedly.

"No, of course not." Richard pushed her gently away. "I'm not a magician. I'm afraid she won't be coming home for a long time."

Rose picked up on Richard's mood and got up, ready to leave. She guessed she'd be walking home again.

"What?" Irina stepped back. "Bethany has to come home. She doesn't belong in that police station. They've got everything wrong."

"I'm sorry, love. The police were right. She did it."

"No. They're wrong. My baby would never kill anyone. Never." Irina remained steadfastly adamant on the subject.

"It's not the police saying it, love. It was Bethany. She confessed."

Rose, who was halfway to the door, stopped in her tracks at Richard's words. She hadn't expected that. She still wanted to believe Irina might be right. "What did—"

Irina's protestations drowned out Rose's words. "No. The police are lying." Irina quickly became hysterical. "They must have forced a confession."

"I was with her." Richard grasped Irina's hands. "There was no coercion. Bethany said, 'It's my fault he's dead.' You can't get plainer than that."

Rose agreed with Richard. It seemed pretty conclusive. There must be more to it. Rose wished she understood *why* Bethany killed her teacher. She decided to leave. Irina and Richard were both too wrapped up in Bethany's confession to notice her. They needed to be on their own.

Relieved to get away, Rose began the familiar trudge home. She really needed a car.

Chapter 13

Rose took her dinner out of the microwave. Jack was becoming rather good at making delicious meals for her to heat up when she got home. She'd really miss him when he went travelling, then returned to university at the end of the summer.

The doorbell rang just as she sat down to eat. Annoyed by the interruption, she picked up the entry phone in the hallway. "Who is it?"

"It's me, Maggie." Rose recognised her voice before she even said her name. She hit the button to open the main door downstairs.

Maggie reached the top of the three flights of stairs to Rose's flat, breathless. "I need to sit down. However do you cope with all those stairs every day?"

Rose laughed, reluctant to point out that her fitness level vastly exceeded Maggie's.

Maggie pulled some sheets of paper out of her handbag. "Take a look at this." She thrust the pages in front of Rose.

Rose scanned the pieces of paper quickly. They listed names and dates. Madison Pearce's name jumped out at her. "What is it?"

"It's a list of attendees for all the school's detentions in the last month," Maggie explained. "See here." She pointed to the first sheet. "The teacher's name and the date are at the top of each section, followed by a list of pupils in the detention."

"That's interesting," Rose said, not meaning it at all. Why had Maggie given her this? Her dinner was getting cold. She'd need to heat it up again after Maggie left.

"Yes, it is," Maggie said excitedly. "Three girls, Madison Pearce, Ava Browning, and Shaz Fletcher are in every single one of Grant Wyvern's detentions. There are others, but it's always these three."

"That is interesting." Rose meant it this time. She paged through the list. Mr Wyvern had supervised four detentions in the last month.

She noticed most of the children in his detentions were girls. "Who gives them the detentions? Would Mr Wyvern have handed them out?"

"No, the name of the teacher who put them in detention is in brackets after each pupil's name."

Rose scanned down the list. There were only two teachers who had sent these three girls to detention. Did they only misbehave in those two teachers' classes? It would be one hell of a coincidence if that were the case. She scanned through the list again. None of the three girls showed up in any other detentions. Her eyes were drawn to the last one on the list, which took place on the day before Grant Wyvern's murder. On that day, the only three people in detention were Madison, Shaz, and Ava. And the supervising teacher was Wyvern.

"Don't you think it's odd that the only teachers sending these three girls to detention were Grant Wyvern and Helen Trenton?" Maggie said.

"And they were nearly all to the detentions supervised by Mr Wyvern," Rose added. "Have you shown this to the police?"

"Not yet. I don't want to get any of the girls or Helen in trouble."

"Yes, I see what you mean. Why don't you leave it with me?" Rose needed to think about it. She could always give it to the police tomorrow if it still seemed relevant. She scanned the list one last time, carefully looking for Bethany's name, but it was notable only by its absence. The detention lists showed no evidence of Bethany being a troublemaker. But equally, Rose couldn't see how this new information would help Bethany.

Rose didn't need to wait long to talk to Madison. She came into the shop the following morning on an errand for her mother. Rose wondered if Jenny was too embarrassed to show her face after the incident with Irina.

"Have you got a minute, Madison?" Rose approached her as she perused the shelves of bread, trying to choose a loaf. She glanced around. Luckily, the shop was empty, apart from the two of them.

"What have I done?" Madison turned towards her, shooting her a wary glance.

Madison's appearance shocked Rose. Her pretty face seemed lined with worry. Rose smiled at her, trying not to let her feelings show. "It's all right. You haven't done anything wrong." Poor Madison. With her teacher dead and her friend facing a long stretch in a juvenile detention centre, it hardly surprised Rose that the recent events had taken their toll on Madison.

Madison picked up a loaf of sliced white bread.

"I like the granary bread best." Rose pointed at another loaf. "It's much tastier."

"Nah. Mum only likes white bread."

"Then how about this one?" Rose picked up a much nicer loaf of white bread than the one Madison originally chose, which tasted of nothing.

Madison took the bread from her, seeming relieved to have the decision taken out of her hands. No doubt she'd blame Rose if her mum didn't like it.

"What do you think about Bethany?" Rose slipped it into the conversation, certain that everybody else was talking about the same subject, so it would appear completely natural.

"She's crazy. I always figured she was weird."

"I thought Bethany was your friend," Rose said.

"Used to be till I found out she's a skanky loser."

Rose hoped that Bethany's other friends might be a bit more supportive. She knew exactly what it felt like to be dropped by people when your circumstances took a turn for the worse. The only good thing was that Bethany might never find out how much Madison had turned against her.

"Will Beth go to prison?"

For all Madison's tough act, Rose saw that she did care, at least a little. "It all depends. Why do you think she did it?"

Madison shrugged. "I dunno. Maybe Wyvern's a dirty perv. Why else would she do it?"

"Has anyone else suggested that?" Rose didn't trust much of what Madison said. But there might be something in her suggestion. If that were the case, then a good solicitor may be able to get Bethany off the murder charge.

"I need to get home. How much is the bread?" Madison swung the loaf of bread agitatedly, making Rose worry that the plastic wrapper might burst open.

"Nothing," Rose said. "You can have it for free."

Madison hadn't answered her question. Was she suddenly so keen to leave because Rose was getting closer to the truth? Somehow, she'd have to talk to the girl again. She must know something.

Madison's eyes lit up. She dived towards the door before Rose changed her mind. Rose guessed she'd pocket the money without telling her mother the bread was a gift.

Hopefully, Debbie would be more forthcoming about Bethany's state of mind. If Irina was correct, the two girls were virtually inseparable. If anyone knew what Bethany really thought about Grant Wyvern, Debbie would. She simply had to work out how to engineer a meeting with her, without knocking at her house. She needed to get her without her parents being around because that would be guaranteed to make her clam up.

As it turned out, Debbie came looking for Rose. The shop was really busy, so it took a few minutes before Rose noticed Debbie skulking in the corner, pretending to read the packaging on a packet of biscuits. Rose kept half an eye on the teenager whilst dealing with her other customers. If she scanned everything through the checkout really quickly and dispensed with her usual chat, Debbie might still be here after the other customers left the shop.

As the final customer finished paying for her shopping, Rose looked up. Debbie no longer stood by the biscuit shelf. Worried, Rose glanced around the shop, then quickly came out from behind the checkout to search for her. She regretted not asking Debbie to wait.

"Can I help you?" Rose sighed with relief as she located Debbie loitering in the farthest aisle.

Debbie turned around. Her eyes widened with fear as she glanced around her, checking for other customers.

"Do you know what's happening with Beth?" Debbie's voice was little more than a whisper. "Madison said you would know. No one will tell me anything. It's been awful."

"The police are still investigating," Rose said kindly. The police had already made up their minds about Bethany, but she wouldn't tell Debbie that. Nor would she tell her of Bethany's confession. If the girl knew anything useful, Rose needed to draw it out of her.

"Madison said Beth did it, but she wouldn't. I'm sure she wouldn't."

"How did Bethany get on with Mr Wyvern?" If Bethany had any problems with her teacher, she would surely have discussed the issue with Debbie.

Debbie shrugged her shoulders. "Ok, I s'pose. Beth kept trying to impress him because of the girls' cricket team. He only made her reserve, and she wanted to be in the team proper."

Immediately, Rose picked up on what she said. "Did that make Bethany angry, only being reserve?"

"Of course it did, but not with Mr Wyvern."

"Then who was she angry with?" Rose glanced at the door, hoping no new customers would come in until Debbie finished talking.

"Madison. She was furious with Madison, and I don't blame her." Debbie looked up, catching Rose's eye and instantly turning away.

"Bethany is brilliant at cricket. She should be team captain, not the reserve. Madison kicked her in the shin really hard during the team trial. It bled all over the place, and poor Beth could hardly walk, let alone run. She did the best she could, but only ended up as reserve."

"That's awful," Rose said. "But surely Mr Wyvern spotted Bethany's talent. If she'd explained about the accident..."

"It wasn't an accident," Debbie interrupted. "Madison did it deliberately. She can't bear anyone to be better than her. And Bethany did try complaining to Mr Wyvern."

"What happened?" Rose asked.

"He said the selection process had to be fair. Otherwise, he'd get half of the girls' parents complaining, and Beth didn't perform on the day it mattered."

Would that have given Bethany enough motive to stab her teacher? Rose doubted it, but it would depend on how desperately Bethany had wanted to be on the team. "Surely, she was upset with Mr Wyvern when he refused to change his mind?"

"Not really. It only made her try harder. Madison's behaviour towards her upset her more. She was really nasty, gloating about getting Beth's place on the team. She kept telling Beth she wasn't good enough and Mr Wyvern would drop her completely as soon as he found someone better to be reserve."

"Was it just Madison winding her up?" Rose wondered if the other girls might have driven Bethany to stab Mr Wyvern. "Was Bethany unhappy?"

Debbie made a face. "Ava Browning was the ringleader. I bet she told Madison to kick Beth. Ava's a nasty bully. Madison and Shaz do what she says. They don't mean it—well, not so much as Ava does." She gave a hollow laugh. "We're reading *Macbeth* at school. They started calling Beth MacBethany. She hated that. So we called them the three witches."

"It must have affected Bethany, being bullied. How did it make her feel?"

"Pretty crap sometimes, but it didn't make her kill Mr Wyvern, if that's what you're getting at. Beth wouldn't do that. Anyway, she was in other teams, so she didn't mind so much. Her dad was more upset than Beth. I think he would have loved to murder Mr Wyvern. Beth was more hurt by Madison turning against her. They used to be friends before Ava Browning came along."

Rose wouldn't have been surprised if Richard had stabbed someone, but the police had checked his story about being in San Francisco on Friday. Being thousands of miles away completely ruled him out. There must be some other reason for Bethany to get angry with Grant Wyvern. "What about the other girls on the cricket team? Did they like Mr Wyvern?" If anything untoward occurred between Mr Wyvern and any of the girls, Debbie might be able to shed some light on it.

Debbie let out a nervous laugh. "Most of them liked him. He was quite good-looking." She blushed.

Rose guessed that Debbie was among Mr Wyvern's fan club. "Would Bethany have been going to talk to him about the cricket team on Friday?"

Debbie shrugged again. "She may have been going for some extra coaching. Madison was having an extra lesson on Friday at lunchtime. Perhaps Beth was planning to join in."

Rose wondered why Madison hadn't mentioned seeing Mr Wyvern shortly before his death. "Did he do that sort of thing often?"

"Not much," Debbie said. "But Madison got really upset last week when one of the other parents criticised her batting technique. Mr Wyvern offered to help her. He was really good like that. He liked his teams to win."

"Yes, that was good of him," Rose said. Did these extra lessons include anything inappropriate, or was that simply schoolgirl rumour? She needed to talk to Madison again and get the truth out of her this time. "I hear Mr Wyvern gave a lot of detentions. Didn't that make him unpopular?"

Debbie laughed. "No. Most of the time it was girls in the cricket team, and they spent the whole detention discussing team tactics."

"Were you in the cricket team?" Debbie didn't come across as the athletic type, but Rose needed to check.

"No way. I don't like sport much. I wish PE wasn't compulsory. I'd much rather go to the library and read a book if only they'd let me."

That explained why Debbie's name wasn't on the detention list that Maggie gave her. Either that or Debbie was a very well-behaved girl. "Did you ever watch Bethany play cricket?"

"Not much." Debbie gave a huge yawn to show how distastefully boring she found that activity. "Can you tell Beth I'm thinking of her," she said, seeming unsure of herself again. "Tell her I know she's innocent."

Rose smiled, trying to reassure her. "I won't be allowed to see her, but I'll pass your message on to her mother, so I'm sure she'll get it." Bethany was lucky to have Debbie as a friend. She doubted that anyone else would still be on her side.

Debbie looked at her gratefully. "My mum says you're better at solving murders than the police. Please find out what really happened."

"I'll try." Rose blushed, not realising she'd gained that reputation. She supposed she'd been through more than her fair share of escapades since she moved to Hale Hill. Her enquiring mind—some would say *nosiness*—meant she often became more involved in other people's problems than she intended. She hadn't meant to get tangled up in this mess with Bethany. She'd try to help her, but she couldn't work miracles. And, short of a rather large miracle, Rose didn't see much hope for Bethany King.

Chapter 14

Rose's friend and neighbour, Tanya Hunt, arrived home at the same time as Rose.

Tan gave her a hug. "I hardly ever see you now since I started my new job."

Rose smiled. She was thrilled when Tan recently decided to get out of prostitution and retrain for a more respectable career. She now worked for the hairdresser, Chantal Williamson, in Hale Hill. "Are you enjoying the job?" They climbed the stairs together towards both of their flats.

"I love it." Tan beamed at her. "The hours are regular, I get paid to talk nearly all day, and I finally get to go to college, day release on Wednesdays."

"That's fantastic," Rose said, really meaning it.

"Come in," Tan said when they reached her door. "We can catch up properly over dinner. I'm making spag bog."

Rose didn't need asking twice. Tanya's spaghetti Bolognese tasted amazing, mostly thanks to the sun-dried tomatoes she added to the recipe.

"Everyone at work is talking about that girl who stabbed the teacher." Tanya gathered up some ingredients and began to chop an onion.

"Bethany King." Rose felt sorry for Irina. She'd hate the idea of everyone talking about them, but it came as no surprise to Rose. It formed the sole topic of conversation among her customers in the shop.

"You know her? Of course you do. I forgot that you know everyone who comes in the shop."

"She's a nice girl," Rose said. "Something must have driven her to it."

"Teacher probably abused her then." Tanya started to fry the onion and walked across the kitchen to get some minced beef from the fridge. "Believe me, I'm well aware of what men can be like."

Rose gave a faint smile. Tan's previous career made her well acquainted with the worst kinds of male behaviour. "We can't assume that." The poor man was dead, unable to defend himself from malicious gossip, although Rose berated herself for already assuming the exact same thing. "Bethany hasn't said anything to lead us in that direction."

"Well, if he did anything like that, she'll probably get off, especially with her being underage, so she'd better say something soon."

Rose wished Bethany would start talking. She didn't seem to care about defending herself.

"Maybe there's no reason." Tan read her mind. "Like the Boomtown Rats' song. Maybe she just doesn't like Mondays." She passed Rose a tin of tomatoes. "Open that, will you?"

The tin opened with a ring-pull. Rose removed the lid easily. "It happened on a Friday."

"Can't be that then. Who doesn't like Fridays? Everyone's looking forward to the weekend. Two days off."

Rose had almost forgotten what a day off was. She worked long hours running the Hale Hill Stores. Her son, Jack, was home from uni for the summer. For a short while, he'd taken the pressure off by working part-time in the shop. But now, until Alfie recovered from being shot in the shoulder, Jack worked all his shifts and a lot more besides. It still meant Rose working fairly long hours again. Perhaps, when Jack returned to university, they should get some part-time help.

"I've just remembered. I meant to visit Alfie."

"You can do that after you've eaten. I'm sure he won't be going anywhere. And if anything was wrong, Billie would phone." Tan sat down and poured two glasses of red wine. "Get some of this down, you. You need to relax."

Tan was right. Alfie's daughter, Billie, would have let her know if there was a problem with her dad. "All right, I'll pop out and visit him later." Rose wished she'd bought something to take with her, chocolate or grapes or something. Too late now. All the shops were shut on Sunday evening, and she wasn't opening up Hale Hill Stores specially.

As Rose rang Alfie's doorbell a couple of hours later, she remembered another reason she needed to visit him. His daughter, Billie, was a lawyer. Rose wanted to get her opinion about Bethany's situation.

"Come in. Dad will be pleased to see you." Billie welcomed Rose into her father's house.

"How are you, Alfie?" Rose wished again that she'd bought him some grapes or chocolates.

"All the better for seeing you," he said.

"So you're ready to come back to work, then?" Rose joked.

"No way," Billie said firmly. "He's not going anywhere until I say so."

Alfie laughed. "See what I have to put up with, Miss Bossy Boots here."

"I bet you love it." Rose laughed.

"Do you want a tea or coffee?" Billie asked.

Rose followed her into the kitchen. "How is he, really?"

"He appears to be all right." Billie filled the kettle. "I was a bit worried about the PTSD returning, but probably having me here has taken his mind off everything else. I'm not sure what's going to happen when I go back to New Zealand."

"I'll keep a close eye on him," Rose promised.

"Thank you. I appreciate that."

"You've heard about Bethany King and the stabbing at the local school." Rose changed the subject.

"Yes, that poor girl."

Rose looked at Billie. Most people's sympathies lay with the dead teacher. Yet Billie immediately sided with the murderer. "Why do you say that?"

"She's thirteen. She's just screwed up her whole life. Don't you feel sorry for her?" Billie asked.

"Yes, but most people say she deserves what's coming to her." Rose thought of Jenny Pearce's attitude towards Irina. Billie couldn't have been more different.

"Thirteen-year-old girls don't generally go around murdering people without a very good reason," Billie said. "Not unless they're really evil. You know her. Is she evil?"

The memory of one of Bethany's many visits to the shop flashed into Rose's head. The happy-go-lucky girl of a few weeks ago didn't seem capable of swatting a fly, let alone murdering a grown man. "No, definitely not."

"I thought not. In which case, it stands to reason that this teacher must have done something to her. He might be an abuser. Has to be something big like that to make her resort to murder. So yes, I do feel sorry for her. Part of me hopes I'm wrong. The other part of me hopes I'm right." Billie poured three cups of tea. "It's not my area of law, but I believe something like that could help her get a reduced sentence," she said. "Or even get her off completely. But I'm sure her solicitor knows that."

"The trouble is, Bethany's not talking. She's so traumatised, she'll barely speak a word."

"Will she talk to her parents?"

"She's barely talking to anyone right now." Rose wondered if Bethany's father scared her. From what she'd seen so far, he very much lacked the temperament and social skills to make Bethany open up to him. And he wouldn't allow Irina to visit, although she'd probably fare no better. Irina was a wreck. Mother and daughter would likely spend all their time huddled in each other's arms, sobbing. "Bethany's parents aren't helping," she admitted. "Richard's aggressive and controlling, and Irina's a bundle of nerves."

"I see. Perhaps they should leave it to the professionals. Has she been assessed by a psychiatrist?" Billie pushed a plate of biscuits in front of Rose.

"Bethany's not crazy."

"I didn't say she was." Billie placed the hot drinks on a tray. "Although anything like that might help her defence. She's clearly traumatised. Someone needs to get to the heart of the issue. Why did she kill her teacher?"

Alfie was lying on the sofa when the two women came in with the tray of tea. "Billie, you should have opened a bottle of wine for our guest."

"Don't worry, Alfie, I can't stay long. I need an early night."

"And you can't drink wine," Billie said firmly to her father. "You're on too much medication."

Alfie looked forlorn. "Yes, miss." He mock-saluted her and turned to Rose. "She's stricter than my old army major. She gets that from her mother."

Rose gulped down her tea. She didn't want to get stuck in the middle of a family argument. Besides, she hated walking home on her own late in the evening.

Chapter 15

Bill Gizzard stood at the lectern in the middle of the stage, shuffling on the spot for a few moments, waiting for everyone in the vast school assembly hall to settle. He hated this sort of thing. Not the public speaking bit. He regularly took school assemblies and he actually rather enjoyed being the centre of attention. No, it was the pressure of trying to sound caring and sympathetic that he couldn't bear. Some of the pupils, and the majority of the teachers, were still upset over Friday's events. He needed to find some sensitivity to deal with them. Unfortunately, he didn't really possess any of that. In his day, a stiff upper lip was maintained at all times. In his opinion, that worked much better than all this talking and crying that was so encouraged these days.

His audience wasn't settling at all. He needed to stamp his authority on the proceedings. Gizzard banged his fist on the lectern. "Silence." His rich baritone voice permeated the far end of the school hall, with no need for a microphone.

Immediately, everyone stopped talking, and a sea of faces stared upwards at him.

"I'm sure you've all heard by now what happened on Friday," he began. They would need to live on another planet not to be aware of a murder in the school. "The vicious murder of Mr Wyvern in the school gym shocked the whole country. I sincerely hope we will never see such a tragedy in this school again. Taylor Park school does not condone violence of any description, and the school will take steps to ensure that all teachers and students can feel safe here."

He took a breath, scanning the rows of pupils in front of him. They didn't appear to be over-traumatised. Perhaps the handful of pupils who were still upset had been kept at home by their parents today. He was more concerned about the teachers. Some of them knew Grant Wyvern well, and his sudden death had hit them hard. A few of them asked for time off this week. That wasn't an option. The kids needed normality. He needed his staff to step up and carry on as usual.

"I realise some of you are angry, some of you are frightened, and many of you are grieving the loss of a popular teacher. Rest assured you are safe in this school. And, if any of you are struggling, we have a specialist grief counsellor, who will be available all week if you wish to talk. She will be taking over the deputy head's office from ten o'clock this morning, so please make use of her services." Retaining this woman for the week would cost the school a small fortune. He'd be miffed if she didn't earn her keep, however superfluous he considered her to be.

"Mr Wyvern was an exceptionally talented and dedicated teacher." He glanced across at Helen Trenton, seated at the edge of the stage with some of her colleagues. She worried him most of all the teachers. Apparently, she and Grant had been close. But she seemed to be holding it together so far.

He continued. "Since joining Taylor Park, he built the PE department into a force to be reckoned with." He wished some of the more academic teachers would do the same with their own departments, then they might get a few pupils into Oxbridge each year. That would be a far more desirable achievement. "The performance of our sports teams has improved tremendously during this time, particularly the year eight girls' cricket team, who have delivered stellar results this term." When Gizzard was young, girls would never be allowed to play cricket. The fact that the girls' results totally overshadowed that of the boys provided a constant source of embarrassment to him.

A hand flew up at the back of the hall, catching his eye. He couldn't quite see who it belonged to, the child being obscured by taller children sitting in front of her. The girl stood up and started to speak before he got the chance to shut her down. He saw her clearly now. Sharon Something-or-other. He failed to remember her surname.

"Sir, who's going to take over coaching the girls' cricket team now?" Shaz Fletcher asked.

Mr Gizzard glared at her. If she'd been sitting closer, the look he directed at her would have bored a hole through her head. "Show some respect, girl," he boomed, not daring to use her name in case he'd got it wrong. "It's only been three days. That question is completely inappropriate at this time." He noticed now the girl wore a black armband. What a pity that sentiment wasn't mirrored by her behaviour. She should be expressing her sympathy for Mr Wyvern's demise, not asking ridiculous questions about the cricket team, which in the scheme of things took on an extremely low level of importance. Scanning the hall, he noticed that many of the girls wore black armbands, sporting them like fashion accessories. He noted too that none of the boys seemed to be following the craze.

A shaky voice piped up from the side of the stage. Sally Knight, the other PE teacher in the school. "Sir, I'd be honoured to take over coaching the team."

Gizzard nodded at her. "Thank you, Miss Knight."

"But, miss." Sharon's voice screeched from the back of the hall. "You don't know a thing about cricket."

Miss Knight turned a bright shade of scarlet. "I'll learn," she said. "I'm sure Mr Wyvern would be happy for me to take charge."

Sharon sat down, whispering something to the child next to her.

"No talking during assembly." Gizzard's first instinct was to give her a detention, but he bit his tongue just in time, mindful of trying to be sympathetic under the difficult circumstances.

He wondered if he should say a prayer for Grant, but he didn't know any, other than the Lord's Prayer, and he didn't fully remember even that well-known one. Besides, with so many different religions represented among the pupils, whichever prayer he chose would prompt complaints from some of the parents.

"Let us all bow our heads for a minute's silence while we remember Mr Wyvern." It was a cop-out, but at least no one would complain about that. He realised after several seconds that he'd forgotten to time the minute. Never mind, he would just guess. It wouldn't hurt the kids if it turned out to be a few seconds too long. In fact, he'd wanted to do two minutes' silence, but children's attention spans these days were ludicrously short, and the dignified silence would undoubtedly deteriorate into wholesale whispering if it continued for too long.

"Thank you," he said when he guessed sufficient time had elapsed. "Assembly dismissed."

Chapter 16

Richard parked in his driveway, giving a huge sigh to try to relax himself before he went into the house. The bail hearing had been a disaster. The judge, a crotchety old tosspot, flatly refused bail. It was all over in minutes. Secretly, Richard was pleased. If Bethany really had murdered this teacher, he didn't even want to look at her, let alone have her in the house all day and every day. Then there was the money. Mrs Roberts warned him that bail might be set quite high. She suggested about fifty thousand pounds. Obviously, he would only have to pay the money if Bethany absconded. But he hardly knew his daughter anymore. He had no idea what Bethany might do. What if she ran away? He wouldn't blame her if she did, given the chance. To be honest, he felt like doing the same thing himself.

So the judge's pronouncement came almost as a relief to him, except that now he would have to break the news to Irina. He wished he'd let her attend the hearing. At least then he wouldn't need to have this difficult conversation. She was going to be devastated.

His phone rang before he'd plucked up the courage to get out of the car and face Irina. He answered, listening incredulously to the second piece of bad news to come his way this morning.

"What do you mean, you're letting me go?" Richard fought the urge to throw the phone out the car window. He knew exactly what it meant. At least his boss might have phoned him to break the news personally. Instead, he'd delegated it to some minion in human resources. This wasn't the Monday morning he'd planned, although he'd half been expecting this bombshell since the San Francisco trip.

It was always a risk that he'd lose his job, with a hostile takeover in the offing, but he excelled at his work, so he really believed they'd keep him on. This brutal rejection shouldn't be happening. It was all Bethany's fault. The moment his colleagues saw the item about the stabbing on the TV news, Richard realised he was doomed, even though, at that stage, they hadn't been able to connect the news to him. He cursed himself, yet again, for not keeping quiet about it. As a minor, Bethany's identity couldn't be reported. The company may never have found out. But he'd needed to give a reason for leaving San Francisco several days early. And, when it was so vital for him to attend those meetings, when they needed his expert opinion to assess the financial consequences of the takeover, his excuse needed to be something spectacular for the company director to allow him to leave. He should have made up something else, but he hadn't been his normal self at the time.

"How much notice do I need to work?" Right now, it would be really useful if they put him on 'gardening' leave, standard practice at his company. They never liked to risk anyone downloading any vital information about the business, then going to work for a competitor. Stupid, really. If anyone planned to do that, they'd do it before they handed in their notice.

"We don't expect you back in the office."

Good. That was what he wanted. It would give him time to sort out this mess with Bethany and to search for a new job. "I'll come in and clear out my desk later this week," he said.

"Don't worry. We'll send your stuff on."

They really didn't want him back in the office, not even to say goodbye to his colleagues, not that he'd be able to face them now. Perhaps this was for the best. Even so, Richard felt deflated as if he'd taken a massive punch in the stomach. He'd given that company five years of hard graft. He certainly regretted it now. Perhaps if he'd worked shorter hours and spent more time with his daughter, they wouldn't be in this awful mess.

"How much severance pay will I get?" He found it easy to be mercenary under the circumstances.

The HR officer reeled off an amount. It was too small, much too small. He would need to find another job fast. Was he even employable now? What would happen when his next potential employer found out what his daughter did? Would they throw his application in the bin before they'd even interviewed him? He'd soon find that out the hard way, and he dreaded it. The only thing he dreaded more was telling Irina. Perhaps he wouldn't have to. Perhaps it would be best to protect her until he'd got a new job lined up, until they'd somehow got Bethany home again.

He remembered he needed to tell her about Bethany being refused bail. That was one piece of news he couldn't protect Irina from. He definitely wouldn't tell her yet about losing his job.

Chapter 17

As soon as they finished lunch, Ava led Madison and Shaz out onto the school grounds.

"This heat's unbearable." Ava flopped onto the grass in the shade of their favourite tree. "It's like being in hell."

Shaz laughed. "You should know. Anyway, they reckon it's going to be thirty degrees by the end of next week, and it's the cricket area finals." She brushed a piece of dirt off the grass with her hand before sitting down daintily on the cleanest patch she could find.

"Not much point now, is there?" Madison pulled at a piece of long grass, twisting it around her fingers. "We're not going to win any matches with Miss Knight coaching. She doesn't know anything." She threw the mangled piece of grass away, picking some more. "I wish Mr Wyvern were still here."

"I didn't think you even liked Wyvern," Ava said. "You're always going on about how awful he is."

"Well, I didn't mean it," Madison snapped.

"Ok, calm down." Ava spotted the tears welling up in Madison's eyes. She didn't want her friend to go into a full-blown meltdown. "We're all upset about Wyvern." She put her arm around Madison. "I can't believe Bethany did that to him. She's such a weirdo. I'm glad they've locked her up."

Madison sniffed back her tears, finding a tissue to blow her nose on. "It must be horrible for her," she said. "I could never cope with going to prison."

"She deserves it," Shaz said. "Ava's right. Bethany's a weirdo."

"We need to win the cricket next week. Let's do it for Mr Wyvern." Ava's left leg felt numb. She shifted position on the grass, rubbing her leg vigorously to restore the circulation.

"But Mr Wyvern won't be there to help us," Madison whined.

"Of course he will," Ava said. "He'll be with us in our heads. When you go into bat, you'll remember exactly how he told you to do it. I bet you can hear his voice inside your head right now."

"I suppose so." Madison looked so pathetic, sprawled on the grass, on the verge of tears.

"I know so." Ava sat up. She needed to motivate Madison so she wouldn't fall apart because they really needed to win the area finals. "Every time you run, or go to catch a ball, you'll hear Mr Wyvern cheering you on. It doesn't matter what Miss Knight says. We're still Mr Wyvern's girls. We'll simply carry on playing exactly like he taught us."

Chapter 18

Irina and Richard sat in silence in their living room. The TV was switched on, but Irina didn't have the faintest idea what they were watching. She guessed Richard didn't either. He'd barely looked at the screen. Irina wished he'd talk to her. She'd never seen him like this. The situation with Bethany had hit them both hard.

It devastated her when Richard told her the unexpected and unwelcome news this morning. She'd really thought Bethany would be coming home with him. But as soon as her husband walked through the door, she sensed something was dreadfully wrong. Now, Richard couldn't even look her in the eye. He might feel slightly better if he talked about it. She certainly would. She'd love to talk to him properly, spilling out all her worries about Bethany's future. But every time she tried, he snapped at her and told her to shut up.

Irina stared at the small screen, trying to work out what was going on. It appeared to be some sort of reality TV show, that one in the jungle. She wasn't certain, as she'd never watched the programme before. Richard normally hated this sort of thing, too. The contestants were being forced to eat live bugs, which made her stomach squirm. She got up and switched it off as neither of them was watching it. The silence between them deafened her. Even watching bug-eating might be preferable to this. She closed her eyes and tried to imagine being somewhere else, but the only picture in her head depicted Bethany, covered in blood.

Suddenly, a thudding sound made her open her eyes. "What was that?"

"What?" Richard stretched his arms as if he had just woken up.

"That noise. It came from outside." Irina shivered. The slightest thing made her jumpy at the moment. She was glad to have Richard with her.

"I can't hear anything. Who turned the TV off? I was watching that."

So he had been asleep. He certainly hadn't been concentrating on the TV. Irina got up and switched it back on, turning the volume down, in case she heard the noise outside again. It was getting dark, so she drew the curtains across, starting with the double patio doors next to the TV, then moving across to the other side of the room. The living room was situated in the corner of the house, designed to be dual aspect. The patio doors opened onto the side garden and gave a fabulous view of Brackford in the distance, as they lived at the top of a hill. The large window at the front of the house overlooked the driveway and the front garden.

"What's that?" Irina took a step back. Some sort of gunky stuff slid slowly down the outside of the window. It reminded her of the vile mixture that had been served up with the wiggling bugs on TV. Immediately, she felt a little sick. "Richard, come and look at this, please? It wasn't there before." She stepped away from the window. Her nerves made her stomach churn, even more than watching the bug-eating had done.

Richard finally got up and came over. "That's an egg," he exclaimed as soon as he saw the mess on the window. "Someone's chucked a sodding egg at our window. How dare they?" He quickly pulled on his shoes, which had been discarded earlier at the end of the sofa.

"You're not going out there, are you? What if there's someone outside?" Irina didn't want Richard to get hurt. Most of all, she didn't want to stay in the house on her own.

"Of course I'm going outside, and if I catch whoever threw that, I'll sodding kill them." He ran towards the front door.

Irina froze. They should call the police, but neither of them wanted that. They'd spent enough time with the police this weekend to last them a lifetime.

Richard opened the front door, spotting no sign of anyone in the garden. He ran into the road, looking both ways, hoping to catch someone running away. There was no one in sight. Immediately, he felt cheated. Only a moment ago, he was all fired up and ready to give chase. He would have loved to vent his frustration on the culprit. Instead, he felt let down and miserable.

At least Irina would be pleased that he'd found no one outside. He turned back towards the house. "Bloody hell." He stopped in his tracks. Someone had sprayed the front wall of the house with red paint. *MERDERER*. Ignorant scumbag. They couldn't even spell properly.

He returned indoors, fuming.

Irina came into the hallway to meet him. "Was anyone there?"

Richard smiled. He didn't want her to worry. "No, they've long gone. Nothing to worry about. Go back and watch TV."

He hurried out to the garden shed. No way would he risk Irina seeing that graffiti. He quickly found what he was searching for, a can of black spray paint. He wouldn't take long to spray over that word, then Irina would never see what had been written. He would get contract cleaners in to remove all the paint professionally tomorrow. It worried him that whoever did this might come back and repeat the offence. He couldn't protect Irina forever. Damn Bethany. Right now, he wished she'd never been born.

Chapter 19

Rose took the bus to Irina's house as soon as she finished work. After a busy day, she was tired. It had rained on and off all afternoon, and the clouds overhead remained an ominous shade of grey. As she slogged up the hill from the bus stop, the heavens opened, and within seconds, the rain came lashing down more like a winter storm than a summer shower. She really wished she owned a car. Of course it would be easier if Irina would come to the shop, but after the incident with Jenny, understandably, Irina didn't want to risk a repeat experience.

She did a couple of quick sums in her head, trying to work out if she could afford to buy a cheap car. Since Jack had come home from university for the summer, she'd let him take over a lot of her shifts at the shop, as well as his shifts covering for Alfie while he recovered from his injury. It had freed up some time for her to put more work into her jewellery business. Rose made bespoke pieces of jewellery in her spare time. The business was really starting to take off, with multiple orders from satisfied customers, as well as word-of-mouth recommendations. She'd been earning an extra few hundred pounds each week. As soon as she got home, she'd check her bank balance to see how much she had saved.

Rose was relieved to find Richard's car missing from the driveway. Rose much preferred to talk to Irina without him present, being under the distinct impression that Richard saw her as an interfering busybody. She laughed out loud. Perhaps he was right, but Irina had asked for her help, and it was difficult to say no.

"Come in. You're soaked." Irina ushered her into the kitchen, then immediately left her. She quickly came back and handed Rose a large, fluffy towel. "I'll make you a hot cup of tea."

Rose took the towel gratefully and rubbed it over her drenched hair. "I've spoken to some of Bethany's friends."

Irina broke off from making the tea and turned towards Rose.

"Madison thinks Mr Wyvern's a pervert. Has Bethany ever mentioned any problems with Wyvern?"

Irina gave her a worried look. "No. No, she's never said anything like that."

She looked as if she intended to say something else. Rose waited for her to fill the silence. "It's just…" Irina paused again.

"It's just, what?" Rose prompted her.

"I'm not sure." Irina shook her head. "She's been quiet lately, like she's got something on her mind, but won't tell me. It can't be that, can it? Surely, she'd have told me. My poor baby."

Irina seemed close to tears. Rose didn't fancy her chances of ever getting that warming cup of tea. "It might be nothing. Teenagers go through phases like that, where they don't want to talk to their parents much. Jack certainly did."

"But—"

"Apparently, Madison was having some extra cricket coaching at lunchtime on Friday," Rose said, changing the subject. "She may have seen something when she left." She planned to talk to Madison again soon.

Irina looked puzzled. "Madison doesn't need extra coaching. She's quite good."

"I heard that one of the parents criticised her batting technique at their last match." It occurred to Rose that, if Madison didn't need coaching, perhaps the meeting had been for other reasons entirely. Perhaps Madison's opinion of Grant Wyvern had some truth in it.

Irina swallowed, looking embarrassed. "That was Richard. He got upset that Bethany only made reserve this time. Then the team lost, and he was convinced they would have won if Bethany was playing. He takes these things far too seriously. I hate it when he does that. It puts too much pressure on Bethany. He really laid into Madison, verbally, I mean. He told her exactly what he thought about her batting just because she missed one ball."

"If Bethany was only the reserve, why did you go to watch?"

"She was supposed to be playing because Madison called in sick. But then Madison showed up at the last minute and insisted she was fine to play." Irina sighed. "Richard thought she did it deliberately to upset Bethany."

Rose easily imagined Madison doing exactly that but didn't want to say so. Irina got back to making the tea, so Rose tossed some scenarios around in her head. Was it possible that Madison hadn't wanted to play to avoid Grant Wyvern? Jenny might have persuaded her at the last minute not to let down the team. What if Wyvern was abusing more than one team member? Or might Bethany and Wyvern have argued on Friday? If Bethany's father was pressuring his daughter to perform, but Wyvern had criticised her ability or even threatened to throw her off the team, perhaps Bethany had inherited some of her father's temper and had reacted badly to it.

"Debbie says to send her love to Bethany." Rose remembered to pass on the message. "She doesn't believe Bethany is guilty."

"She's not guilty," Irina snapped back.

They were the only two people in the world to truly have faith in Bethany's innocence. Rose worried that Irina was deluding herself. With so much evidence stacked up against Bethany, Irina would fall hard when the verdict went against her daughter in court. But that day was a long way off yet.

Rose glanced out the kitchen window. The rain had abated. "I should go home before the weather gets bad again."

It was a relief to leave Irina. Rose felt guilty for having doubts about Bethany. She tried to be open-minded, but the evidence so far all pointed towards Bethany's guilt. Her best hope probably lay in proving that there were mitigating circumstances. That led her back to Madison's accusation that Grant Wyvern might be abusing some of the girls.

It puzzled Rose that someone as confident as Madison would show up for an extra coaching session if Wyvern was abusing her. Then again, the incident with Richard King at the cricket match clearly upset her. Perhaps that confidence was simply an act to hide the insecure little girl who lay beneath the surface.

Chapter 20

"Madison," Jenny shouted up the stairs, where her daughter selfishly monopolised the bathroom as she usually did first thing in the morning. "I can't find your sports kit."

Madison ambled down the stairs. She looked as if her eyes were still half shut. She normally needed a bomb underneath her on a school morning to get her moving, but this week she was being particularly bad. Jenny supposed that was understandable. This business with Mr Wyvern and Bethany King had shocked everyone.

"Where's your sports kit? Don't you normally do cricket practice on Tuesdays?"

"It's cancelled." Madison's sullen face told Jenny exactly what she thought of that.

"I thought Miss Knight offered to take over," Jenny said. They'd had a long conversation yesterday evening about Miss Knight's lack of credentials to coach cricket. At least she volunteered, which Jenny pointed out was rather good of her. Madison didn't see it that way.

"She's not starting until next week. She says we can't play cricket today, as a mark of respect to Mr Wyvern. She doesn't know what she's talking about," Madison sneered. "We've got an important match next week. Mr Wyvern would want us to practice so we can win."

That's all Jenny ever heard over the last few days. Mr Wyvern this, Mr Wyvern that. Normally, Madison did nothing but complain about him. Death had elevated the teacher to the status of a saint. "I still need your kit." She'd meant to wash it over the weekend but completely forgot. At least she'd have time to do it now.

"I lost it," Madison admitted.

"Madison! You should be more careful. I can't afford to keep buying you a new kit."

"It's not my fault," Madison retorted quickly. "Someone took it."

"So which was it? Did you lose it, or did someone take it?" Jenny was disinclined to accept either excuse but gave Madison the benefit of the doubt.

"Someone took it, ok? It's not my fault." Madison started to pout as if she were about to cry.

Jenny wrapped her arms around her. "It's all right, darling." There had been enough tears already since Friday. She didn't want any more. Silently, she cursed Bethany King. Jenny wanted her normal, happy daughter back. There was no point in pushing Madison about the missing sports kit. Not right now. She'd phone the school later this morning. If someone took it, let the school sort out the problem.

Chapter 21

"Hey, wait for me," Shaz shouted at Ava's back, running to catch up. They often met up on the walk to school as they both lived nearby and came from the same direction.

Ava turned and waited for her friend. "Hurry up, Shazza. You're going to make us both late."

"Like you care." Shaz admired Ava Browning, precisely because she wasn't afraid of anyone.

"Did you bring your stuff for cricket practice?"

Shaz lifted up the bag containing her sports kit. "Are you sure we should be practising today? Miss Knight cancelled it, out of respect for Mr Wyvern, she said."

"That's rubbish." Ava stuck one finger up in a rude gesture of defiance. "We're doing it for Mr Wyvern. He would want us to win next week's area final. Only reason Miss Knight cancelled is so she's got time to mug up the rules for cricket."

"I guess so." Shaz wasn't sure, but if Ava intended to take a stand on this, she would too.

"Anyway, it's only going to be you, me, and Madison."

"How's Madison?" She didn't seem herself yesterday. Shaz wondered if Ava had noticed how Madison nearly burst into tears when they were talking about Mr Wyvern.

"She's fine." Ava stepped sideways to avoid a pothole in the pavement.

Shaz tripped slightly on the pothole, too busy worrying about Madison to concentrate on where she was going. "I'm not sure if she is. Didn't you see yesterday, when we were talking about Mr Wyvern, she struggled not to cry?"

"She'll get over it," Ava said harshly. "He's just a teacher."

"Yeah, but she knew him from before he came to Taylor Park." Shaz realised that Madison had told her the whole story in confidence, but she couldn't stop herself from blurting it out. "You know Miss Trenton is best friends with Madison's mum?"

"What's that got to do with it?" Ava slowed her pace, concentrating on Shaz's story.

"Miss Trenton and Mr Wyvern were engaged."

"Really?" Ava stopped walking abruptly, turning to face Shaz. "What happened? Did Miss Trenton dump him?"

Shaz squirmed under Ava's intense gaze. She knew she shouldn't be telling Ava any of this, but if she stopped now, Ava would hound her relentlessly until she dragged the full story out of her. "Actually, it was the other way round. Mr Wyvern dumped her, and guess what, he did it two weeks before the wedding. Can you believe that?"

"What a scumbag. But I don't get it. Why is Madison upset? She should be pleased. Sounds like Bethany did Miss Trenton a huge favour."

Shaz had thought exactly the same thing. "She's confused." No other explanation made sense to her. "She used to really like Mr Wyvern, but she feels loyal to Miss Trenton."

"Do you think there might have been something going on with Madison and Mr Wyvern?"

"No, of course not. She would have told us." Shaz was certain Madison would have told her, probably asking her to keep it from Ava. She'd blown it now. If Madison found out that she'd broken her confidence and told Ava about Miss Trenton being dumped, she'd never trust her with a secret ever again.

"She saw Wyvern on Friday at lunchtime," Ava retorted. "I know because she texted me, asking me to tell Bethany that Mr Wyvern wanted to see her."

"And did you?"

"Did I what?" Ava stared at her, puzzled.

"Tell Bethany."

"Yes." Ava's face fell as the horrible truth dawned on her. "If I hadn't passed on that message, Mr Wyvern would still be alive."

"It's not your fault," Shaz said. "It's Bethany's fault. You weren't to know what would happen."

"I just wish it hadn't happened."

Shaz gave her friend a hug. For once, Ava Browning looked vulnerable. "You should tell the police, about the text, I mean."

Ava pulled away from the hug. She shook her head violently. "I ain't no grass." She snorted with derision and headed off towards the school, walking so fast that Shaz struggled to keep up.

Shaz remained silent. Ava would calm down soon. She certainly hoped so, or it was going to be a long day.

Chapter 22

Richard jumped up to answer the doorbell as soon as it rang. "Try to keep out of the way, love. They won't stay long." Irina had been worried about someone coming to view the house, but the estate agent insisted they were really keen. It might be for the best if they sold up now. If the worst happened, they may be forced to move away and rent somewhere for a while until he found another job, which would dictate where he wanted to live. Finding a job would be much easier if he was flexible on location. They wanted to sell anyway and, whatever happened now, he didn't see how they'd be able to stay living in this area for long.

He opened the door and forced a smile at the stranger. "Mr Jones?" On reflection, Richard wished he'd asked the estate agent to conduct the viewing. What if this man worked out who they were? What chance would they have of selling the house then?

"That's right. I've come to view the house."

"Come in. Do you live locally?" Richard really wasn't in the mood to make small talk, but he wanted to sell the house. Now that the idea of moving away from Brackford had planted in his brain, he couldn't get things moving quickly enough.

"No, but I need to move to this area for work." Mr Jones followed him into the kitchen.

"It's a lovely area. Very good train links to London, and Brackford is nice, too. Do you have children? There are some good schools in the area." Damn. Whyever did he mention schools? He could hardly recommend Taylor Park. Mr Jones was sure to have heard of it. It had been all over the news in the last few days.

"No, no kids yet. What about you?" Mr Jones asked.

"No, me neither." No way would he admit to having a daughter. He resolved to stop asking personal questions. The potential for it to backfire didn't bear thinking about. "The kitchen gets the sun in the morning, and there's a lovely view of Brackford Woods."

Mr Jones walked around the kitchen, ignoring the view out the window and instead opening all the cupboards. "Can I see the bedrooms, please?"

"Of course." Richard tried to hide his annoyance that his carefully made plan of showing him everything downstairs first would have to be changed. He led the way up the stairs, hoping Irina hadn't gone to their bedroom to keep out of the way.

"This is the main bedroom." He poked his head in to check Irina wasn't lying naked on the bed or anything equally embarrassing. "It has an en suite with a whirlpool bath and a shower." Perhaps he would take a long bath when Mr Jones had gone. The whirlpool jets might help his muscles to relax.

"I hoped it would be bigger." Mr Jones sounded disappointed.

Richard's face fell. So far, the buyer seemed a lot less keen than the estate agent led him to believe. If he wanted a bigger bedroom, why had he bothered showing up? The estate agent must have given him the brochure with all the dimensions. "We find it very roomy," he said.

Mr Jones seemed to have lost interest in this room.

"Would you like to see the other bedrooms?" Richard asked.

"That would be great."

Richard led him out onto the landing. He opened the door to the next room, ushering Mr Jones inside. "This is the smallest bedroom." It was quite roomy for a third bedroom, in Richard's opinion, with space for a pull-out sofa bed for visitors, as well as Richard's desk and computer, and Irina's sewing table. A partially cut out dress pattern was strewn across the table next to the sewing machine. Richard wondered whether the dress would ever get finished now. "I use the room as a study, and my wife uses it as a sewing room."

"It's certainly multipurpose." Mr Jones scanned the room slowly, taking everything in. "It's a three-bedroom house, isn't it? Can I see the third bedroom?"

"Of course." Richard led him along the landing. The sign on the bedroom door turned him cold. He'd forgotten about that. *Bethany's Room, Keep Out.* He opened the door quickly, hoping Mr Jones hadn't spotted the name. If he stood in front of the open door, he might be able to hide the incriminating sign. He certainly hoped so because right now he longed for the floor to swallow him up. He pulled himself together. Bethany's name wasn't public knowledge. At least, not unless you had a child at Taylor Park school. The name would mean nothing to Mr Jones.

Mr Jones' interest perked up. "Interesting choice of decor. I suppose we could paint over it."

Richard recalled major arguments with Bethany over her choice of colour. She'd wanted to paint the room black. In the end, he'd agreed to purple simply to end Bethany's constant whining on the subject. Black wasn't normal, was it, especially for a girl? Had that been an indication that she'd been having murderous thoughts? If only he'd got her some help back then, things might have turned out differently.

He was so deep in thought, he hadn't noticed Mr Jones using his phone to take photos of all of Bethany's stuff. "What are you doing?" He definitely wasn't taking photos of the whole room, which might be forgiven if he was genuinely interested in buying the house, especially if he'd got pictures of the other rooms he'd seen. "Stop that." This was Bethany's personal stuff. He had no business taking close-up photos of it. Richard tried to grab the phone off of him, but Mr Jones moved too quickly.

"Whoa, calm down, mate. I need some photos of the house to show the wife."

"I'm not your mate. Get out of my house." Richard's blood was close to boiling point. It was so obvious now. Mr Jones was a sightseer, wanting a tour of the house where Bethany lived. He bet Jones wasn't even his real name. How could he have been so stupid? "I said, get out." Richard put his fists up. He'd like nothing more than to punch the man's face in, but he'd settle for him leaving.

"Ok. I'm going." Mr Jones ducked past Richard and made a run for the stairs.

Richard followed him out, keen to make sure he left the premises as quickly as possible. As soon as the wretched man drove off, he would phone the estate agent and take the house off the market.

Rose was tidying up the shop, ready to hand over to Jack for the Monday evening shift. She liked to leave everything as perfect as possible. At nineteen, Jack was a typical teenage lad. He didn't do tidying, so Rose always had a job on her hands to clear up after him when she came in first thing in the morning. She never complained. Jack was a godsend at the moment, and the customers loved his friendly manner and winning smile.

The bell over the shop door tinkled and Rose looked up, expecting to see Jack.

"You'll never guess what I found out this afternoon." Maggie Mahoney started talking the moment she walked through the doorway.

"What?" Rose was intrigued by Maggie's excitement.

"Helen Trenton, remember, the teacher that you met on Friday? Well, she only used to be engaged to Grant Wyvern."

"Used to be? What happened?"

Maggie leant up against the checkout. "They both used to work at another school before they came to Taylor Park."

"Really, which one?"

"Clayborne Grammar, in Basildon," Maggie said.

"Ok, go on."

"They split up only a couple of weeks before the wedding. Can you imagine? It must have cost them a fortune, and the embarrassment…"

"Yes, it must have been awful for them," Rose said. "Which one of them broke it off?"

"Nobody knows." Maggie shrugged her shoulders. "Apparently, Helen claimed that she did, but Grant said it was him. I suppose neither of them wanted to admit they'd been dumped at the altar."

"Not quite at the altar," Rose said.

Maggie laughed. "Near enough. All the guests would have arranged to come, and everything would have been booked and paid for by then, the venue, the catering, the dress. They must have lost a forrrr-tune!" Maggie waved her hands in horror.

"I expect it must have been very upsetting for them, too." Rose sympathised with the couple. It had been devastating when she and Philip split up after twenty years of marriage, even though the split was entirely his fault. She wanted to kill her husband when she discovered him conducting a long-term affair with her supervisor at work. Not that she ever would have done it. She wondered if Helen Trenton felt like that, too. Immediately, she shook the thought from her head. If they'd hated each other that much, they wouldn't have ended up both taking a new job at the same school.

"Yes, I'm sure it must have been," Maggie said.

"It's funny that they both moved to the same school. Did they get on well at Taylor Park? I suppose it's a large school, and they were working in different departments."

"Yes, Helen teaches English."

"So did they get on?" Rose asked.

"As far as I'm aware. I only saw them together a couple of times in big staff meetings. They weren't even sitting together, so it's hard to tell."

"No rumours of any trouble between them?" Rose knew that Maggie didn't miss much. If the two teachers had been at each other's throats, she probably would have heard about it. She wondered how she might arrange to bump into Helen Trenton again. She certainly had a few questions to ask her now.

"It must be a bit of a shock, having all this thrown at you when you haven't been in the job long." Rose sympathised with her friend. "Apart from the murder, how's the job going?"

"It's good." Maggie smiled. "I shouldn't say this, but Friday's drama has helped to relieve the tedium. The job isn't normally so exciting. For instance, this morning, I had Jenny Pearce phone me up. Gave me a right earful, she did. Madison lost her sports kit last week. Reckons someone stole it. As if anyone would want to take smelly sports clothes. The fuss she made about it, you'd think it was all my fault."

"So you'd rather have a violent murder than an irate parent?"

"Absolutely, yes." Maggie laughed.

Rose doubted that the dead teacher's family would think the same way, but maybe she should cut Maggie some slack. Grant Wyvern had been a colleague, albeit not a close one. Joking about it probably helped Maggie to cope with the shock of what happened.

Chapter 23

DI Paul Waterford reversed his Audi into the last remaining space in the mortuary car park. Nigel Todd had finished the post-mortem on Grant Wyvern. He'd postponed this one as there had simply been no one available to do it over the weekend. It should be an open and shut case, so other post-mortems had taken priority. There seemed to have been a spate of unexplained deaths over the weekend, keeping the on-call pathologist busy.

"I'm going to grab a coffee." Nigel greeted him as he walked into his office. "Do you want one?"

"That depends on whether you want me to look at the body." Even after several years of watching post-mortems, the smell still made Paul queasy. He found it best not to eat or drink until afterwards.

"No need," Nigel said. "Milk, no sugar, right?"

Paul smiled. "Perfect."

He wished they could find a way to get through to Bethany King. She'd barely spoken since she'd been arrested. The poor girl seemed terrified, and understandably so. Even though she'd confessed, he wouldn't be doing his job properly if he didn't find out why she'd done it. Wendy appeared to be making progress with her but at a painfully slow pace. They'd charged Bethany with the murder and planned to transfer her to a young offenders' institution as soon as they found a vacancy somewhere suitable. Moving Bethany would undoubtedly slow progress even more, especially if she found it difficult to settle in somewhere new.

Nigel soon came back and handed him a coffee. "Careful, it's hot."

"So what have you discovered that you couldn't tell me over the phone?" Paul didn't usually mind coming to visit Nigel for post-mortem results. In fact, he preferred it. He got much more information in person than he would have done via a phone call, when there wasn't always time to think of the questions he needed to ask.

"Normal healthy male. Nothing much to find, except the knife injuries. The slightly odd thing about it is that there were three stab wounds, two of them very close together in the chest, but the third one at an odd angle in his side, right here." Nigel pointed to the side of his waist.

"Could Wyvern have seen Bethany coming and moved, so she missed her target?"

"That's highly unlikely." Nigel rubbed his brow thoughtfully. "That wound was fairly superficial compared to the other two. Yes, he would have bled out eventually, but he could still have overpowered a teenage girl in the first few minutes. Grant Wyvern was a well-muscled man, looked like he spent a lot of time doing weights in the gym, and I do mean a *lot* of time. Abs to die for."

"Ok. I get the picture."

"One of the other wounds went deep, with the entry point disturbed, probably when the knife got pulled out. With the knife removed, he would have bled out in a couple of minutes. But that wound in his side is odd."

"What do you mean, odd?"

"I mean exactly that." Nigel took a pen in his right hand. "If you're stabbing someone multiple times, you're likely to have vaguely similar wounds close to each other." He demonstrated stabbing the pen through the air in front of him. "The perpetrator gets into a rhythm, so to speak, and repeats the same movement."

"So, the odd one?" Paul prompted.

"The angle's wrong. It's like someone has stabbed upwards from below."

"Someone short, or someone sitting down?" Paul suggested.

"They'd have to bring the knife upwards and from one side." He thrust the pen forward to show Paul what he meant. "It's an unnatural way to stab someone."

Paul wondered if any method of stabbing someone would be natural. "So the two smaller wounds wouldn't have killed him?"

"They might have finished him off eventually, if the bleeding wasn't stopped, but he's a fit, strong man. If the first attempt was one of those shallow wounds, he could easily have fought off his attacker, especially if it was a teenage girl."

"So you're saying the first wound was the deep one?" Paul looked puzzled. "Why would they then add a couple of minor wounds afterwards?"

"Exactly. If it was a mistake, they would have stopped after the knife went in the first time. And a frenzied attack wouldn't have petered out like that on the second and third stab. Maybe by the ninth or tenth, yes, if they'd gone that far. But not the second and third. It doesn't make sense." Nigel took a gulp of his coffee. "Anyway, you've got the perpetrator in custody. Ask her to explain her state of mind when she did it."

"I wish," Paul said. "She's hardly said a word since we arrested her."

"It's the shock, I expect." Nigel shook his head sadly. "She probably thought it was a good idea at the time. Now she's realised the rest of her life is screwed. It's a lot to take in, even when you're older, but at that age…"

"Yes, you're probably right." Paul hoped Nigel's observations would give them some ideas to help get Bethany talking. Perhaps she needed reassuring that everything would be all right. Except that would be a giant, barefaced lie. It would be a long time before everything was all right again in Bethany King's world.

"Have you seen this, guv?" Wendy McKay shoved her phone towards DI Waterford as soon as he got back to the station.

"What is it?" He took the phone from her, unsure what he was looking at.

"It's the Brackford Bugle website. They've got pictures of Bethany King's bedroom."

Paul swiped through the photos. The first one gave a good view of the purple walls. The second showed one of the posters stuck on her wall, of some famous rock star that apparently all the girls liked. Then a simple photo of Bethany's bed, with its dark-coloured duvet. For a normal teenager, the choice of decor didn't seem out of the ordinary. He guessed the local newspaper would be making a big thing out of the dark colours, trying to relate it to her state of mind. They'd already put that question to a psychologist, who stated that it didn't provide evidence of anything. "We've already searched the room and found nothing of any use." He skimmed through the report. Mercifully, the newspaper didn't mention Bethany's name.

Wendy grabbed the phone and swiped back to the photo of the singer. "That's Luke Stone," she said.

"So...?" The name sounded familiar, but Paul wasn't exactly sure who Luke Stone was.

"Don't you remember, last year. Luke Stone was tried for murder?"

A lightbulb flicked on in Paul's brain. Yes, he did remember. Stone was tried for stabbing one of his old teachers. "He got off, didn't he?"

"Yes, he had a good lawyer, but everyone thought he'd done it," Wendy said. "The newspaper's making out that Bethany copied him, and because he got off, she obviously assumes she will too."

"Wow." Paul read the paragraphs below the photos, more thoroughly this time. "You've spent the most time with her," he said. "What do you think? Is that possible?" Surely, no normal person would stab a teacher simply because their favourite singer committed a similar crime. He didn't buy it. There must be more to it than that.

"The thing is, Stone stabbed that teacher three times," Wendy said.

"He was proven innocent," Paul interrupted.

"Yes, but three times, guv? The same as Bethany."

Paul flinched. The press didn't have that piece of information yet. Perhaps they should hold off releasing it as long as possible. If he remembered correctly, the prosecution in the Luke Stone case reported that Stone murdered the teacher because he'd abused him at school. Could anything like that have happened to Bethany? Because, so far, he was completely stumped as to a motive. And wanting to imitate her favourite pop star wasn't it, whatever the Brackford Bugle inferred.

Chapter 24

Richard King tossed the Brackford Bugle into the bin in disgust. He didn't want Irina getting hold of it and reading those lies. How were they allowed to print such rubbish? He shook his head sadly. It would only be a matter of time before this ridiculous theory got into all the tabloids. He blamed himself. How could he have been so stupid, showing that journalist around the house? If only he were here now, Richard would punch his face in. Didn't the man realise Bethany was his little girl? Of course he realised. He simply didn't care.

He walked up the stairs to Bethany's room, opening the door cautiously as if she might be in there and tell him off for not knocking. At first sight, everything looked innocent enough. The dark purple wasn't ideal. Thank God he hadn't let her paint everything black. But even if he had, wasn't that perfectly normal? When he'd been a teenager, he'd gone through a goth stage for a full year. It didn't do him any harm.

Quietly, he looked in on Irina, who was still in bed, having taken a sleeping pill last night. How would he ever manage to protect her from the press? This was just the beginning. He had the horrible foreboding that things were only going to get worse. What would they do when the case went to trial? He wasn't sure how to cope with it. Quietly, he closed the bedroom door. With a bit of luck, Irina would still be asleep when he got home.

He had an appointment this morning with an employment agency in central London. He couldn't waste any time in looking for a new job as the insultingly low payoff he was getting from his old employer would rapidly disappear, especially if he had to fund overpriced solicitors for Bethany for long. Normally, he was good at interviews, but today his nerves kicked in early. He pulled himself together. No one at the agency could possibly realise who he was, and even if they did, he wasn't Bethany. He hadn't done anything wrong.

Irina woke up with a jolt. The red luminous digits on their alarm clock said 11:15. She hadn't intended to sleep that long. The sleeping pills the doctor prescribed must be too strong.

She rolled out of bed and pulled on her dressing gown before slowly walking into the bathroom. Gradually, that blissful few minutes between sleep and total alertness, when her life was still perfect, and her daughter was still at home, gave way to the stark reality of Bethany's arrest as she remembered the tragic event that took place on Friday.

As she splashed some water on her face and cleaned her teeth, she thought she heard noises outside. She turned off her electric toothbrush to listen. There it was again.

Back in the bedroom, the noises grew louder. Perhaps something was going on next door. They were always having work done to their house. She tried to blot out the sound while she got dressed. The kitchen, situated at the back of the house, would probably be quieter.

Irina was right. The kitchen was a haven of peace, too peaceful. She took her cup of tea into the living room and turned on the TV, switching the channel to Food Network. Cookery programmes were her favourites, and at least on this channel, there would be no news, no horrible reminders of Bethany's predicament.

She picked up a framed photo from next to the TV. Richard's brother had taken it. A younger Bethany was walking between herself and Richard. A tear came to her eye. The three of them were holding hands and smiling. What had gone wrong?

She turned her attention to the TV. Who'd have thought it possible to make a cake by mixing melted ice cream and flour? She tried to concentrate, but it was useless. She needed to get out of the house. Some fresh air and a walk to clear her head might make her feel better. The stress of worrying about Bethany must be to blame, although the sleeping pill couldn't have helped because she didn't normally feel this fuzzy-headed.

Irina kicked off her slippers and found some shoes. She simply had to get out of the house. If she kept her walk short, there would be less chance of meeting anyone.

As she opened the front door, Irina blinked in astonishment, trying to focus on the scene in front of her.

"There she is." A shout came from the crowd of people standing in her front garden. It didn't take more than a couple of seconds for her to slam the door shut and lock it firmly. She shrank back from the door, resisting the temptation to run to the back of the house. Taking a deep breath, she steeled herself to peer through the spyhole in the door. She gasped at the sight outside. It was as she'd seen it in those brief seconds when the door was open, only worse. There must be at least two dozen people milling around in her front garden. She squinted through the spyhole, but it distorted her view, making it impossible to recognise any of them, although she thought she'd recognised Jenny Pearce when she'd opened the door.

The sounds of people talking drifted through the closed door, but she couldn't make out what they were saying. She wanted to tell them to go away and leave her alone but would never pluck up the courage to open the door again. What were they doing here? It must be connected with Bethany, but didn't they realise that Bethany wasn't here? She couldn't stay any longer listening to them moving around outside, so she fled to the relative safety of the kitchen. Her phone lay on the worktop, charging. Quickly, she dialled Richard.

Richard didn't answer. What to do now? She couldn't cope with this on her own. She scrolled down her list of contacts. Rose Marsden's number came directly after Richard's. Rose would know what to do. Irina dialled her number, willing her to answer because she simply couldn't do this on her own.

Chapter 25

"What's going on, Mum?"

Jack looked annoyed. Rose guessed her son had probably still been in bed in the middle of the morning, but she needed him to look after the shop for her.

"I'll only be a couple of hours." Maybe a bit longer if she missed the next bus and needed to walk. She'd forgotten how far away Irina lived.

"It sounded urgent. What's up?" Jack tossed his uncombed hair out of his eyes. Rose noticed that he'd done up his shirt buttons out of sync, too. He'd certainly perfected the just-got-out-of-bed look.

"It's Irina King. It sounds like she's got a crowd of people outside her house." They were probably journalists. The press was bound to be after the story. "She can't get hold of her husband, and she's terrified to be on her own, so I said I'd pop over."

"Are you sure you want everyone to see you siding with a murderer's mother?" Jack asked.

"She hasn't done anything wrong. It's not her fault. I expect it's a bunch of journalists harassing her. Someone needs to tell them to go away."

Jack laughed. "Well, she's picked the right person. I'm sure you'll tell them exactly where to go. But seriously, Mum, be careful."

Rose hurried out to catch a bus to the other end of Hale Hill.

Chapter 26

A crowd of people spilled out of Irina's front garden as Rose walked up the hill from the bus stop. She tried to count them, but they kept moving around, and the front garden wasn't even in full view yet. There must be over thirty of them. It came as no surprise that Irina felt intimidated. Rose was too.

As she got closer, she recognised a few of them. They weren't all press. In fact, she wasn't entirely sure that any of them were journalists. What on earth were they doing here, apart from trampling Irina's flower beds and dropping litter on her driveway? A couple of them were pressing their faces up against one of the front windows. Someone else rattled at the side gate into the garden. Another person crouched by the front door, shouting through the letterbox. This wasn't a crowd of journalists. It was a mob.

She wished now that she'd insisted on Irina calling the police when she spoke to her on the phone. But she'd flatly refused. Rose didn't entirely blame her for that. She'd probably had enough of the police in the last few days and never wanted to see a police officer ever again. But this was worse than she'd imagined. Rose considered turning around and walking straight home, phoning the police on Irina's behalf, but that would be the coward's way out. She stared at the crowd of people. Jenny Pearce stood next to the house, with Madison right beside her. What were they doing here? And Ava Browning had her face pressed against Irina's window. Shouldn't she and Madison both be in school? She recognised a few other people, all local residents. It made Rose angry to see everyone turning against Irina at a time when she most needed their support.

Rose clenched her fists and marched through the group of people towards the front door.

"Excuse me." Rose pushed past a couple of women blocking her route and stretched over to reach the doorbell. "You'll get your nose stuck if you stay there any longer," she snapped to the old man peering through the letterbox.

He got up, glaring at Rose blackly.

Rose heard the key turn in the lock. To be on the safe side, she planned to dive inside and lock the door behind her as soon as Irina opened up. She addressed the crowd of people. "You should all go home. Leave the poor woman alone. It's not her fault, and you should all be ashamed of yourselves for harassing her."

The door opened a fraction. "It's ok. It's me," Rose said. The gap became larger. Rose quickly slipped inside, not waiting for a response from any of the crowd behind her. "Lock the door," she urged Irina.

Irina didn't need telling twice. She slammed the door shut as soon as Rose stepped inside. "I'm so glad you're here. I was so scared."

"Why don't we sit down with a cup of tea and decide what to do," Rose said calmly.

Irina tried phoning Richard again while Rose made the tea. It would be best to warn him about the demonstrators in the garden. There was still no answer. She couldn't even leave a message.

"Where's he gone?" Rose placed the steaming cup of tea in front of Irina.

"He's seeing an employment agency. His company is being taken over and he wants to leave."

"When will he be back?" Rose asked. Richard really needed to re-evaluate his priorities. Planning a career move in the middle of his daughter's major crisis struck Rose as a crazy idea. He should be focusing on Bethany.

"He didn't say, but I don't suppose he'll be too long."

"Have you heard anything more about Bethany since yesterday?" Rose hoped Bethany's solicitor had made some progress already.

"No. It's hard to get any information about what's going on."

Rose wondered if that was completely true, or whether Richard was being selective about how much he revealed to Irina.

Richard still hadn't arrived home by the time they'd finished their tea, but at least Irina seemed more relaxed. "I'm going upstairs to check if they've gone." Rose would get a better view from the upstairs windows without the protesters noticing her.

"I'll come with you," Irina said. "I don't want to stay down here on my own."

Rose only suggested it as an excuse to nose around upstairs on her own. "You'll be ok in the kitchen." The protesters would be mad to try to break into the house with both of them here. Irina would be perfectly safe downstairs, but Rose understood her fear. As she walked towards the kitchen door, Irina glued herself to Rose's side like a shadow.

Before they could head upstairs, Irina's phone rang.

Irina tugged at Rose's arm. "Please, can you answer that?" She stared at Rose imploringly. "I don't want to speak to any strangers."

"It's probably Richard," Rose said.

"No. It's the landline. Richard never phones me on the landline. Please, Rose."

Rose headed into the living room and picked up the phone. She didn't understand why Irina couldn't have simply let it ring out. The caller would get bored, eventually. "Yes."

"Mrs King?"

"Who is this?" Rose asked.

"This is Detective Constable Wendy McKay from Brackford police. I couldn't get hold of your husband. I'm phoning to say that we're going to interview Bethany again this afternoon. Is one of you able to be present at three o'clock? Otherwise, we can appoint an appropriate adult for Bethany."

"Yes, someone will be there." Rose needed to get back to Irina, so she didn't waste time explaining who she was. Wendy obviously didn't recognise her voice, despite meeting her a couple of times a few weeks ago in connection with those awful prostitute murders.

Rose found Irina in the front bedroom. "Come away from the window," Rose advised, skirting around the edge of the room so she could peep around the curtain and avoid being seen. There were still plenty of people outside, although she was sure the numbers had dwindled. She stepped away from the window. "Richard's going to get a shock when he comes home. It's a pity he won't answer his phone."

They returned to the safety of the kitchen. "I'll stay until Richard gets back," Rose promised, hoping that wouldn't be too long.

Richard revved the engine of his black four-wheel-drive Porsche in frustration. Three traffic lights in a row had turned red on him. He just wanted to get home. Fat chance of that, at this speed. A car like this should be flying along, not crawling in heavy traffic. What a waste of a decent car. Not that he would have it much longer. His ex-employer was sending someone to collect the car later today.

The interview with the agency hadn't gone well. The woman interviewing him had a son who attended Taylor Park school, and she recognised his name immediately. She spent half the interview asking him personal questions about Bethany, none of which he answered, and the other half informing him that, under the circumstances, his prospects might be difficult, at least until after the trial, as that would inevitably take up a great deal of his time. Then the woman had the nerve to tell him that she would be uncomfortable recommending him to any of her clients and he should try other employment agencies. Apparently, no one wanted to employ the father of a murderer. Richard gave a despairing laugh. Did they believe he had the family gene, that he might be a murderer too? The way he felt towards the interviewer right now, perhaps he did possess the murderous gene. She shouldn't be allowed to write him off like that. It was blatant discrimination. Unfortunately, he wasn't aware of a law that specifically said employers couldn't discriminate against families of killers and, if he made a big deal of it, he would only draw more attention to himself and Bethany.

He stopped the Porsche, indicating right, waiting for a break in the traffic so he could turn onto his road. The stream of cars coming towards him seemed never ending. His thoughts drifted to the coming months. What would they do for money if he couldn't get a job? He cursed Bethany. The fees for her lawyer would rapidly bleed their savings dry, and it looked as if he'd need to take a big pay cut to stand any chance of employment. He started doing the calculation in his head of how much he'd need to earn to cover the mortgage and other essentials.

At last, he spotted a gap in the traffic. He gunned the Porsche into action, swinging the car across the road. Nearly home. He'd earned a stiff drink but not before lunchtime. He wasn't ready to stoop that low yet.

Seconds later, he slammed his foot on the brakes. "What the...?" Who were all these people in his front garden? His mind had drifted off, working out the cost of their monthly bills, so he'd nearly run one of them over. The car skidded slightly before the ABS braking system kicked in. Richard watched the scene in slow motion as a bunch of scruffy-looking people scattered in all directions. He couldn't stop himself from slamming his fists on the steering wheel. Bloody journos. They must be. He wished he had run them over.

"What the hell are you doing here?" he shouted at no one in particular as he got out of the car, slamming the door angrily.

"We're protesting." A big chunk of a man with long brown hair stepped in front of Richard.

Richard resisted the sudden urge to punch him. "Well, go and protest somewhere else," he snapped. He reconsidered hitting him, but, weighing up the odds, decided he'd come off worse in a fight.

"We were hoping you'd go somewhere else instead, mate. Your family's lowering the tone of the neighbourhood. You need to move house."

The sun glinted on his glossy hair, which was pulled back tightly into a ponytail.

Richard found himself wondering which shampoo the man used to make his hair so shiny and tangle free. "We're not going anywhere. Now shove off, or I'll call the police." He would almost be better off if they were journalists. At least then, he might be able to make some real money selling his story. But protesters? People demonstrating against him in his own front garden. He wasn't going to stand for that. He stepped around ponytail-man and made his way towards the front door, worried now about Irina. If she'd tried to leave the house this morning, all this would have terrified her. He speeded up, desperate to check on her. If they'd hurt her, he'd... He didn't know what he would do. Wanting to inflict violence, and actually doing it, were two very different things. If only Bethany had realised that.

He locked the door behind him as soon as he was safely inside.

"Irina, I'm home," he called from the hallway.

Irina ran out from the kitchen and flung her arms around him, almost knocking him off balance. "I was so scared. I'm glad you're here."

Richard was about to hug her back when Rose Marsden appeared in the kitchen doorway.

"Richard." She nodded at him. "Irina asked me to come over because she was frightened of being on her own. She wouldn't let me phone the police, but I think you should."

"Why didn't you phone me?" he addressed Irina, ignoring Rose.

"I phoned twice. You didn't answer."

Richard sighed. He'd forgotten he'd switched off his phone for the interview. He needn't have bothered. The whole morning was a waste of time. "Sorry, love," he said.

"Please don't phone the police," Irina begged.

"I have to." If anything happened. If these so-called protesters damaged anything, the insurance company would want to be reassured that he'd taken steps to protect the property.

"On Friday, at the police station, they made me feel constantly guilty. I don't want to feel like that again."

"If they try to blame you for this, I'll be having words with them. We need them to make these people stop. Otherwise, they'll come back tomorrow, and the next day, and the next."

Rose gave a slight cough. "I'm going home, Irina. Phone me if you need me."

"She won't." Richard scowled at her. "She's got me to take care of her."

Rose decided to walk home, being uncomfortable waiting for a bus within view of the crowd outside the Kings' house. Richard hadn't been particularly grateful to Rose for helping Irina, so she was glad to get away. Under the circumstances, she didn't really blame him for the way he acted. They must both be going out of their minds with worry.

She was still surprised by Bethany's confession and wondered if the police might have bullied it out of her, but DI Waterford was a good sort. She'd had dealings with him before and found him very fair-minded.

It's my fault he's dead. It was a slightly odd way to confess. Wouldn't she be more likely to say: *I did it*? It occurred to Rose that she may have meant something slightly different. Did she encourage someone else to kill Grant Wyvern? Or perhaps she witnessed the stabbing and did nothing to stop it.

Rose was less than halfway home when the bus passed her. What a pity she hadn't waited for it. Then she could be home in a few minutes. Never mind. She needed the exercise, and it wouldn't do Jack any harm to mind the shop a little longer. He'd earn extra money for his travel fund.

Her mind wandered back to Friday. Bethany was caught red-handed, literally, with the knife in her hand and blood on her clothes. Rose questioned again whether she might be overthinking things. The simplest explanation usually proved to be the right one. Perhaps, for Irina's sake, she wanted to believe the best of Bethany. If only she could talk to her.

Suddenly, she remembered. That phone call. She'd completely forgotten to tell Irina about it. She'd been so focused on the crowd of protesters outside the house that the phone call completely slipped her mind. Then Richard arrived home and was less than welcoming, all but throwing her out of the house. Someone needed to show up at the police station to support Bethany. She checked her watch. Two thirty already. They were due to interview Bethany at three. Quickly, she phoned Irina. No one answered.

In the distance, a bus chugged up the hill towards her. Without hesitation, she ran across the road towards the bus stop. All the buses on this road went to Brackford. It would stop right outside the police station.

A few seconds later, she was sitting in a bus, heading towards Brackford. She just hoped DI Waterford would let her stand in for Bethany's parents. And she hoped Richard wouldn't kill her for doing so. The opportunity seemed too good to miss.

Chapter 27

Rose asked for DI Waterford when she arrived at Brackford police station at two minutes to three. He came downstairs to meet her.

"I'm here for the interview with Bethany King." She avoided looking Waterford in the eye. "Her parents can't get here in time, so I'm going to fill in as the appropriate adult, if that's all right with you." None of what she said was a lie. She wouldn't mention it was her fault that neither Richard nor Irina King could make it, that neither of them were aware of the interview taking place.

"Yes, I suppose so." Waterford smiled. "It might make Bethany open up a bit more, not having her parents present." He led the way into a large, empty interview room. "Do you want to wait here? We'll join you shortly. Bethany is still in discussion with her solicitor."

Rose sat down and surveyed her surroundings. This room was a step up from the stark, functional room she'd expected. A large beige sofa took up most of one wall, and the carpeted floor gave the room a warmer, homelier feel. Rose recalled hearing something about a 'soft' interview room. This must be it. No doubt they were trying to put Bethany at ease.

A few minutes later, the door opened, and a bunch of people piled into the room: Bethany, a professional-looking lady, who Rose surmised must be the solicitor, DI Waterford, and DC Wendy McKay.

Bethany sat on the sofa next to Rose. Rose smiled at her, receiving a faint glimmer of recognition before Bethany shied away from her eye contact to gaze down at the floor in front of her. At least she didn't question her presence, but that did nothing to calm Rose's nerves. She shouldn't really be here, and when Richard found out, she'd probably regret her bloody-minded cheek.

DI Waterford made the introductions for the benefit of the recording. The solicitor's name was Veronica Roberts. Rose made a mental note of it, in case anything occurred to her later that might help Bethany's case.

"How are you today, Bethany?" Wendy McKay spoke softly, smiling constantly.

Bethany grunted without saying anything. Her appearance shocked Rose. Everything about her seemed unkempt, and the worry etched on her face aged her by at least ten years. But the way she rocked from side to side, refusing to engage properly with anyone, upset Rose even more than her physical appearance. She appeared to be severely traumatised, hardly surprising under the circumstances. Even so, Rose didn't expect her to be this bad. No wonder Irina was so worried about her daughter.

"We'd really like you to tell us how you feel, Bethany, so we can help you," Wendy continued.

Bethany opened her mouth as if to speak, then thought better of it.

"How about I ask you three questions? Is that ok with you?"

Bethany nodded, almost imperceptibly.

The silence in the room was oppressive. Rose wondered if they should try playing some music, anything to relax Bethany a bit. This atmosphere would make anyone tense.

"Ok, here's question number one."

Rose held her breath, not wanting to disturb the silence that punctuated Wendy's questions.

"How did you feel on Friday morning?" Wendy looked at Bethany.

Bethany continued to stare at the floor.

It wasn't an easy question to begin with. If Wendy asked her that same question, Rose would have taken several minutes to give a very complicated answer. She could only imagine how twisted and complex Bethany's answer would need to be, if she even remembered Friday in her current semi-fugue state.

"You only need to tell me in a few words. One word even. How did you feel on Friday morning?" Wendy prompted.

Bethany raised her eyebrows a fraction, making her forehead wrinkle, but still said nothing.

"Were you happy, bored, angry?"

"You're leading my client." Veronica Roberts banged her fingers on the keys of her laptop.

Rose wondered what she was typing.

"Shall we try question two, Bethany?" Wendy continued to smile, not seeming to notice that one of her three questions had been completely wasted. "How did you get on with Mr Wyvern?"

The room fell silent again, waiting for Bethany to answer. She lifted her head a fraction. "Ok," she mumbled.

Rose wondered if she dared ask DI Waterford if she could speak to Bethany alone after the interview. Perhaps the girl would be more likely to talk one-on-one. Bethany offered no further explanation. Wendy's second question had been wasted, too. She was asking the wrong questions.

"Bethany, where did you get the knife?" Rose blurted the question out, unable to help herself.

Paul Waterford glared at her angrily. He looked as if he was about to admonish Rose when Bethany spoke.

"It was already there."

Chapter 28

Rose stared at Bethany, who quickly reverted to gazing at the carpet. No one else in the room seemed to react to what Bethany said.

Wendy carried on, after a stern glare at Rose, which either meant that she wanted Rose to stay quiet and not interfere again, or she wished for Rose to burn in hell eternally. Rose wasn't quite sure which.

"Bethany, why did you stab him three times? Did you think the first wound hadn't killed him? Is that why you stabbed him deeper and deeper?"

The room fell silent. Bethany didn't look likely to say anything else.

Rose hadn't known about the three stab wounds. That was bad news for Bethany. The stabbing may not have been pre-meditated, but it must have been a frenzied attack. That would definitely count against her.

"Bethany?" Wendy prompted gently.

Bethany had shut down. Any further questioning would be pointless.

Rose leaned towards her. "Bethany, if there's a reason why you did this, you need to tell us so we can help you." Out of the corner of her eye, she noticed Wendy about to speak. DI Waterford raised his hand to stop her. Rose ignored them and carried on. "I'm sure there's a very good reason. You can tell me."

Bethany looked up, momentarily catching Rose's eye. "I thought..." Bethany paused.

Rose stretched across the table and squeezed her hand. "It's all right, Bethany. You're doing great. What did you think?" Rose kept her voice calm and soothing, despite her natural instinct being to give Bethany a good shake and tell her to get on with it.

"I thought it would help. I didn't mean to." Bethany burst into tears.

Mrs Roberts stood up. "My client's distressed. Can we stop for the day, please?"

DI Waterford nodded. "Interview suspended at three forty-seven." He switched off the recording.

Bethany's words played over and over in Rose's head during the bus journey home. Whatever had she meant? Was she referring to stabbing Grant Wyvern? But that wouldn't have helped him. What could she have done that might have helped him? Rose drew a blank.

As Rose walked towards Hale Hill Stores, she realised she'd completely forgotten to phone Jack to tell him she'd been delayed.

She'd turned off her phone to avoid being interrupted during Bethany's interview, although she admitted to herself it was more from the worry that Irina or Richard might phone her. She noted three missed calls from Jack. She would have some explaining to do.

"Mum, where have you been? I've been worried about you." Jack rounded on her as soon as she entered the shop.

"I'm sorry. I should have phoned. I've been at the police station with Bethany King."

"They let you visit her?" Jack looked surprised.

"It was meant to be one of her parents," Rose confessed sheepishly, "but they weren't there."

"And you were? Why? What were you doing at the police station?"

"It just sort of happened." Rose decided not against admitting to Jack how she'd taken advantage of her momentary forgetfulness. It was lucky she had been present. At least now the police knew the stabbing had been a spur-of-the-moment action on Bethany's part. The fact that she hadn't taken the knife into the gym with her proved the murder wasn't premeditated, a big point in Bethany's favour.

Jack looked at her suspiciously as if he doubted her explanation.

"You should go home," Rose said, wrestling with her guilt. "I'm sure you've got other things to do." Jack hadn't planned to spend the last few hours working.

"I'll come back at seven."

"Thank you." Rose was grateful. The shop stayed open until ten o'clock, six days a week, only closing early on Sundays. She never felt safe working the late shift. So, while Alfie recuperated from his injury, Jack worked every evening. He wasn't getting much of a social life. Rose's guilt piled up higher. Somehow, she'd make it up to her son. On the other hand, the relief that his working hours prevented Jack from mixing with the wrong people easily overrode her guilt. Only a few weeks ago, his two dubious new friends had almost killed him.

As soon as Jack left, Rose's thoughts returned to Bethany. Why had there been a knife in the gym? Someone must have taken it in. And, if not Bethany, who else would? No one would expect to find a knife like that in a school gym. Apparently, it was a Swiss army knife, not the sort of implement a teenage girl would own. The metal detectors were supposed to prevent knives from getting into the school. So where did it come from?

They should have put some of these questions to Bethany as soon as she'd told them about the knife. But Wendy shot herself in the foot when she promised to only ask three questions. Bethany firmly held her to that promise and refused to speak further, quickly returning to her uncooperative, fugue-like state.

Wendy was furious with Rose, despite the fact that she'd gained them some useful information, more than Wendy herself had managed. Rose wondered what Wendy's third question would have been. No doubt she'd ask it tomorrow.

The old-fashioned bell above the shop door tinkled, signalling a customer entering. Rose smiled as Clint approached her. The elderly man was one of her most regular customers, although definitely not the biggest spender.

"Is everything all right, Clint? You're late today." He normally showed up at 11:00 a.m., like clockwork, not late afternoon.

"Everything's grand, thanks. I went to the protest this morning."

"What protest?"

"The one at Bethany King's house. I saw you there, coming out of the lion's den, so to speak. At least you don't have to solve this murder cos we all know who did it."

Rose hadn't noticed Clint outside Irina's house. She wished she'd got a proper look at all the protesters. How many of her other customers were in Irina's front garden this morning?

"Those protesters are really upsetting Irina."

Clint didn't seem to care. "Well, it serves her right for not bringing her daughter up better. If she'd taught her right from wrong, this never would have happened."

Rose shuddered at the lack of compassion. "Is that what people think?"

Clint laughed. "That, and more. You should see the trolls on social media. I don't really do social media myself, but my granddaughter showed me. She goes to the same school as Bethany King. I reckon she had a lucky escape. It could have been her who got stabbed."

"Perhaps it's best if you don't go spreading these opinions further. There are always two sides to every story. Something must have driven Bethany to do it."

"Yes, but my granddaughter said Bethany was weird. Maybe she did it for fun."

Rose was quite sure that Bethany didn't find anything fun now. "How well does your granddaughter know Bethany?"

"Shaz is in the same class as the King girl."

"Shaz? Is that Shaz Fletcher?" Didn't Irina mention that she used to be one of Bethany's friends?

"Yes, that's her. How do you know her?" Clint asked.

"I don't, but I'd very much like to meet her. Why don't you bring her in one day soon?" If she could talk to Shaz, it might shed some light on Bethany's state of mind and the reason for her horrific actions.

"I might just do that. Anything for my lovely Rose, although you'll be hard pushed to get two words out of her these days. She certainly doesn't talk to her mum much anymore. I suppose that's a normal teenage thing. She used to be such a sweet girl."

Jack showed up at seven o'clock as promised to take over the shop for the last few hours of the evening.

"You look tired," he said to Rose. "Go home and take it easy. I cooked some dinner. I left yours in the fridge so you can heat it up in the microwave."

"Thanks, love." Sometimes, Jack acted like the best son in the world. A nice meal and a good rest in front of the TV would do wonders for Rose's tired feet. "I'm planning to drop in on Alfie on the way home." Rose had been neglecting him since he came out of hospital. At least Billie, his daughter, would be taking good care of him, but Rose wanted to check on Alfie herself. Getting shot in the shoulder was a big deal, and Rose worried about the effect it may have on him. "I won't stay there long. I can't wait to sample your cooking."

Chapter 29

Richard spent most of Thursday morning on the phone with employment agencies. The answer was always the same, merely dressed up differently each time. We don't have anything that fits your skill set at the moment, but we'll be sure to inform you as soon as we do. Reading between the lines, Richard assumed they meant that their clients didn't want to employ a murderer's father. If this carried on for long, he could lose everything he'd worked so hard for because of his daughter's stupid mistake. This wasn't his fault, dammit. Perhaps he should search for jobs further afield. The court wouldn't allow the media to release Bethany's name due to her age, so how would the employment agencies realise she was his daughter? If that bitch who'd interviewed him on Monday had phoned around her contacts in other agencies, he'd kill her. Of course he didn't believe any of them when they said that the job market had recently tanked due to the state of the economy. He refused to be fobbed off with excuses.

Irina brought him a cup of coffee. "Have you had any luck?" She put her arm around him.

He shrugged her away, nearly knocking over the coffee as he did so. Irina still didn't know he'd lost his job. He'd made up some reason for giving the company car back, unable to bring himself to tell her the truth. She had enough to worry about already. "I'm going out for a walk." Richard turned his head away from Irina to avoid seeing the disappointment written on her face.

The protesters were back. As soon as he opened the front door, they started chanting in unison. "Out, out, out. Murderers out."

"Get off my property," he shouted, "or I'll call the police." They carried placards today. Some of them weren't polite, but at least it beat graffitiing the house. He still hadn't got that paint mark removed. There didn't seem to be much point. It would only encourage them to do it again. "I said, get off my property."

The protesters started to drift onto the road. They seemed to have grown in numbers since yesterday. Richard didn't recognise any of them, but then his job meant working long hours. To be honest, he probably wouldn't even recognise his own neighbours. He scanned the small crowd. Most of them were women and children, with a few older people. He didn't think they'd be a big threat to Irina if he left her alone for half an hour. He really needed some fresh air, and a good fast walk to work off some of the anger that these people stirred up inside him.

As he pushed past them, a couple of women separated from the crowd and started to follow him down the road. One of them shoved a microphone in front of him.

"Mr King, Richard, how is Bethany?"

"No comment." He lengthened his stride, his long legs eating up the distance, making the women jog to keep up.

"Has she said why she did it?"

Richard clenched his fists. He'd come out for a walk to work off his tension, not to become even more stressed. He wished Bethany would tell them why she'd done it because he couldn't for the life of him fathom it out. But she stubbornly refused to talk. He stopped suddenly, pivoting round to face the women.

"I have nothing to say." Richard didn't see the camera until the last moment. He pushed his hands up in front of his face a split second after it flashed. "Leave me alone," he shouted. "Leave us all alone." He set off at a run, quickly leaving them behind and ducking down an alleyway as soon as he turned the corner.

He stopped to get his breath back. Was this what life would be like from now on? He wasn't sure he could handle it. He didn't relish the prospect of tackling those protesters a second time when he got home. Perhaps he should phone the police again. With a bit of luck, they'd arrest the whole lot of them before he got back. He reached into his pocket, realising with dismay that he'd left his phone at home.

Chapter 30

Rose finished work early today and handed over to Jack after lunch. She'd promised she would look in on Irina and take her some bread and milk as she had run out, although she didn't see why Richard couldn't do the shopping if Irina was too scared to leave the house.

She decided to walk, needing the exercise as she hadn't found time for her usual morning runs lately. As she trudged up the hill towards Irina's house, it shocked her to see the number of protesters congregated outside. She counted at least twice as many, compared to her last visit. The peaceful protest had escalated into something more frightening, with most of them carrying antagonistic placards and shouting. No wonder Irina didn't want to go out.

For a moment, Rose worried about going past them. She took a deep breath to calm her nerves. There was only one thing to do: march up to the door and ignore everyone. It took some time after she rang the doorbell for anyone to answer. As she heard the rattling of the security chain being unlocked inside, she began to feel vulnerable, despite most of the protesters staying out on the road. She willed Irina to hurry up and let her in.

The moment the door opened, the protesters let rip, some shouting obscenities, and others chanting *out, out, out*. Someone shouted, "murderer's mother." The rest of the crowd took it up, repeating it again and again.

Rose glanced around quickly to see who was winding up the crowd. A bunch of girls were screaming the words and waving at the rest of the protesters to indicate they should shout louder. Rose recognised one of them instantly. Ignoring the half-open door, she marched over to Shaz. "What on earth are you doing? You should be ashamed of yourself. Don't you think these people have enough to worry about without you intimidating them?"

"It's their fault," Shaz said defiantly. "Her parents should have taught her not to murder people."

"Go home," Rose said, "or I'll report you to the school. You're supposed to be unwell."

She walked back to the front door. Irina had shut it again but must have been watching out for her through the spyhole because it flew open as soon as Rose got close.

"Come in, quickly," Irina said. She shut the door and locked it as soon as Rose stepped inside.

"How long have those people been here?"

"They're here all day, every day. The police have been twice, but I don't want the police here, and the protesters come back, anyway, as soon as the police leave. I haven't been out all week." Irina looked to be close to tears. Her eyes were red as if she'd spent much of the morning crying.

"That's awful. Doesn't Richard do anything?" It disgusted Rose that these people got away with making Irina's life hell as if it wasn't hellish enough already.

"He's not here half the time. He's been sitting in on Bethany's interviews. One of us has to be there. He won't even let me visit her." Irina burst into tears. "He says I upset her because I'm too emotional."

Rose gave her a hug. "Has Bethany said anything more?"

"Not much. Richard says she hardly speaks. I keep wondering if she might talk to me instead."

"Is Richard at the police station now?"

Irina nodded.

Rose held up the bag with Irina's bread and milk in it. "I'll put this in the kitchen."

Before she could move, the doorbell rang, followed by a thumping on the door knocker.

Irina froze, looking terrified.

"Maybe it's Richard, forgotten his keys," Rose suggested.

"He's not due back yet, and he never forgets his keys. Can you see who it is, please?"

Rose went to the front door. Most of the protesters were women or pensioners. Even so, she took the precaution of looking through the spyhole first. The man outside looked harmless enough, as far as she could see through the distorted spyglass, but she refused to take any chances. She fastened the security chain on the door and opened it, peering at the man through the small gap.

"Are you Mrs King?"

Rose didn't recognise the man, but she quickly picked up on the underlying current of anger. "Who are you?" Initially, she'd wondered if he might be a journalist, but something about him didn't fit with that.

The man glared at her, looking as if he might explode. "I'm Danny Wyvern. Your daughter murdered my brother."

Immediately, alarm bells rang in Rose's head. She tried to shut the door, but he wedged his foot in the gap. There was no way she could let him anywhere near Irina. She took a second to compose herself.

"Firstly, I'm not Mrs King. Secondly, I'm pretty sure you shouldn't be here. And thirdly, until it's proven in a court of law, you don't know for sure who killed your brother." Rose felt dreadful. She wanted to express her sympathy for his loss but guessed he'd interpret any such condolences as an admission of guilt.

"Everybody knows she did it. Let me speak to Mrs King. Is she here?"

"I'm very sorry for your loss." Rose couldn't stop herself from expressing her sympathy for the poor man, but, despite that, he scared her. She doubted he'd control his anger if he ever came face-to-face with Irina or Richard. "Please leave," she insisted.

"I'm not going anywhere." Danny Wyvern sounded determined. "Mrs King can't stay in the house forever. I'll wait as long as it takes. She needs to understand that her daughter's actions have consequences."

Rose was sure Irina already knew that and hoped Wyvern didn't mean anything sinister by it. She kicked at his foot, trying to dislodge it so she could shut the door. Her efforts were useless. "I'm phoning the police." She pretended to reach into her pocket for her phone, which she knew was in her handbag in Irina's kitchen, but she didn't want to leave this man alone with only the security chain to keep him out. Even though he wasn't a big man, his well-muscled physique would probably break the security chain if he gave the door a hefty shove.

Luckily, he pulled his foot out. "Tell Mrs King I'll be back for her." He spat at the door as Rose slammed it in his face and locked it.

"Who was at the door?" Irina asked as soon as Rose came into the kitchen.

Rose hesitated, unsure whether she should keep Danny Wyvern's identity from her. No, she decided. If this man posed a potential danger, Irina needed to be told, even if it frightened her.

"You're not going to like this." Rose couldn't find an easy way to tell her. "The man at the door said he's Grant Wyvern's brother." She gave Irina a couple of seconds for the information to sink in.

It took several seconds. Her expression turned from puzzlement to horror. "What does he want?"

"I'm not sure. I doubt if he really knows, either." Rose was still trying to work it out. Did Danny Wyvern want retribution? Or did he simply want to understand *why* his brother died? Only Bethany knew the answer to that, and she wasn't saying.

"Is he...? Do you think he might be dangerous?"

Rose didn't think the frightened expression on Irina's face could get any worse, but it had. She didn't need to answer the question.

"I wish all this would end," Irina said. "I wish I could go back to work and pretend it never happened."

"Perhaps you can. Go back to work, I mean." She didn't think Irina was ready for that yet, but it wouldn't hurt to give her some hope.

"How can I, if I'm too frightened even to leave the house?" She put her head in her hands in despair. "Richard never wanted me to work. It looks like he's going to get his own way, after all."

It seemed to Rose that Richard King usually got his own way. "I wish I didn't have to work." She realised instantly that her statement was untrue. She'd be bored stiff.

"When Bethany first started school, I got so lonely stuck in the house on my own all day. I don't need to work as a cleaner. Richard earns plenty of money. It's not even the best job, but the people are lovely and I get to talk for a few hours a day. Besides, I like cleaning. What am I going to do with nothing to get me out of the house?"

Rose often wondered why Irina kept her job at the hospital for so long. She realised how lucky she herself was. When she first split from her husband, Philip, working in Hale Hill Stores saved her. She had people to talk to all day, and she made some good friends, too. Perhaps she should appreciate that more.

Irina calmed down slightly. Even so, Rose didn't see how she could leave her until Richard came home. They really should report the Wyvern brother to the police. He needed warning off. The police might talk to him before anything happened, before he did something they all might regret.

Suddenly, a banging on the front door startled them. A loud rattling noise followed. Irina jumped. The terrified expression returned to her face.

Rose ran into the hallway. "Sorry," she called out. "I left the chain on."

Richard peered through the gap, cursing loudly.

She closed the door to remove the chain, tensing as if plucking up the courage to let a rabid dog enter the house.

"It's bad enough having to deal with all that lot outside," Richard snapped. "But I can't even get into my own house now."

Rose stepped back to allow him in. "We had a visit from Grant Wyvern's brother, Danny. That's why the chain was on."

"What the hell did he want? He shouldn't be coming here. He'd better not be making trouble."

"He threatened to harm Irina. She's very upset. You should report it to the police before something happens."

"I think you should go home and stop interfering. I need to talk to my wife."

Rose couldn't wait to get out of there. "I'm just leaving. I only waited for you because Irina was frightened." Even though Richard must be extremely stressed, he ought to be more polite. She was trying to help. At least she'd given him her opinion. If Richard chose not to listen, he'd only have himself to blame and, if Danny Wyvern attacked him, she wouldn't shed any tears. She hoped that Irina would be all right.

Richard kicked his shoes off and slouched on the sofa. "I've had just about as much as I can take from Bethany. She barely says a word. She's not even trying to help herself. The stupid girl is wasting everybody's time."

"She's frightened," Irina said. "Wouldn't you be?"

"Yes, and I'd be explaining like crazy what happened and why it wasn't my fault."

Irina sat down next to him. "Perhaps we should both visit her tomorrow."

"I'm not sure that I want to go at all. I feel like washing my hands of her. I'm paying a fortune for her solicitor. She charges by the hour, you know. Bethany is costing me an arm and a leg, and it's completely unnecessary. She needs to start talking soon before we run out of money." Richard shook his head. That might happen a lot sooner than Irina realised. He couldn't bring himself to tell her about the state of their finances, not yet. That would mean admitting he'd lost his job, and he wasn't ready to do that. Thanks to Bethany, their lives were falling apart.

"You can't give up on her." Irina pleaded with him. "Let me make you a coffee. You'll feel better when you've relaxed."

Richard stood up. A cup of coffee wouldn't fix anything, and it certainly wouldn't help him to pay the bills. "If you want me, I'll be upstairs in my office." He didn't need Irina fussing over him. Maybe with some quiet time alone, he'd come up with a brainwave, something amazing to get them all out of this awful predicament in which Bethany had landed them.

Richard sat at his desk and switched on the computer. There was no point in looking for jobs. He'd already exhausted that avenue for this week. Nothing new would be posted online until Monday now. It would be more productive to spend his time researching cases like Bethany's. Irina was wrong if she thought he'd given up already. Whatever happened to Bethany would impact his own life, and Irina's. He'd be proactive and find a solution to this mess before Bethany sucked them both under with her.

He clicked on the internet icon. Immediately, he found himself staring at a large picture of himself.

"What the...?"

The photo must have been taken on this road. He recognised the house in the background, about four doors down from here. In the photo, he held his clenched fists in front of him as if he was about to punch someone. The memory of his encounter this morning slowly returned. The reporter. She'd flashed a camera at him when he left the house for a walk. They'd deliberately used the photo completely out of context to make him look bad. He hadn't been preparing to punch someone—although, if that reporter walked into the room now, he certainly would—he'd been putting his hands up to block his face from the camera. What a pity he hadn't been quicker.

Richard looked down at his hands now. They'd formed themselves into fists, exactly like the photo. His shoulder muscles had tightened and pain ripped across his back. He needed to do something to get rid of this tension.

He clicked on the photo, noticing the headline, *Has This Man Raised A Killer?* Were they allowed to post rubbish like this? It didn't take long for him to scan the report. There was no mention of him or of Bethany. The report was a general piece discussing whether poor parenting helped to turn children into murderers. Clearly, whoever wrote it didn't have kids. Didn't they understand how difficult parenting was? Didn't they realise how many hundreds of other influences a child got subjected to every day? Other children at school, television, internet: they all conspired to make any attempt at parental control completely ineffective. They were monsters that swallowed your children whole, then spat them back out as unrecognisable baby monsters who played a totally different game from the one you thought you'd started with them.

A stabbing pain in his temple made him shut his eyes against the bright light from the screen, and he slumped over his desk with his head in his hands. None of this was his fault. How could it be? How much worse could things get? A small voice in his head told him it might get very much worse. This was only the beginning.

Chapter 31

"What have you got for me, Kevin?" DI Paul Waterford wanted to get home at a reasonable time today. He hoped Kevin wasn't bringing him trouble.

"It's Danny Wyvern, guv. I've been doing some digging." Kevin looked pleased with himself.

"Go on." Since Paul had taken Kevin under his wing earlier this year, he was turning into a good detective. He was glad he persevered with him instead of trying to get him transferred.

"Turns out he's an environmental activist. He's been arrested plenty of times, but nothing has ever stuck. The closest we got was last year, when he assaulted someone during a demonstration at that toxic waste site in Deacon Road. But the victim dropped the charges the next day, so we had to let him go."

"Interesting," Paul said. "Keep an eye on him. He's already made threats against Irina King. But I can't see how else he's wrapped up in this, aside from being the victim's brother."

"Do you want me to bring him in?"

"Not yet. Until we've got some evidence, best that he doesn't know we're interested in him."

"Yes, guv."

Chapter 32

Paul Waterford sat in his office, trying to make sense of the Bethany King case. The background checks into Grant Wyvern had come up with some interesting stuff. Rose Marsden suggested he contact Wyvern's previous school, Clayborne Grammar. It turned out he'd been accused of molesting a young girl. He'd been suspended for two weeks, but the investigation found no proof, and he'd always denied the accusation. He'd left that school a few months later to go to Taylor Park.

Mud sticks, and Paul guessed it had been impossible for him to continue teaching at Clayborne Grammar school. Or perhaps he'd run away for another reason. If he'd got away with it the first time, sooner or later, Wyvern would try the same thing again. And if he'd picked on Bethany, that would explain everything because something big must have happened to cause Bethany to snap like that. Paul wished she'd tell them. They'd tried everything, short of asking her outright. And, if they did that, any good lawyer would accuse them of leading the witness.

Paul glanced at his watch. He'd promised to meet Clarke at Brackford hospital in an hour for her first scan. No way could he risk being late. He still had some serious making up to do. Over the last few days, he'd tried really hard to summon up some enthusiasm about becoming a father. Both of them wanted children. He should be overjoyed right now. But this case constantly cast a shadow on that joy. The daily interviews with Bethany were increasingly harrowing, and every new piece of information rendered him even more terrified of bringing a baby into the world.

He didn't usually get so emotionally involved in a case, but this case was unlike any other he'd dealt with before. He took a deep breath, telling himself not to be so stupid. Any child lucky enough to have Clarke as a mother would grow up absolutely fine. He needed to stop worrying and enjoy the moment. And the sooner he wrapped up this case, the sooner he could get on with his personal life. He'd do the best he could for Bethany King, but he mustn't let this case destroy him.

The only person who'd got anything useful from Bethany was Rose Marsden. He could hardly ask her to sit in on all the interviews instead of Bethany's father. But Richard King completely lacked patience and seemed to wind his daughter up more than anyone else.

Perhaps he could engineer a meeting between Bethany and Rose, something informal that appeared to happen by chance. If the two of them could have a proper chat outside of the official interviews, he bet Rose would get the complete story out of her. He'd have to set it up soon because Bethany would be transferred to the juvenile detention centre any day now. They had finally managed to find a suitable place for her.

Chapter 33

Jenny Pearce was the last person Rose expected to come into the shop. After the upset between her and Irina a few days ago, Rose imagined Jenny would be too embarrassed to show her face so soon.

She walked straight up to the checkout. Rose forced a smile.

"I came to apologise." Jenny looked sheepish. "I shouldn't have upset Irina the other day. It's not her fault what Bethany did. Will you tell her for me, please?"

Rose wondered why Jenny didn't apologise directly to Irina, but perhaps that was a step too far. "I suppose I could, when I see her. She hasn't been in the shop since. She's too worried about the protesters outside her house. If you really want to help her, then persuade them to stop." She knew Jenny was one of them. Was she being too subtle, or should she point out that Jenny herself was responsible for Irina being terrified to leave her house?

"I'm sorry." Jenny's face was swamped with guilt.

Rose wasn't sure if Jenny's apology was for upsetting Irina in the shop or protesting outside her house. She changed the subject. "How's Madison?" She'd given Jenny something to consider. Maybe it would make a difference.

Jenny shook her head. "She's not taking this business with Mr Wyvern well. Helen is really worried about her."

"Helen?"

"Helen Trenton. She's a teacher at Taylor Park, but she's a good friend, so she knows Madison well. She used to live next door to us until a couple of years ago."

"That's nice that she can keep an eye on Madison at school," Rose said. "Why is she so worried?"

Jenny sighed. "Apparently, Madison's been difficult at school this week. It's hardly surprising, is it?"

"Was she particularly fond of Mr Wyvern?" Rose got the impression when she'd spoken to Madison that the girl didn't really like the teacher much.

"I'm not sure. He coaches the girls' cricket team, so she sees a lot of him. They're doing ever so well this summer. There's a good chance the team will make it to the national finals." Jenny beamed with pride. "At least, there was a good chance. Not much hope now that they've lost their coach. I expect that's partly why Madison's so upset. She's excited because they've nearly qualified for the championships. There's just one more match to go. Once she sets her heart on something, she takes it very badly when it doesn't work out."

"Madison came into the shop at the weekend. I got the impression she didn't like Mr Wyvern." If Madison had expressed her opinion to her mother about Wyvern being a pervert, Jenny gave no indication of it.

"She certainly didn't use to like him." Jenny shrugged. "But that was because of Helen. He and Helen were engaged, you know. The rotten scumbag dumped her two weeks before the wedding. Can you believe it? What sort of man would do that? I shouldn't say this, but I'm not sorry he's dead."

"That must have been hard for Helen. I wouldn't blame Madison for being upset with him for doing that," Rose said.

Jenny laughed. "I don't think it was all sympathy for Helen. My diva daughter was going to be a bridesmaid. She was really looking forward to it and Helen had let her pick out the bridesmaid's dress."

"That must have been disappointing."

"Disappointing? That doesn't begin to cover it. Madison was inconsolable. The bridesmaid's dress was only hired, so she never got to wear the dress. I'm not sure if she ever completely forgave Grant for that."

"And what about Helen? Did she ever forgive Grant?" It couldn't have been easy with the two of them working at the same school, seeing each other every day. Had Helen wanted him dead?

"Helen's moved on. I'm sure Madison has too."

"I'm sure she has," Rose said. "Children are much more resilient than you think." She hoped she was right about children being resilient. Never mind Madison. Bethany would need all the resilience she could muster to get her through the coming months or years, and she didn't appear to be bearing up very well so far. "I'm sure Irina would like it if you dropped in on the way home to apologise in person."

Jenny backed away a couple of steps. "I don't think I could do that. What if she doesn't want to see me? Please would you talk to her for me?"

"Of course I will." Why did everyone always expect her to do their dirty work for them? It would do Jenny good to have to grovel for Irina's forgiveness. It didn't look like that would happen anytime soon. At least her conversation with Jenny had been enlightening, giving her several things to think about. If only she could work out what they all meant.

Chapter 34

Paul Waterford sat at his desk, trying to make sense of the Grant Wyvern murder case. He wrote down what they knew so far.

Bethany confessed, and all the evidence pointed to her, but they had no idea why she did it.

Helen Trenton had flagged up with the headteacher that same morning that Bethany's behaviour was becoming a concern. Was it possible Grant Wyvern was abusing her?

Wyvern had been accused of molesting a girl at his last school, but nothing was proven.

Helen Trenton had been engaged to Wyvern. He broke it off before the wedding.

Bethany had only been made reserve in the girls' cricket team. Was that really enough to make her murder the teacher in charge?

Paul screwed up the piece of paper and lobbed it into the waste bin.

His gut feeling told him Wyvern must have done something to Bethany to provoke such a huge, out-of-character reaction, but he had no proof. If only Bethany would tell them. Rose Marsden was coming in to talk to her, strictly off the record. Rose was good with people, and Bethany knew her. Perhaps she could get the teenager talking when everyone else had failed.

Rose arrived at the police station promptly. Paul led the way to Bethany's cell, embarrassed and disgusted that she was still being held here. A police cell was no place to detain a child, especially at weekends, with the custody suite full of noisy drunks. She'd been here far too long. No wonder she'd withdrawn into herself and refused to talk. But, until now, they had been unable to find a place at a juvenile detention centre. The nearest one they'd found with a vacancy was over two hundred miles away, too far for her parents to drive every day, and definitely too far for Paul and his team to continue the slow interview process. It would be far better to move her to a local institution. Thankfully, it looked as if a vacancy would come up in the next few days at a place less than ten miles out of Brackford.

"How long will I be allowed to talk to Bethany?" Rose asked.

"I'm not sure." Paul shouldn't really be doing this, not without the permission of Bethany's parents. If he weren't so desperate, he'd never resort to bending the rules like this. "Twenty minutes at most. Might be less." If either of the parents showed up, or if the DCI got wind of his stunt, he'd have to pull Rose out quickly. He'd already warned the custody sergeant, who luckily owed him a favour.

He unlocked the cell. The loud clunking noise of the lock, that sound that made grown men despair when the door banged shut behind them, sounded particularly poignant to Paul, mindful of the cell's occupant.

"Bethany, you've got a visitor," he said, smiling to make his voice sound more cheerful.

Bethany was slumped on the bed.

"Will you be all right if I leave you?" he whispered to Rose.

Rose nodded. Paul gave her a final smile, then locked them both in.

"Bethany, hi, it's Rose. Can I come and sit next to you, please?" Twenty minutes wasn't long to make an impact, especially if Bethany wasn't in the mood to respond.

Bethany glanced up.

Rose gave her warmest smile. "I've come to help you."

Bethany shrugged her shoulders, almost imperceptibly.

"Would you like to get out of here? I bet you'd love to go home, see your mum and dad."

"Dad's angry with me."

Rose took her hand and squeezed it. "He's angry with himself, love, because he hasn't managed to fix everything yet." Richard King hated not being able to control everything. "But he still loves you." Rose certainly hoped that was true.

"When can I go home?"

The sinking feeling in the bottom of Rose's stomach, knowing that it may be several years before that happened, made her nauseous. It wouldn't help to tell Bethany the truth now. She'd find out soon enough.

"We need to understand what happened. As soon as you tell us everything, you'll be one step closer to going home."

Bethany started to cry. "It's horrible in here. I hate it. I want to go home now," she whined.

Rose put her arm around Bethany and gave her a hug. Even if the police were to let her go today, which was highly unlikely to happen, this experience had taken its toll on her already. It might take many months of counselling even to begin to return her to normal. "Well, why don't you tell me everything, then the police will check what you said to make sure it's true, then you'll be able to go home. Why won't you tell them, Bethany? What are you frightened of?"

Bethany erupted in a fresh flood of tears.

"Bethany?" Rose prompted her gently when the tears began to subside.

"I... I saw it on TV once, but I only remembered after, then it was too late."

Rose hugged the shaking girl tighter. "What did you remember, Bethany?"

"I shouldn't have pulled the knife out. That's why he bled to death. If I'd left it, they could have saved him."

"So you didn't mean to kill Mr Wyvern? That's good, Bethany." Her remorse, and the fact that she didn't intend Mr Wyvern to die, would count in her favour and get her a reduced sentence.

Bethany shook her head violently.

"It's ok, Bethany. That's good. Now, can you tell me why you went to the equipment store in the gym?"

"I was looking for Mr Wyvern."

A giant knot formed in Rose's stomach. Had Bethany gone purposely to stab her teacher? "Why were you trying to find him?"

"Because he was looking for me. He wanted to see me."

"How do you know that?"

"Someone told me."

"Who told you, Bethany?" As far as she knew, no one ever admitted to sending Bethany to the gym.

"I can't tell you. She'll kill me if I tell on her."

A loud *thunk* startled Rose as the heavy lock on the door clicked open. Paul Waterford stood at the door. "Sorry, Rose, you have to leave."

Rose put her hand up. "Just five more minutes." She needed to find out who sent Bethany to find Mr Wyvern.

"Now," Paul said firmly.

"Don't worry, Bethany. It will be ok. You simply need to tell the police everything," she said as Paul ushered her out of the cell.

Paul locked the door behind them.

"I was making progress," Rose said. "Please, can I go back in?"

"Richard King has shown up. Someone's bringing him here to see Bethany. We need to hurry, or he'll see you. I'll take you to my office, so you can debrief me. Then I'll smuggle you out when Mr King is with Bethany. If we get a move on, he'll never find out you've been here."

"Unless his daughter tells him." They both knew that wouldn't happen.

Paul led Rose up some stairs and ushered her into his office. "Stay here until I get back," he ordered.

Rose took the time to gather her thoughts. It really sounded as if Bethany only meant to wound Wyvern, but then why were there three separate stab wounds? And would she have inflicted a fourth if she hadn't been interrupted? Even if she'd left the knife in place, he probably wouldn't have survived, not with the other two wounds as well. More importantly, why did Bethany seek out Mr Wyvern? Who was this mystery person who told her to find him? And why was Bethany so scared of her?

DC Kevin Farrier interrupted her with a cup of tea. Paul must have briefed him to keep an eye on her. Rose accepted the tea gratefully despite it being almost undrinkable machine brew.

Paul returned, breathing more heavily than normal, from running up the stairs. "Sorry about that."

"Why is Richard King here?" Rose asked. "I thought he only came to sit in on the interviews."

"He's getting impatient. He's got it into his head that he can make Bethany tell him everything."

"That's awful. I bet Bethany doesn't tell him a thing." Rose was glad she'd been able to talk to Bethany before Richard made her completely clam up.

"He's entitled to see his daughter. Don't worry, I've left Wendy to supervise. She can step in if he starts losing his temper."

"I'm sure Bethany would rather see her mum." Rose wondered why Irina hadn't visited since that first day. No, she knew why. Richard wouldn't let her. He really did like to control everything.

"So what did you talk about?"

Rose took a sip of her disgusting tea, which was even worse than she remembered the last time she'd sampled it. Paul gave her a list of questions earlier to ask Bethany. Rose pretty much ignored them, preferring to see where the conversation took them, rather than trying to force it in a particular direction.

"She seems to think that, if she'd left the knife plugging the wound, then Mr Wyvern would still be alive."

"Even if she'd done that, he lost a fair bit of blood from the first two wounds, and the third one pierced his heart. It's unlikely they could have got him into surgery in time to save him," Paul said.

"But it does mean that she didn't intend to kill him. Surely that must count for something?" Rose hoped that at least it might give Bethany a reduced sentence.

"Probably not much." Paul looked grave. "The fact that she stabbed him three times counts against her, despite her saying she didn't want to kill him. Actions speak louder than words. She must surely realise that stabbing someone like that would be potentially fatal. She's not stupid."

"Poor Bethany." She seemed so remorseful. Was that genuine concern over Grant Wyvern's plight, or was it her own predicament that made her so upset?

"So what else?"

"Someone sent her to the gym to find Mr Wyvern."

"Better than going to look for him off her own back," Paul said. "Who told her? We'll have to check with them."

"She wouldn't say." Rose could have got a name out of Bethany, if only Paul hadn't dragged her out of the cell early. "It was definitely somebody female, if that helps."

"Doesn't narrow it down much. Anyway, no one's come forward to confirm that story." Paul looked sceptical. "Why should we believe her?"

"I don't think she's lying," Rose said. "Whoever told her to find Wyvern, Bethany's frightened of them. That's why she didn't want to say."

"How frightening can they be? I mean, to spend a few extra years locked up rather than stand up to them?"

Rose had asked herself the same question earlier. "I wondered if it could be a teacher." She surely wouldn't be that frightened of a child, but an adult might have threatened her.

"We've already interviewed all the teachers. None of them admitted to that," Paul said.

"They wouldn't, would they?"

"Probably not, so we'll interview them again, but I'm not holding out much hope. Bethany needs to tell us exactly what happened and why. Otherwise, we've got nothing to help her with."

"I'm sure she wouldn't have done it without a very good reason." Rose hoped she was right about that.

"What about my list of questions?" Paul asked.

"I hadn't got round to asking any of them." At least being dragged out of the interview early gave her the perfect excuse. Otherwise, she'd probably be in trouble now.

He sighed loudly. "Perhaps we can try again tomorrow, if she hasn't been transferred by then. We're expecting a place to come up for her any time now. In the meantime, let's get you out of here before Richard King finishes visiting his daughter. I imagine he'll lose patience with her quite quickly."

Paul escorted her down the back staircase. "How do you do it?" he asked.

"Do what?"

He stopped halfway down the stairs and turned to face Rose. "Deal with this. You seem to spend so much time with Irina King. Doesn't it get to you?"

"Of course it does, sometimes. But surely you must be much better than me at coping with murders. I bet you're hardened to them by now."

"This one's different." Paul turned away from Rose's eye contact. "My wife's pregnant."

"That's wonderful news!" Rose smiled at him.

"Is it? What if I'm a lousy father? What if our child turns into a murderer?"

"Of course they won't. Most children grow up to be perfectly all right. Look at my Jack."

"He's turned out well. You must be so proud of him."

"Yes, I am. But what I'm trying to say is that I was never the perfect parent. I didn't get everything right, but Jack still grew up into a lovely young man."

"You must have done something right," Paul said.

Rose laughed. "And so will you. Parenting's hard. You'll make loads of mistakes, but that's ok. You need to stop worrying and enjoy the ride. Happy parents make happy children."

"Thank you. Now, we'd better get you out of here." He turned and carried on walking down the stairs.

Rose followed. "When's the baby due?"

"January. I haven't told anyone yet, so please keep it to yourself."

"Of course I will. Anyway, congratulations, and please stop worrying."

Paul punched in a code to unlock the door leading into the car park, holding it open for Rose to exit.

"You'll make a great dad," Rose said as she left.

Chapter 35

Irina rushed to greet Richard as soon as he opened the front door. "How's Bethany?"

Richard brushed her aside. He'd had to fight his way to his own house through a crowd of protesters, all shouting abuse at him. The police were useless. They should have got rid of them by now, but every time the police cleared them, they came back. "They only let me visit for fifteen minutes." That had been more than enough. She'd spent all her time sobbing, but he knew not to tell Irina that. She'd barely said a word. It didn't help that the young woman detective remained in the room with them. If only he'd been allowed to see her alone, he'd have got her talking, one way or another.

"But does she seem all right? Did she say anything?" Irina bombarded him with questions.

"Let me sit down and relax for a minute. I need a drink."

"I'll get you a coffee," Irina offered.

Richard had been imagining a large glass of whisky, but he supposed coffee would be more appropriate, given that it wasn't even lunchtime yet. Bethany was going to drive him to drink. He seriously wondered how much more of this he could take, especially if the protesters outside his house didn't let up. He still hadn't found a job yet, either. That was also down to Bethany. The seemingly endless rejections sapped his usual confidence. He didn't know what he was going to do. Perhaps he needed to get away for a while. Away from Bethany, away from these protesters, perhaps even away from Irina, who constantly reminded him of Bethany. A couple of weeks away would recharge his batteries. He immediately baulked at the cost. One week. That was all he could afford. One week to take a break from reality and pretend none of this was happening. He needed to do it for the sake of his sanity. He wished there were an easy way to break the news to Irina.

Rose woke up agitated. The red LED digits on her alarm clock glowed 5:17. The first thought in her head was Bethany. She'd gone to bed, churning the problem around in her head, and consequently took a long time to fall asleep. Her brain must have kept churning, but instead of revolving around like a cement mixer, muddling everything up into a big mess, one thing now leapt out at her clearly.

She lay on her back, staring at the ceiling. It was starting to get light outside, so she could see every mark on the white surface.

Was there anything in it, this thought spinning around in her head? The police assumed that Bethany stabbed Grant Wyvern and were focusing on *why* she had done it. To their credit, they were trying hard to find a motive that would reduce Bethany's sentence. That was the professional view. That was what all the evidence pointed towards. Rose shouldn't be ignoring it.

But something Bethany said kept coming back to Rose, again and again, until she simply couldn't let it go. She'd been looking at everything all wrong.

Chapter 36

"What you mean, you're going away? Surely the company isn't making you travel at a time like this?" Irina's face expressed her sheer horror at the prospect of Richard leaving her on her own.

"No, it's not work." Richard immediately regretted telling her that. She'd given him the perfect reason to take off for a week and get away from this mess. He should have simply said his boss insisted he go. He was such an idiot. "I need to get away from here and clear my head. I can't take any more of this. I'm sorry."

"And you think I can take it? I need you, Richard. Bethany needs you. Surely you understand that."

The first tears began to roll down Irina's cheeks, making Richard feel more guilty than he already did. "Then come with me. We both need a few days' holiday." Irina coming with him would mess up his plans. He longed for solitude and a complete break. Taking Irina along would mean that all they talked about would be their daughter.

"Then who will take care of Bethany? We can't desert her, not now. I don't understand how you can leave her." The floodgates opened properly as tears flowed thick and fast.

Truthfully, Richard was worried sick about leaving Irina, but he really needed to get away from here to put everything into perspective. The whole situation was eating him up, making him feel more useless and depressed than ever. He'd be no use to his family if he carried on like this.

"Bethany is moving to the juvenile detention centre in the morning, so it will be harder to visit. We should leave her for a few days to settle down. After all, she's going to be in there for a long time."

Irina flew at him, raining feeble punches onto his chest. "No, she isn't. She's innocent."

Richard took her hands gently, holding Irina's wrists to stop the barrage of punches. "But the evidence shows—"

"The evidence is wrong. Our daughter would never do that. I'm her mother. Do you think I don't know?"

Richard pulled Irina into a hug. It was pointless arguing with her. He didn't know how he could make her accept the inevitable, and she really needed to, or she wouldn't survive the coming months. Perhaps she needed a break even more than he did. He didn't need to be alone all day and night. He'd find his solitude on the golf course. "Come with me. A holiday will do you good."

Irina burst into a fresh flood of tears. "How will it look to the press when they find out we've gone swanning off on holiday?" she said when she got her tears under control.

Richard hadn't even considered that, but he didn't really care. The press had already vilified Bethany, already convicted her in their pages. He didn't imagine how going away for a few days could make anything worse.

"I'm going out for a bit. We both need to calm down." He bent down to kiss her on the cheek. "It will be ok," he said, telling her what she needed to hear, even though he no longer believed it himself. Nothing would ever be ok again.

The protesters continued to march up and down outside. They never seemed to leave now, at least not until it got dark, which was late in the evening at this time of year. Richard hated that they were prisoners in their own house. He and Irina had already stopped using the living room at the front of the house and spent most of their time in the large kitchen/dining room at the back. Richard was thankful that he'd insisted on installing a small TV in the kitchen when they'd first fitted out the room, in case they wanted to watch TV while they ate. They now consumed a diet of daytime soaps and chat shows. Anything to take their minds off Bethany.

He started the car. The noisy engine in Irina's small hatchback made him long for the velvety purr of his company Porsche. He wished he'd negotiated to keep it as part of his severance package, not that he could afford the insurance without a high-paying job.

As he eased the hatchback out of the driveway, the protesters parted like the Red Sea. For a moment, he allowed himself a small fantasy about gunning the engine and mowing down a bunch of the demonstrators. But it was only fantasy, although he understood now how Bethany might have snapped if she'd been provoked enough. He was beginning to feel the same way.

A few minutes later, he eased the car into a parking space outside Hale Hill Stores. He took out his phone. He couldn't take Irina's car to the airport. She would need it to visit Bethany in his absence, assuming she could pluck up the courage to go out on her own. He could get a train to the airport. Now all he needed was to find a cheap flight. He wasn't even sure where he wanted to go. Scotland might be nice. Somewhere remote with a good golf course. But everyone in Scotland would have seen the news. And he wouldn't be able to turn on the TV without seeing the case being discussed on some news programme or other. Perhaps in a different country, they wouldn't take much interest in his daughter's crime. Spain was full of good golf courses. Five minutes later, he'd booked a cheap package holiday in Alicante on his phone. The hotel boasted its own golf course, which would meet his needs perfectly.

Rose was busy stacking shelves when Richard entered the shop. He glanced around. To his relief, he saw no other customers.

Rose looked up as he approached. Richard relaxed, happy to be greeted by a smile instead of the hostile looks he got from everyone else he met.

He got straight to the point. "I wanted to ask a small favour."

"Ask away." Rose's smile dropped slightly. "Is Irina all right?"

No, Richard thought. Irina was far from all right. He ignored Rose and carried on. "I have to go away for a few days." No doubt Irina would fill her in on the details later, probably making him out to be the worst husband in the world. He didn't care what Rose Marsden thought of him. Nonetheless, he decided not to mention anything about a holiday. With a bit of luck, Rose would assume the trip was work-related until Irina disillusioned her, and he'd be gone by then. "I wondered if you would keep an eye on Irina. I'm not sure how she'll cope on her own, and there's no one else I can ask." Since Bethany turned into public enemy number one, their friends had deserted them. His parents lived abroad, and Irina's parents had died several years ago.

"Of course," Rose said. "I can visit after work every day, and she has my phone number if anything urgent comes up."

Richard let out an enormous sigh of relief. Although he resented Rose's interference, he also admired her, the way she stood by Irina and agreed to his request without a moment's hesitation.

"Thank you. Thank you so much." It removed a huge weight from his mind. Of course he'd gone away and left Irina many times, travelling for his job, but this time was different. Thanks to Bethany, Irina needed a great deal of support. He didn't know what he would have done if Rose said no. "I'm leaving tomorrow morning and I'll be away for a week," he told her.

Rose gave him her phone number in case he had any concerns about Irina and couldn't get hold of her. Richard doubted he would use it. He hadn't told Irina he planned to switch off his phone and not speak to her all week. Otherwise, she'd be calling him constantly, and his plan to get away from this mess would be a waste of time and money. He felt less cruel about that plan now, confident that Rose would take care of his wife for him so he could take care of himself.

Chapter 37

DI Paul Waterford and DC Kevin Farrier headed straight to the school administrator's office on Monday morning.

"We need to speak to Helen Trenton." Paul tried to catch her at her home twice over the weekend, but she'd been out both times.

"Why don't you wait here." Maggie Mahoney pointed at the chair in front of her desk. "I'll check her timetable, then I can fetch her for you. You know what kids are like. She'll never hear the end of it if I let you drag her out of class."

Paul didn't know what kids were like, but the more time he spent on this case, the more he worried that he wouldn't be up to the job of being a dad. After Rose Marsden gave him her pep talk, he'd bought Clarke some flowers and spent a very positive weekend, discovering he was genuinely enthralled at the prospect of a baby. But it didn't take much to set his fears going again despite Rose's insistence that he should ignore them.

Helen Trenton appeared a few minutes later. "Inspector." She smiled at DI Waterford and gave a cursory nod towards DC Farrier as she closed the door behind her. "I hope this won't take long. I've left Maggie to keep an eye on my class and I'm not sure she'll cope with them for long."

Paul reckoned that Maggie Mahoney would cope with a bunch of rowdy teenagers rather better than the nervous teacher standing in front of him. "I'm sure it won't take long."

Helen sat in the empty chair behind Maggie's desk. "I told one of your officers everything I could after it happened. There's really nothing I can add to that."

"Tell me about your relationship with Grant Wyvern."

"I don't have one." She answered too quickly. "We were just colleagues." Her hands grasped the edge of the desk.

"I heard you were engaged to be married." Paul watched her reaction. He should make her come out from behind the desk so he could read her body language more easily. But, even with her attempt to hide behind Maggie's computer, Paul picked up on the tension triggered by his question.

Helen gave a nervous laugh. "That was ages ago."

Kevin, who was taking notes, paused and stared at her pointedly. "Not much more than a year, isn't it? So you're over it already and became the best of friends again?"

"I didn't say that. Yes, I'm over it, but we weren't friends. I mean, we were just colleagues. We didn't socialise or anything like that. We..." Helen cut her gabbling short.

"It must have been hard for you bumping into him every day." Paul smiled warmly, trying to put her at ease to encourage her to talk further.

"Like I said, I'm over him. We really didn't see much of each other. I teach English. Grant teaches..." She corrected herself. "Grant taught PE. There's not much crossover."

"It must have been humiliating, being dumped," Paul said, deliberately rubbing it in. "Some might say that's a motive."

Helen looked up at him, incredulous. "You don't think...? I didn't murder him. Of course I didn't. Bethany King did that. In any case, I wouldn't. I loved him once, so I could never kill him, no matter what he did to me." Helen's eyes glinted as she tried to hold back her tears.

Paul decided to change tack. Helen Trenton most definitely wasn't over her ex-fiancé. That much was obvious. "What do you know about this accusation at Clayborne Grammar school? One of the pupils alleged that Grant Wyvern touched her inappropriately."

"Well, she made it up. He didn't do it, and the inquiry proved it."

Helen sounded adamant. Did she know that for sure, or was that love talking? She was still engaged to him at that time. Naturally, she would have wanted to believe the best of the man she loved.

"Did you see Bethany King on the morning of Grant Wyvern's murder?"

"No. Not that I recall."

"So you didn't send her to the gym equipment store or tell her that Wyvern wanted to see her?" Paul put on his serious face deliberately to make her worry. If anyone was likely to break down and confess, it would be Helen Trenton. She was a bundle of nerves.

"No, definitely not. I would have remembered that. And, like I said, I didn't have much to do with Grant, so how would I know if he wanted to see Bethany?"

"Why did you express concern about Bethany King on Friday morning? We know you asked Bill Gizzard to add her to the list of troubled pupils to discuss in your weekly meetings." Poor Bethany. Her problems then were nothing to what they were now.

Helen seemed to relax more with the spotlight turned away from her. "She was becoming very quiet and withdrawn in class, not her usual self at all. I wondered if she had problems at home."

"And did you ask her what was worrying her?"

"No."

"Really?" Paul was incredulous. "So instead of asking her directly what the problem was, a bunch of teachers who hardly knew her were going to get together without her being present and speculate."

Helen looked embarrassed. "I suppose now that you put it like that, it does seem silly."

"Silly? It's madness." It made Paul angry. If only Helen had spoken directly to Bethany on Friday, this tragedy might never have happened.

Helen folded her arms defensively. "I can't help everyone. The school has too many pupils and not enough teachers."

"Where were you when Grant Wyvern was murdered?"

Helen answered quickly. "In my classroom with Madison Pearce, one of my pupils. She came to hand in her homework, and we discussed why she was late giving it in. Then we discussed the subject of the essay. It turned into quite a long conversation." Helen gave a weak smile.

"Why was the homework late?" Paul queried.

"I can't remember. The shock of Grant's murder made that whole day a blur," Helen explained.

"And yet you remember being with Madison?" Paul pressed her. His gut instinct told him she was holding something back.

"Of course. I've just forgotten some of the finer details, that's all."

"What was the essay about?" Kevin chipped in.

Helen hesitated. "As far as I remember, something to do with *Romeo and Juliet*."

Paul didn't believe a word she said. She'd hesitated for much too long. She must have set the essay topic. And she must have been marking them only a few days ago. She ought to remember more than that.

"You have to understand that I teach a lot of children, and each school year is reading different books."

The way Helen was over-explaining convinced Paul she wasn't entirely telling the truth. And, if she lied about her alibi, that cast doubt on everything she said. Perhaps she knew more about Wyvern's indecent touching incident at Clayborne Grammar than she let on. Paul let it go. Was he simply clutching at straws, trying to find something to help Bethany? Maybe nothing could help the poor child.

Chapter 38

Clint came into the shop at his usual time of 11:00 a.m. with a young girl following reluctantly behind him.

"This is my granddaughter, Shaz," he said to Rose.

Shaz had already perked up and zoomed in on the display of chocolate bars.

"No school today?" Rose asked.

"I didn't feel well this morning."

Rose cast an expert eye over Shaz Fletcher. She recognised truanting when she saw it. She was willing to bet there was absolutely nothing wrong with Shaz.

"I'm looking after her so her mum can go to work," Clint said.

"I don't need a babysitter. I'm thirteen," Shaz protested.

Clint smiled. "Think of it as a nice excuse to spend time with your favourite grandad."

Shaz shrugged. "S'pose so."

"I need to pop down the road for five minutes on an errand," Clint said. "Do you mind if I leave Shaz with you for a few minutes?" He winked at Rose.

"Of course." Rose guessed there was no errand. Clint brought Shaz to meet her deliberately, and she didn't intend to waste the opportunity.

"That's a shame about your friend Bethany," Rose said.

"She's not my friend. She's a saddo."

"I thought you were friends."

Shaz shrugged her shoulders. "Used to be. Not anymore."

Rose guessed that most of Bethany's friends would deny even knowing her at the moment.

"She shouldn't have stabbed Mr Wyvern. And she's made my best friend Ava feel awful, too, for sending her there."

"Ava Browning sent Bethany to find Mr Wyvern?"

"No, I shouldn't have told you that. I promised." Shaz seemed flustered.

"It's all right, Shaz. You won't get into trouble. Why did Ava do that?"

Shaz eyed her suspiciously. "You have to promise not to tell."

"Cross my heart." Rose smiled at her warmly. "I promise you can trust me."

"She got a text. It's not Ava's fault."

"Who sent the text, Shaz?" Rose asked softly.

Shaz hesitated. "I dunno."

Rose knew she was lying. She moved on to a different question. "Do you know why she did it?"

"I dunno, but I don't blame her. Wyvern's a perv."

"Really?" It was one of the many things Rose had been wondering about, one of the few things that may help Bethany's case. "Why do you say that?"

"I dunno. Madison said so. You should ask Miss Trenton. They both used to teach at another school before they came to Taylor Park. I bet she knows."

"How about you, Shaz? Did Mr Wyvern ever do anything to you?"

"No way. He wouldn't dare. I'd have kicked him where it hurts if he did. That would be gross. He must be nearly as old as my grandad."

Rose tried not to laugh. Mr Wyvern was probably no older than Shaz's father, but, to the average thirteen-year-old, every grown-up looked ancient.

"Did you like Mr Wyvern?"

"Not really. He gave us loads of detentions."

The bell on the shop door tinkled, signalling Clint's return.

"You two been having a nice chat?"

"Yes, thank you." Rose smiled at him. Shaz hadn't told her anything new. It kept coming back to the same big question. Did Grant Wyvern abuse Bethany?

As soon as Rose got home from the shop, she took out her jewellery-making equipment. She'd finally decided that she really must get herself a car, and she needed to make a few more pieces to sell in order to afford something reliable. She tried to focus, but her mind kept returning to Madison. Was the teenager still upset with Wyvern for jilting Helen Trenton? Was that why she'd accused him of abusing girls? That was exactly the sort of stupid rumour an immature teenager would start in order to lash out at someone who'd upset her.

She opened her notebook, where she kept the details for all her designs. All her jewellery pieces were bespoke, and she loved designing them as much as she liked to admire the finished product. Hopefully, she'd finish her current piece, an intricate beaded necklace, by the end of the afternoon.

Perhaps Madison hadn't only lashed out verbally at Wyvern. Had he upset her enough for her to murder him? If Debbie told the truth about Wyvern giving Madison some extra coaching on Friday at lunchtime, she could have been at the scene just before Bethany arrived. Perhaps they'd done it together. This entire problem was very much like the necklace. One minute she looked at it and all the pieces fitted together perfectly. Then she would notice pieces that weren't quite right.

Rose had just finished laying everything out ready when the doorbell rang. She considered ignoring it, but the ringing was persistent. With an enormous sigh, she got up to answer the door.

Maggie Mahoney gasped for breath after walking up three flights of stairs to Rose's flat. "Someone let me through the front door, so I came up." She paused to take another breath. "I still can't imagine how you do this every day. It's like climbing Everest."

Rose laughed at her exaggeration. "It keeps me fit." Perhaps Maggie should visit more often. The exercise would do her good.

"I'd love a cuppa," Maggie said.

Rose didn't have the heart to say no. She mentally parked her necklace. She could get back to it later.

Maggie followed her into the kitchen. "How's Irina getting on?"

"As well as can be expected, I suppose." Sadly, that wasn't very well at all. "She's still struggling with the situation."

"It can't be easy when your daughter's a murderer." Maggie eased her ample frame onto one of Rose's dining chairs.

"Actually, I wondered if it could have been Madison Pearce who murdered Wyvern," Rose said casually.

"Madison?" Maggie looked incredulous. "But she's got an alibi. She couldn't have done it."

Rose wished she hadn't voiced her theory so soon. "What alibi?"

"She was with Helen Trenton, handing in her English homework."

Rose felt deflated. It was a stupid theory, anyway. Madison would have been covered in blood and would probably have run into Bethany on the way out. The most likely scenario was still that Grant Wyvern tried something inappropriate with Bethany, and she defended herself with whatever was at hand, which happened to be a Swiss army knife. Perhaps she would try to talk to Madison again. Rose felt sure the girl was holding something back, even if she couldn't have murdered Wyvern.

Chapter 39

The protesters were out in full force when Rose arrived at Irina's house the following evening. She was getting used to them now, so she zigzagged through the crowd to reach the front door, refusing to speak to anyone. The number of people was as high as ever, although the chanting and the placards were a bit half-hearted at this end of the day. And at least, since the police had intervened more firmly, arresting a couple of the worst troublemakers, they were mostly making their protests heard from the road, not the garden. But the front garden wasn't huge, so they remained too close for comfort and as there was no fence along the frontage, to allow for easier parking, the protesters had a tendency to drift onto the driveway quite frequently. It must be awful for Irina, knowing they were outside almost constantly. For once, Rose longed for a massive thunderstorm to drive them away.

Irina led Rose into the kitchen. Immediately, Rose spotted a comfy armchair in front of the small TV on the wall.

Irina noticed Rose gazing at the chair. "Richard put it in here. We mostly stay in this room now. It's not pleasant in the front room, with all those people outside."

"That's awful." They Kings shouldn't be made to feel so bad in their own house. At least the kitchen was a good size, probably big enough for two armchairs, but Rose noted that Richard had only brought in one comfortable chair, which did nothing to improve Rose's opinion of him.

"How's Bethany? Have you had any news?"

"They moved her this morning to a juvenile detention centre. It's a better place for her. She gets a proper bedroom instead of a police cell, and everyone is under eighteen. But it's further for me to travel." Irina forced a weak smile, clearly trying to make the best of things.

"At least you've got the car." Rose saw it parked on the drive when she came in, as close as possible to the front door. Irina was taking no chances with the protesters.

"Have you eaten yet? I'd love some company if you've got time to stay."

Rose remembered the chilli con carne that Jack said he'd left for her to heat up. "Of course. I can help you cook. If you'd like." She could take the chilli to work tomorrow and heat it up for lunch in the microwave at the back of the shop.

"You've been working all day. Please, sit down."

"Where did Richard go?" Rose didn't think to ask him yesterday, not that she was all that interested.

"Spain." Irina chopped an onion, moving her fingers so quickly Rose wondered if she'd accidentally chop one off. "Alicante. He's gone to play golf."

"Golf?" Perhaps it was some business thing. Lots of deals were brokered on the golf course, weren't they?

"Yes. He needs to get away from it all. This thing with Bethany is really upsetting him. He needs a break."

Irina clearly wanted to defend her husband, but her voice betrayed her bitterness. Rose couldn't tell if the tears streaming down her cheeks were real or induced by chopping onions.

"Not work then?" If Richard needed a break from the situation after only a few days, how on earth would he cope with the many months ahead? And what about Irina? This was destroying her. She needed Richard's support.

Irina shook her head sadly. "He lost his job. His company made him redundant when they found out about Bethany. Please don't say anything. He doesn't want anyone to know. He hasn't even told me. I only found out when I overheard him on the phone."

"Surely that's not legal, getting rid of him for that reason. He could take them to a tribunal," Rose said.

"It's difficult." Irina put some pieces of chicken in a pan with the onions. "The company is being taken over, so redundancies are inevitable anyway, Richard says. He'd have a hard job proving that they let him go because of Bethany. He might end up spending a fortune on legal fees and still lose. And the publicity the case would attract might mean that other employers wouldn't want to touch him."

Rose realised that Irina was probably right. She'd been in a similar position herself a few months ago, fired for punching someone at work. There'd been a very good reason as the woman in question, her supervisor, was having an affair with Rose's husband, her soon-to-be ex-husband. There were no guarantees, the solicitor told her, apart from a large legal bill at the end, which Rose hadn't been able to afford. Richard would stand a better chance of winning his case than she would have done, but it would still be uncertain and stressful. "It's still an awful thing for them to do," she said.

Irina poured a generous glug of wine into the pan, watching it sizzle as it boiled off.

"That smells delicious." Rose had worked up an appetite walking here.

"It's nearly ready." Irina chopped some fresh herbs.

Rose salivated as Irina dished up the fresh pasta and chicken with a creamy herb and white wine sauce. If it tasted as good as it smelled, she'd teach Jack how to cook it.

Rose had lost track of the time. It was almost dark outside. She didn't like taking buses after dark, not in this area. Perhaps, if she hurried, she could catch a bus in the next few minutes before it grew properly dark.

"Please, stay." Irina picked up the bottle of wine and moved to top up Rose's glass, even though she had barely drunk any of it.

"No, really, I must go home." Rose stood up. Irina was ridiculously needy. If she got any worse, Rose would end up staying here twenty-four seven until Richard got back from his trip. She really had to learn how to say no.

"Please," Irina begged. "I don't want to be on my own all night. I'm scared." She began to cry. "I wish Richard hadn't gone away. I've been worrying all day that he might not want to come back."

"Of course he will." Rose put an arm around Irina to comfort her, but she continued to sob. Rose's heart went out to her. She'd had a dreadful time of it already. How could her husband leave her in this state? "I'll need to go home and get my overnight bag." She hated the thought of putting on dirty clothes in the morning and not having her toothbrush and face creams. "Can you lend me your car? Then I can get back in less than twenty minutes."

"Yes. Of course you can borrow the car." Irina immediately stopped crying. "Please hurry back. I can't bear it here on my own."

It didn't take long for Rose to throw a few things into a bag. As she drove back to Irina's house, she cursed herself for being so soft. Now she'd probably end up staying with Irina every night until Richard came back. He had better come back. Was Irina being paranoid, worrying that he might not? Perhaps things were worse than she'd let on. Having a daughter arrested for murder would be enough to end many marriages. Whatever happened, Rose couldn't stay with Irina permanently. She needed to help her stand on her own two feet. She resolved to make this a one-off.

Rose accelerated up the long hill towards Irina's house. It was completely dark now and this stretch of road lacked any street lighting, so she flipped her headlights onto full beam. A flash of light ahead made her dip the lights immediately. There must be another car coming. She tried to remember exactly how much further she had to go. The houses all looked similar in the dark, and she didn't have Irina's car parked in the driveway to guide her.

Suddenly, she slammed her foot on the brakes as something flew across the road in front of her. At first, she thought it might be a deer or a large dog, then she clearly identified the dark shape as a person running. The car skidded towards the pavement and, to Rose's horror, the front wing hit the runner, knocking them to the ground.

Rose jumped out of the car. "Are you all right?" she shouted. The runner got up and ran along the road away from her before she reached the off-side of the car. "Hey, are you all right?" Rose yelled again. He, or she, didn't look all right. Dressed in dark clothes from head to foot, the figure blended into the shadows, but they must have injured their right leg as, even in the darkness, Rose noticed how badly they were limping.

After a few seconds, she lost sight of them. Shortly after that, an engine starting up and the frantic screech of rubber on tarmac announced the mystery person's departure. What, or who, had they been running from? It occurred to Rose that there may be someone lurking out here. She got back into Irina's car quickly, locking the doors. As her eyes adjusted to the darkness, she recognised her location. Irina's house was just around the next bend. She could have walked it in less than a minute. She started the car, wondering if she should report the accident. Perhaps in the morning, after she inspected Irina's car for damage in daylight.

Chapter 40

"Oh my God." Rose spotted the flames as she rounded the bend and, getting closer, was horrified to find Irina's house on fire.

Rose quickly pulled herself together and phoned Irina. No answer. There were no lights upstairs, but Rose remembered Irina and Richard's bedroom was at the back of the house. Surely Irina wouldn't have gone to bed yet, not when she expected Rose back so soon. Rose phoned the fire brigade, stressing that her friend may be trapped inside.

She ran towards the house. The front window was smashed, and the living room seemed to be where the fire was strongest. Had someone thrown something through the window? Suddenly, it all made sense. The person she hit earlier must have been the arsonist. That's why they'd been so desperate to run away.

Fierce flames leapt out the window. The fire had worsened even in the couple of minutes she'd been standing here. Despite the darkness, she spotted the cloud of black smoke thickening above the rooftop. She couldn't wait for the fire brigade to find Irina.

Rose raced across the garden and tried the gate at the side of the house, shoving it with her shoulder, but it stayed firmly locked. The high gate seemed sturdy but was topped with shards of glass to prevent intruders from climbing over and, in any case, Rose saw nothing she could stand on to help her climb up. The fencing in the back garden was even higher and, from memory, much of it bounded the neighbouring gardens. The gate might be the only way in. She ran back out onto the road, hoping to find someone with a ladder. The two closest houses looked deserted. Either the neighbours were asleep or had gone out. It would take too long to find out. She still hadn't heard the fire engine's sirens. She had to think of something, fast.

Seconds later, Rose had an idea. She jumped into Irina's car and drove into the front garden, ploughing over the corner of a flower bed before stopping directly in front of the gate. What a pity the gate was too narrow to ram it open with the car, but she would have hit the corner of the house instead. Never mind. Rose made another plan.

She searched the car and found what she needed: a jack and a blanket. She slid the jack under the gap beneath the gate, then grabbed the blanket and climbed onto the car. The glass shards looked nasty. Silently, she cursed Richard for putting them there. If she folded the blanket enough times, it should be thick enough to protect her when she climbed over.

Rose peered over the top of the gate. No sign of Irina in the garden. With a huge effort, she heaved herself up, using her arms to push herself above the gate. She flipped one leg over, straddling the folded blanket on top of the gate. Her weight pushed down onto the sharp glass. Quickly, she felt for the wooden strut she had seen on the inside of the gate and wedged her foot sideways onto it to ease the pressure. Then, holding tightly onto the gatepost, she swung her other leg over, causing a momentary wobble. Aware that the gate might not be as strong as she'd imagined, Rose sped up before the whole structure collapsed beneath her. She jumped down, bending her knees as she landed before stumbling backwards onto the hard concrete.

Rose let out a scream of pain. Her foot must have landed on the jack, invisible in the dark, twisting her ankle slightly. Leaning against the gate, she rubbed it until the initial sharp pain began to subside. The heat from the fire sent sweat streaming down her face. She didn't have time to waste. The pain in her ankle felt bearable. Hopefully, it would hold up. She pulled the blanket from the top of the gate and picked up the jack.

The fire hadn't yet spread to the back of the house. Rose tried the back door, which led straight into the kitchen. Locked. She peered through the glass door. Two mugs sat on the kitchen table. Did that mean Irina hadn't gone to bed? Her obsession with cleaning meant she would never leave dirty mugs out overnight. Quickly, Rose pressed her face up against the window and used the torch app on her phone to see into the kitchen. She panned the light around the room, stopping abruptly. A single leg poked out from under the table. Rose moved to get a better view, but the rest of Irina's body was obscured by the island unit in the centre of the kitchen. She needed to get inside.

The glass in the door would be toughened, making the window her best bet for access. Rose wrapped the blanket around her arms and smashed the window with the car jack, frantically bashing the glass until she had cleared a large enough space to climb in. She threw the blanket across the windowsill to protect herself from the jagged edges of glass and hauled herself through the gap, crawling onto the draining board before carefully dropping to the floor, landing carefully on her uninjured leg.

"Irina." Rose crouched down to examine her friend, checking for a pulse before shaking her to try to wake her up. Irina stirred slightly. Smoke was filling the room, billowing under the door into the kitchen. It made Irina cough. Rose prioritised getting both of them outside quickly before the smoke got to her too.

Rose had spent enough time at Irina's house lately to have noticed where she kept the back door key. She went straight to the cupboard under the sink. The hook was empty. Rose switched her torch on again, frantically scanning the cupboard's contents, in case it had fallen off the hook. A slight breeze came through the broken window and she thankfully gulped in the fresh air. How would she ever manage to get Irina, in her semi-conscious state, out through the window? It was impossible.

She took a step backwards, trying to think. Her foot landed on something hard, making her gasp with pain as she tweaked her ankle again. Her torch picked up a glint of silver on the floor beneath her. Rose quickly bent down to retrieve the key. Irina must have picked up the key and been on her way to the back door, but been overcome by the smoke before she could escape.

Dragging Irina outside was a harder slog than Rose expected, although she was grateful for the air coming through the open back door, ensuring they both could breathe. As soon as they were in the garden, Rose stopped for a rest. She was exhausted, but her concern for Irina forced her to battle on.

Irina was waking up in the fresher air. "Where am I?" Her reedy voice was immediately lost in a fit of coughing.

"It's all right." Rose phoned the fire brigade again. Where on earth were they? They should have arrived by now.

"The fire engines will be with you shortly," the operator informed her. "They had some trouble with a road blockade. The police have nearly cleared it."

"I've got my friend out of the house." Rose listened to Irina coughing. "She needs an ambulance. And we're trapped in the back garden." There wasn't a hope in hell of getting Irina out over the side gate. She cursed herself for not finding the key to the gate while she was in the kitchen, but she wasn't going back for it now.

The fire had spread rapidly towards the back of the house, even in the short time Rose had been here. The arsonist must have used a large quantity of accelerant for it to burn so quickly. One end of the roof was a ball of flames, and pieces of burning debris floated through the air, sending sparks flying upwards into the smoke-filled sky. It wouldn't be safe to stay in the garden for long. The heat would soon become too intense, and it was only a matter of time before sparks set fire to the wooden fence that surrounded the small garden.

"Can you get up?" Rose needed to move Irina away from the house.

"I think so, if you help me." Irina's voice came out thick and raspy, a far cry from her usual soft lilt.

Rose helped Irina to her feet. She was shaky, but she could walk if she leaned on Rose.

"Wait," Irina pulled back. "I need to get my stuff."

"What stuff?" She dragged Irina away from the house.

"Bethany's things, and our photos. All my memories of Bethany are inside. I can't leave them."

Rose gripped her arm tightly to stop her from heading towards the house. "You can't go back in. It's not safe." The kitchen door may still be retarding the flames, but the smoke would incapacitate her long before she found anything. Besides, everything she wanted would probably be upstairs or in the living room at the front of the house. It would be suicidal to go back in. Irina wasn't thinking straight. "The fire brigade will be here soon. They'll save Bethany's things." Rose felt bad promising Irina something impossible, but better that than letting her die in a burning house.

She wondered about the blockade the emergency services operator mentioned. Her first thought, that a road might be closed for overnight repairs, quickly gave way to more sinister imaginings. Someone deliberately set fire to the Kings' house. Could that same person have blocked a vital road en route from the fire station? Did any of the protesters really hate the Kings enough to attempt to kill them? She pictured some of the protesters: Jenny, Madison, Clint. She couldn't see it. Who had lost the most from Bethany's actions? Danny Wyvern? He'd certainly been angry, but Rose also knew never to underestimate a woman. Could Helen Trenton have been responsible? It had been far too dark to be certain whether the person she hit with the car was a man or a woman.

A fresh round of coughing from Irina brought Rose's attention back to the task in hand.

"I'm scared," Irina rasped when the coughing subsided. "It's really hot. What if the building falls on us?"

Rose thought that unlikely, although they may be hit by pieces of burning debris from the fire. Her answer was drowned out by a loud popping noise.

Irina screamed. "What was that?"

"It's all right. It's nothing." It came from the side of the house. Rose guessed it might be Irina's car, but she thought it best not to worry her.

Another pop, closely followed by two more confirmed it. The car tyres must have burst in the heat. If the car had caught fire, there was no way they could exit through the garden gate. Not now.

Chapter 41

"Let's get out of here." Rose helped Irina to the end of the garden and sat her by the back fence before running towards the house, where she had left the jack, the only remaining piece of Irina's car, leaning next to the back door. The pain in her ankle had eased off, but running immediately inflamed it again.

She scooped up the jack, instantly dropping it. The scalding hot metal jack clattered on the paving. She tugged at the blanket, which still lay folded over the broken kitchen window where she had climbed in earlier. Quickly, she wrapped it around the jack so she could carry it without burning herself and hurried back to Irina.

The wooden panelled fencing appeared solid. But the posts were on the inside. That meant she'd be pushing the nail that held the slats in place outwards, instead of hammering against them, driving them in deeper. Both she and Irina were reasonably slim. If she could remove four slats, that would be enough for them to squeeze out. She wrapped a corner of the blanket around the end of the jack and started hammering at the fence.

It was hard work. It took a couple of minutes of solid effort to loosen the first vertical slat enough to prise it off.

"Richard will go mad," Irina said. "He paid a lot of money for that fence."

Rose glared at her, although Irina would never see the depth of her expression in the darkness. There were definitely some advantages to no longer having a husband. Phillip possessed plenty of faults, some of them major ones, but at least he was never as controlling and unreasonable as Richard King.

Rose took a short breather after the second fence slat popped off. The kitchen was ablaze now, and the light from the fire threw their shadows up against the fence. It scared Rose how quickly the fire had taken hold. She steeled herself to carry on, working more frantically this time.

The fourth slat pinged off just as the screech of sirens announced the arrival of the fire brigade.

"Can you get through the gap?" Rose asked, hoping she wouldn't have to hammer off another slat.

"I'll try." Irina pushed her shoulders through the hole in the fence.

"Be careful not to tread on the bits of wood. Those nails are huge. They may be sticking up." Rose shone her phone's torch through the gap to help guide Irina. The battery must be nearly flat by now. With a bit of luck, it might hold out for another minute.

"Where are we?" Rose asked as she stepped through the fence. It seemed to be a car park.

"I'm not sure." Irina sounded concerned.

"But you live here." Surely Irina knew the area. She'd told Rose they'd lived in the house for several years.

"Yes, but I've never had any reason to go round the back of the garden. I think there's a housing estate over there." She pointed to the car park exit. "But I'm not sure how to get back to our road from here."

Rose quickly scanned their surroundings. There was only one exit from the car park and it wasn't in the direction she wanted to go. Finding their way back to the front of the house wouldn't be as simple as following the fence line. "I'm sure we'll manage." Irina still appeared wobbly, so Rose took her arm and headed towards the exit. Behind them, Irina's house lit up the sky like a beacon. They could use it to navigate.

The housing estate was a maze. Every time they turned towards the fire, a dead end thwarted them.

"This is driving me mad." Rose was sure they were going round in circles. They were no closer to finding Irina's road. "I'm going to knock on someone's door and ask for directions."

"It's really late. You'll wake them up."

"I doubt it." Anyone normal would realise there was a fire nearby and be watching the show from an upstairs window. She walked towards a house that was still lit up.

Ten minutes later, they stood outside Irina's house.

Irina stared at her wrecked house, shock rendering her speechless.

A large number of firefighters appeared to be getting the blaze under control. The shooting flames that had taken hold earlier were dying down, replaced by thick, acrid smoke. Water dripped off the front wall. The living room, where the fire started, had transformed into a black skeleton. At the other end of the house, the burnt-out shell of Irina's car reminded Rose what a narrow escape they'd both had.

Rose counted four fire engines and an ambulance lined up along the road. If only they hadn't taken so long to arrive, they could have saved most of the house, but by the time the fire brigade showed up, the whole house had gone up like an inferno. Thank God she'd got Irina out in time.

Irina finally found her power of speech. "What am I going to do?" Her voice was still raspy, reminding Rose that Irina had inhaled a lot of smoke.

"You need to see a paramedic," Rose insisted, leading Irina towards the ambulance. At least it might take her mind off the state of her house. She had no idea what Irina would do now. They would take things one step at a time.

While the paramedics checked out Irina, Rose wandered around. Amazingly, the fire hadn't spread to the neighbouring houses. She found the neighbours standing at the side of the road.

"Maybe this will stop those dreadful protesters," one of them, a tall man who seemed full of his own self-importance, said. "No point in them coming back now."

"Best thing that could happen is if the house gets completely rebuilt and the Kings move away." The overweight woman rubbed her hands frantically through her curly hair as if checking that no stray pieces of ash had flown across the road and set fire to her. "I'm sure house prices have taken a tumble already because of them."

Rose didn't need to listen to this vitriol. "Sounds like you've both got a motive to start the fire yourself," she pointed out.

The woman threw her hands up in horror and backed away from Rose.

"We would never do that," the man said. "What sort of people do you think we are?"

Ones who slag off your neighbours when they haven't done anything wrong, Rose wanted to say. "Where were you an hour ago?" She looked the man directly in the eye.

"I was out." He sounded flustered.

"Do you have any witnesses to that?"

"What are you getting at? I would never..."

Rose ignored him. She didn't really suspect them, although she might suggest to Paul Waterford that the police should pay them a visit. No doubt they would anyway, to ask if they'd seen anything. She marched over to the nearest fire engine, targeting the man who appeared to be in charge.

"The homeowner got out. She's with the paramedics. There's no one else in there."

The firefighter shouted across at one of his colleagues. "Cruise, the house is empty."

His colleague put both of his thumbs up to indicate he'd heard.

"What's your name?" As the firefighter spoke to her, his gaze continued to dart around the scene, assessing the situation.

"Rose. Rose Marsden."

"My name's Blue," he said. "I'm the station commander. Can you tell me what happened, Rose? Did you see anything?"

"I'm sure it was arson. Probably something thrown through the front window." Rose checked her watch. "I saw someone running away when I got here, around forty-five minutes ago."

"Don't worry, our fire investigator will look at everything thoroughly. He'll get to the bottom of it. Sounds like they used an accelerant to do this much damage so quickly. Meanwhile, you need to speak to the police, tell them what you saw."

Rose nodded.

"Any idea who might have done it?"

Rose didn't want to voice her suspicions yet. "No, but there have been protesters outside the house for the last few days. It may have been one of them." She stared up at the house. Firefighters were still spraying massive jets of water at it. "What happens now?"

Blue smiled, pulling a space blanket out of the appliance's cab. "You look cold." He shook out the foil blanket and draped it around Rose's shoulders. "Try not to worry. We'll make sure the fire is completely extinguished. The fire investigator will do a thorough search as soon as it's safe and liaise with the police."

"Thank you." Rose clutched the thin foil blanket around her. She felt like a Christmas turkey.

Blue peered over her shoulder towards the ambulance. "Why don't you go and take care of your friend. The police will be here any minute. I'll send them to find you."

"Richard's going to go mad when he sees this," Irina said as soon as Rose stepped into the ambulance.

"Don't worry about that." At least, when Richard saw the state of his house, it would take his mind off Bethany. Anyway, it served him right for selfishly taking a holiday and leaving Irina on her own.

"We're taking Irina to Brackford General Hospital," one of the paramedics said. "She needs to be examined properly and they'll probably want to keep her overnight." He turned to Irina. "I expect you'll get five-star treatment, seeing as you work there."

"That's good." Rose squeezed Irina's hand. "I need to wait and talk to the police. Phone me when they discharge you and try not to worry."

Chapter 42

Paul Waterford drove towards the Kings' house with a sinking feeling inside, not entirely caused by the large Chinese meal he'd been enjoying with his wife, Clarke. He was supposed to be off duty but had asked to be notified if anything came up regarding the King case. It didn't sound good. Not only did the house fire have all the hallmarks of arson, but the fire engine got held up by protesters blocking the road on the way over. He hoped Richard and Irina King weren't harmed. The last thing he needed was another murder on his hands.

He parked the car at a safe distance and found Blue, Brackford fire station's manager.

"What happened?" he asked.

"Got to be arson," Blue said. "I'd stake my life on it. Most likely a Molotov cocktail through the front window. There's a witness who saw someone running away. She's here somewhere. Her name's Rose Marsden."

Paul wasn't surprised to discover Rose was involved. At least she made a reliable witness. She could wait until he finished with Blue. He stared up at the house, quickly assessing the damage. Plumes of black smoke rose skywards, even though most of the flames had been extinguished. The blaze must have been fierce to gut the house this badly. The burnt-out building reminded him of a blackened skeleton. "Any casualties?" He hardly dared to ask.

Blue pointed towards an ambulance. "Homeowner's in mild shock and has inhaled a lot of smoke. She's on her way to hospital."

Paul nodded. Thank God there were no fatalities. "Give me a shout when you find the cause of the fire."

"Likely to be tomorrow morning," Blue said.

That was what Paul expected. He left Blue to get on with his job and went to find Rose Marsden.

Chapter 43

Rose hugged the thin space blanket around her but realised that shock, rather than cold, was making her shiver. She spotted DI Waterford heading her way. Perhaps he'd have more information on who might have done this.

"Rose. I hear they've taken Irina to hospital. Is she all right?"

"Of course she's not all right." Rose regretted her words as soon as she uttered them. He was only trying to help. "Sorry. It's been a difficult evening. Irina inhaled a lot of smoke. I had to drag her out of the kitchen. But the paramedics think she'll recover quickly. I'm more worried about the effects on her mental health. She's already got more than enough to cope with."

"Yes, I can't see her taking this well. What about her husband? Is he here?" Paul asked.

"He's in Spain, playing golf."

Paul raised an eyebrow. "Has Irina got somewhere to go? When they discharge her from hospital, I mean."

Rose gave a couple of coughs. The wind had turned in their direction, and the thick smoke irritated her throat. "She can stay with me for one night if necessary, then I'll help her find a hotel." She really didn't have space in her small flat for another person, not with Jack living there for the summer, but she could sleep on the sofa tonight if necessary and let Irina have her bed. "Unless you have a better idea." She looked at Paul. "What do people normally do in these circumstances?"

"It would be better if Mrs King stayed with family if she has any. She must be upset."

Rose agreed, although *upset* was a huge understatement. She suspected the hospital would keep Irina overnight. If they discharged her tomorrow, Rose would help her find a hotel. The insurance company would surely pay for one until the house was habitable again. It would worry her if Irina stayed with her. If someone started the fire to harm the Kings, they might try to hurt them again, and it wouldn't be so easy to escape from a third-floor flat.

"And what about you? Are you ok?" Paul looked at the space blanket with concern.

"I'll be fine. I need to get home."

"Let me give you a lift. You can tell me on the way what you saw. Blue, the fire station manager, said you saw something."

"A lift home would be wonderful," Rose said. They could talk in private in the car.

There wasn't very much Rose could tell Paul. "Will you find out who did this?" she asked when he dropped her off outside her flat. Perhaps the police could get forensic evidence, if the fire hadn't destroyed it all by now, but Rose didn't hold out much hope. She told him as much as she could about the arsonist, carefully omitting the part about hitting him with Irina's car. She also explained her theories about Danny Wyvern and Helen Trenton. Hopefully, it would be some help, but she'd never be able to identify the suspect. It had been much too dark to get a proper look at him or her.

"We'll do everything we can," Paul reassured her. "And we know where to find you if we have any more questions."

"How do you cope with so much death and violence?" Rose asked. DI Waterford always seemed so calm, but he must be constantly dealing with other people's suffering.

"We all develop our own coping methods. It's part of the job. Honestly, sometimes I think this job is like a Shakespeare play."

"Too many dead bodies, like *Romeo and Juliet*?"

"Too many tragedies." Paul sighed loudly.

Rose agreed. This was a tragedy.

"Funny you should mention *Romeo and Juliet*." Paul smiled faintly. "Year eight are studying that one."

"No, they're not." Rose remembered her conversation with Debbie clearly, because she had called Madison, Ava, and Shaz the three witches. "They're doing *MacBeth*."

Paul sat bolt upright. "Are you sure?"

"Yes, why?" Rose couldn't think how it would be of any importance to him.

"It's just that Helen Trenton said Madison Pearce was handing in her homework at the time of Grant Wyvern's murder. She told me it was an essay on *Romeo and Juliet*."

"And if she lied, then she has no alibi." Rose's mind buzzed. Could Helen Trenton have killed Wyvern? "Maggie could find out which Shakespeare play they're studying."

"Leave it with me," Paul said.

Rose had no intention of leaving it with the police. She would ask Maggie to find out for her. She watched Paul drive away, wishing she'd had time to discuss Bethany with him, but it was only a short drive from Irina's house to her flat and she hadn't wanted to invite the detective inspector inside. She'd have to find another time soon.

Chapter 44

Rose checked the clock on the wall. Only five thirty. It promised to be a long evening. Jack was meeting up with some university friends in London, so Rose was working until the shop closed at ten. She hated the short walk home at that time of night. It wasn't the best area to be wandering around late. At least in the middle of summer, it would still be daylight, but it still made her nervous being out that late.

The old-fashioned bell above the shop door tinkled, signalling another customer. Maggie Mahoney headed towards her.

"Hi, Maggie." Rose beamed at her.

"I only dropped by for an update." Maggie dumped her substantial handbag on the counter. "Have you heard from Irina?"

"She phoned earlier. She's staying in a hotel, close to where they're holding Bethany."

"That's convenient." Maggie leant on the counter, still breathing heavily from walking the short distance from her house to the shop.

"Yes, she's seen Bethany already." Rose hoped more regular contact with her mother might make Bethany open up more. It seemed to be the only way they'd ever find out what really happened and why. "Have you heard anything more from the police about Wyvern's murder?" she asked Maggie.

"That good-looking inspector chap showed up yesterday, interviewing some of the teachers again."

"You mean Detective Inspector Waterford?"

"That's the one."

"Did he find out anything?" She wondered what might have happened to make him re-interview anyone.

Maggie shrugged her shoulders. "He wouldn't tell me. But he spent ages questioning Helen Trenton."

"Really?" Rose reminded herself she still wanted to speak to Madison again. Perhaps she would have heard from Helen, seeing as the teacher was a good friend of the family.

"I reckon she did him in because he dumped her right before their wedding," Maggie said. "Probably got Bethany to help her."

"But that was ages ago." Rose dismissed the theory. They'd both been working at Taylor Park for several months and, by all accounts, enjoyed a good enough working relationship, although of course no one knew what went on outside of school. Could they have been putting on an act in front of everyone? If so, it must have been an Oscar-winning performance. "Besides, Bethany would never agree to help murder anyone." She bit her tongue as soon as the words escaped her mouth, remembering how Bethany was caught standing over Wyvern's body, still holding the bloodied knife.

"If it wasn't Helen, it must have been Bethany all along," Maggie said firmly.

Another possibility suddenly occurred to Rose. Could the date of Grant Wyvern's murder have been the anniversary of the wedding that never took place? It must be around this time of year. It would give Helen Trenton a strong motive.

Rose still didn't want to accept that Bethany was guilty, at least not unless it was a clear-cut case of self-defence. "We must be missing something," she whispered out loud. If only she had a clue what it might be.

Maggie ignored her, busily digging into her handbag. "I found this pinned on the noticeboard in the staff room." She extracted a small white card, handing it to Rose. "You keep saying you need to buy a car. One of the teachers, Claire Bailey, is selling hers. It's a cheap little runaround, exactly what you need."

Rose quickly read the advert. It was a nine-year-old VW Polo. The mileage looked low for its age, and the price was just about within her budget. "What do you know about this teacher? Is the car likely to be as reliable as she says it is?"

"Claire's lovely," Maggie said. "She teaches biology. Everybody likes her, teachers and pupils. I can't imagine she'd sell you a duffer."

"I'll give her a call tomorrow," Rose said. It wouldn't do any harm to look at the car. It might be exactly what she needed.

"That's great. I'll tell her." Maggie headed for the door.

"Shakespeare," Rose called after her, suddenly remembering she'd meant to ask Maggie about it.

Maggie turned. "What?"

"Just something I need you to double-check. Which Shakespeare play are year eight studying?"

Chapter 45

It was early Thursday morning before Rose saw Madison again. She spotted her perusing the bars of chocolate near the checkout.

"Can I help you?"

Madison jumped. "I'm ok. Just need some chocolate. I haven't had breakfast."

"That's not a proper breakfast." Rose smiled. She would have expected Jenny to give her daughter a healthier start to the day, not forget to feed her and leave her to fend for herself on junk food. She wondered what went wrong this morning.

Madison ignored her and picked out a Kit Kat bar.

"I hear you were handing in your homework when Mr Wyvern got stabbed." Rose made an effort to keep her voice casual, not easy when she was talking about something so serious, but she didn't want to frighten Madison away.

"Yes, I was." Madison tentatively handed the Kit Kat to Rose to be scanned.

"Miss Trenton, wasn't it? What subject does she teach?" Rose knew full well. Maggie had already told her that Miss Trenton taught English.

Madison made a face. "English."

"Don't you like English? I used to love it. I always had my head in a book."

"I prefer sport." Madison fidgeted as she stood waiting. "Reading's boring. At least the sort of books you have to read at school are boring."

"That will be 75p, please." Rose held out her hand while Madison counted out some coins from her purse. "So what boring book was the homework about?"

"Can't remember." Madison stared at the floor, avoiding Rose's eye contact.

"Really? It wasn't that long ago." Madison must know what books she was studying. Rose wondered why she didn't just make something up.

Madison held out her hand for the chocolate bar.

"Are you sure you were giving in your homework?" Why didn't she hand it in during class, as everyone else must have done? "Are you sure you didn't go to see Mr Wyvern? I thought he was going to give you some extra coaching that day."

"Yes. I mean, no." Madison seemed flustered.

"What do you mean, Madison? Where were you?"

"I went shopping. I was in Brackford." Madison snatched the chocolate bar from Rose.

"So why did you lie about handing in your homework?"

"I didn't want to get into trouble. We're not supposed to leave the school grounds." Madison turned away from Rose, too late to hide the tears dripping down her cheeks.

Rose followed her to the door. "Which shops did you go to?" She didn't enjoy interrogating Madison, but the girl had lied and Rose needed answers.

Madison stopped at the door. "Trendy Bitz." She sniffed back some of the tears. "I went to Trendy Bitz, ok?" She opened the door and tried to slam it shut behind her, but the door's slow-release spring mechanism made her dramatic exit fall flat.

Rose knew Trendy Bitz. It was part of a big chain store that sold accessories, such as jewellery, scarves, and hair ornaments. It was exactly the kind of shop Madison would visit regularly. She almost believed Madison's story about going shopping. If it checked out, then Madison still had an alibi. On the other hand, Helen Trenton didn't. What were the chances of Helen still being angry with her ex-fiancé?

Rose thought about Philip. The decree absolute for their divorce arrived in the post yesterday. She hadn't forgiven him yet for rushing through the divorce so he could marry the woman he'd left her for.

She tried to imagine how much worse she'd feel if she'd been jilted two weeks before their wedding instead, like poor Helen Trenton. *Angry* wouldn't even begin to describe it.

Claire Bailey lived on the other side of Brackford. It took two buses to get there, which simply reinforced Rose's decision to buy a car. She'd arranged to view the car at six o'clock, thinking it would be easier to test drive it after the usual rush hour finished. Now she wished she'd come earlier. By the time she arrived home, she'd be starving.

At first sight, Claire's house appeared huge. It made Rose wonder why the woman drove such a cheap car, then she realised the house was split into four flats, each with its own separate entrance.

Claire answered the door quickly. "Thank you for coming." She smiled at Rose. "The car's over there." She pointed at a small blue hatchback on the opposite side of the road. "Shall we go and look at it?" She shut her front door behind her, without waiting for an answer from Rose, and led the way towards the car.

"How long have you owned the car?"

"About five years," Claire said. "It's been so reliable, I'll be sorry to part with it, but my parents gave me some money to buy a new one."

"Lucky you," Rose said kindly.

"Maggie says you live near her."

"Yes, that's right. I mentioned to her I needed a car, then she spotted your advert." Rose walked around the car, noting the good condition of the paintwork and the fairly new tyres. She didn't see much point in checking the engine. She wouldn't have the first clue what to look for. Best to give the car a good test drive, then she'd find a mechanic to check it over if she liked it.

Claire handed Rose the keys and walked around to the passenger side. "Do you know where you're going, or do you want me to direct you?"

"If you can navigate to the main road, I know my way around from there." Rose fastened her seatbelt and started the car. The engine purred satisfyingly.

"Take a left at the end of the road," Claire said.

Rose found the indicators after accidentally switching on the headlights. "You must have known that teacher well," she said. "The one who got stabbed." She glanced over at Claire in time to witness the smile disappearing from her face.

"He was a good friend."

"I'm so sorry. It must be awful for you."

"Dreadful. The police wouldn't let us go home until they'd interviewed all the teachers and that took hours."

Rose was about to say something, but Claire wouldn't stop talking. Recognising her surroundings, she kept driving and listened.

"The worst thing was, I had to break the bad news to my year eight class. I'd only just got them settled and Gizzard—that's the headteacher—came round himself and told me what happened, then said I had to tell the children and keep them in class for the rest of the afternoon. Apparently, he did the same to all the teachers.

"I was pretty shocked myself. I couldn't face telling the children until I'd calmed down, so I kept teaching. Worst class I ever taught. I was trying to explain how the human heart works and all I could think of was whether Grant had been stabbed in the heart and how it would have shut down. My class must have been completely confused, the way I gabbled on. It didn't even make sense to me."

"You poor thing." Rose slowed the car's speed to concentrate on what Claire said.

"Eventually, I plucked up the courage to tell them. I don't know how I did it. It was horrible. Lots of the girls were crying. The boys kept pressing me for all the gory details, which I didn't know and wouldn't have told them, anyway. Some of the girls were in the cricket team Grant coached, so they got really upset. I can tell you, there were lots of tears, including mine. One girl got hysterical. I thought she was completely overreacting, but it turned out she knew Grant from outside of school. I spent most of the time hugging Madison to try to comfort her. We're not really supposed to do that, but I had no choice." Claire's voice shook as she spoke. "I never want to go through that experience again. It was total pandemonium."

Rose waited for her to continue, but she sat silently. "It must have been dreadful." She pushed her for more. "Do the police know what happened?" Rose accelerated across the main road, more relaxed now that the car's owner was no longer concentrating on her every move.

"One of the pupils stabbed him. I couldn't believe it. I always thought she was a nice girl."

Rose waited in case she said more. She didn't want to admit to knowing Bethany King in case it made Claire clam up.

Claire obligingly filled the silence. "The thing is, if the girl hadn't been caught red-handed, I'd have suspected one of the teachers. Grant nearly married one of my colleagues. Thank God he didn't because they were always arguing on the quiet. She pretended to get on with him, but you could tell from the way she looked at him that something wasn't right between them."

"Do you think that teacher would have liked to kill him?" Rose stopped herself from saying Helen's name just in time.

"I wouldn't put it past her." Claire spat the words out. She obviously wasn't a fan of Helen Trenton.

Rose wondered if it was jealousy. Perhaps Claire had been sweet on Mr Wyvern. "Why do you think that? Did they argue recently?" The road ahead was clear, so she accelerated smoothly. The car handled well at speed.

"That's the thing. They argued on Friday morning. Well, more a blazing row than an argument. I only heard part of it. It was embarrassing, so I walked away. She was screaming something about detentions and girls. Poor Grant. I really sympathised with him."

Rose made a right turn. "You'll have to direct me the last little bit to your house," she said. "Or, better still, drop me off at the bus stop."

"Do you like the car?"

"It drives really well. Would you mind if I get a mechanic to examine it?" Rose had already decided to buy the car, as long as the mechanic found nothing major wrong with it. She really needed some transport.

"That's fine. I'm sure they won't find any problems. If you want, you can drive to your house, then I'll drive the car home. It's not that far, and it will save you messing about with buses."

"That would be wonderful." Rose hadn't been looking forward to the bus journey. This way, she could be home in less than fifteen minutes. Then she could try to make sense of what Claire had told her. It was all starting to piece together.

Chapter 46

Richard sat in the taxi, trying to shut out the incessant babble of the driver, who finally finished droning on about the weather and was now interrogating Richard on his holiday destination. It was none of his bloody business and normally Richard would have told him exactly that. But at this hour, he was exhausted from waiting in an overcrowded Spanish airport all day, when his flight got delayed by several hours. He closed his eyes, pretending to be asleep. He simply wanted to get home and relax for the rest of the evening.

The holiday hadn't exactly been a resounding success. He'd wanted to get away from all his problems. He intended to switch off, relax, and pretend none of it was happening, then return refreshed and ready to fight the battles ahead.

Switching off had proven impossible. The off switch wasn't only faulty, it had completely vanished. Whatever he tried, all he could think of was Irina, or Bethany, or his unemployed status, or usually, all three at once. The nights were the worst. Sleep was a rare luxury, what with the heat, combined with incessant nightmares, where a mob of angry protesters surrounded the house before trying Bethany in a kangaroo court in the garden and sentencing her to a hundred years in prison. He'd arrived back in the UK in a far worse state than when he'd left. He probably needed to see a shrink, but no way could he afford that now, not without a job and with Bethany's lawyers gobbling up money as if it were a river of liquid chocolate sliding down their greedy throats.

He'd switched his phone off to avoid contact with Irina, who'd only want to talk about Bethany, and also to avoid the dreaded internet, especially the ignorant, vitriolic trolls on social media. Not that he had a choice, having left his phone charger at home. The battery died before he was halfway to Spain.

"This it, mate? Looks like the neighbours have been having a barbecue."

The taxi driver's deep, throaty laugh woke Richard from his thoughts. He opened his eyes.

"How much?" he drawled, still half asleep.

The fare cost more than he expected. Much more. He cursed himself for not taking the train instead, but he was so tired and he just wanted to get home. Grimacing, he handed over his credit card. He'd start cutting down on his expenses tomorrow.

"What happened then, mate?" The taxi driver stared at him quizzically.

Richard had no idea what he meant, but it was none of the taxi driver's damned business. "Don't forget my suitcases in the back." He turned to open the car door and froze.

This wasn't his house, was it? He looked up and down the road, straining his eyes to check off the familiar houses, cars, and gardens of his neighbours. Directly in front of him, the blackened carcass that used to be his house made him wonder if he was in the middle of a particularly horrific nightmare. He stared at the house, rubbing his eyes, in case the blurriness of sleep was affecting his eyesight. He blinked a few times. The burnt-out skeleton stared back at him. What the hell had happened?

A sudden panic overtook him. Where was Irina? Surely, she hadn't... It didn't bear thinking about.

He should run next door and ask the neighbours. Except that they had treated him and Irina like pariahs as soon as they found out about Bethany. They wouldn't know where Irina had gone. In any case, he wasn't sure he could even get out of the taxi. His legs had morphed into two wobbly columns of jelly.

The taxi driver retrieved Richard's suitcase and dumped it on the pavement. He opened the passenger door. "You getting out or what?"

Richard snapped to his senses. "Sorry, change of plan. Can you drop me off a mile down the road, please?"

The driver picked up Richard's suitcase and slung it in the back of the car with a thud that Richard hoped hadn't shattered his bottle of duty-free whiskey.

"Where are we going?" The driver slammed the door and fastened his seatbelt, clearly put out about Richard's change of destination, or perhaps upset that Richard failed to tip him when he paid.

"Straight on." There was one person who must know where Irina was. He directed the taxi driver to Hale Hill Stores, dreading what Rose would tell him.

Chapter 47

Rose was getting ready to go home. Jack would be here at any moment to take over for the evening. Business had been brisk all afternoon, with a non-stop stream of customers, so she longed to put her feet up with dinner and a nice glass of wine.

Richard flew into the Hale Hill Stores like a whirlwind, nearly knocking Rose off her feet.

"Where's Irina? Where's my wife? And what the hell happened to my house?" He dropped his suitcase onto the floor.

Rose took a deep breath and mustered all her effort to stay calm. Clearly, Irina never managed to contact him. It served him right for not answering any of her calls all week, making her frantic with worry. She stared at the man, despising him with all her heart. Where was he when Irina needed him? "If you'd bothered to return any of Irina's phone calls, you'd know," she said as calmly as she could.

Richard's face glowed a bright shade of beetroot, and he looked ready to explode. She really wanted to tell him exactly what she thought of him, swanning off on holiday, leaving Irina and Bethany to struggle without him. But, realising the two of them were alone in the shop, it might be more prudent to defuse the situation.

"Where's Irina?" To his credit, at least Richard had the decency to appear really worried.

Rose snuck back behind the checkout, wanting to keep a solid barrier between them. She hoped Jack wouldn't show up late today. "Irina's all right. She's staying in a hotel."

"And what about the house?" Richard took another step towards her. "I've just been there. What happened?"

Rose spotted Jack outside the door and relaxed. "Someone chucked a firebomb through the front window."

"They what? Do the police know who did it? Was it one of those awful protesters?" Richard fired questions at her like a machine gun.

"The police are investigating." Rose struggled to stay calm, suppressing an overwhelming urge to punch Richard in the face, even though she'd come off worse in a fight. If he'd been at home, perhaps the fire wouldn't have happened.

"Why didn't anyone tell me?"

Rose stared at him, open-mouthed. "Do you realise how many times Irina tried to phone you? Why didn't you answer?"

"My battery died," Richard said.

The bell above the shop door tinkled as Jack came in. "Is everything ok?"

"Richard was just leaving." Rose hoped he'd go quickly. She didn't want to walk home yet in case he followed her.

Jack joined Rose behind the checkout, making her feel more confident. Jack's recent martial arts training made him more than capable of defending them both if Richard gave any trouble.

"Does this mean you've finished your shift?" Richard addressed Rose.

Rose didn't answer. She didn't want him harassing her as she walked home.

"Because if you have, you can give me a lift to Irina's hotel. I don't have a car, and I let the taxi go."

"I don't have a car, either." Typically self-centred of Richard not to have noticed that. The fact that Rose hadn't yet bought Claire Bailey's car filled her with relief right now. She still needed to get a mechanic to check it over, then sort out the insurance. But when she did own a car again, Richard King would be the last person she wanted as a passenger.

"What am I supposed to do?" Richard glanced down at his suitcase. He looked pitiful.

"I'll call you a taxi," Jack offered.

"I don't have any choice, do I?" Richard said. "The hotel had better not be too far."

Rose refrained from telling him it was close to Bethany's detention centre, nearly a half-hour drive away. She didn't want to be near him when he found out. She hoped the taxi would collect him quickly.

Chapter 48

Sunday morning started pleasantly, but by the afternoon, the temperature had soared to thirty-one degrees.

"Are you sure you want to spend the afternoon watching cricket?" Maggie fanned herself with a magazine. "It's so hot."

Rose didn't really want to watch cricket at all. She'd watched more than her fair share of test matches when she'd been married to Philip and found the sport too slow-paced to keep her interest for long. But she'd make an exception today. She mustered as much enthusiasm as possible in order to convince Maggie. If Maggie pulled out, Rose wouldn't be able to attend the school cricket match on her own, not when she didn't have a child playing in it. That would seem odd. "We can find a shady spot to sit, and I've got some cold drinks to take with us. It will be a lovely, relaxing afternoon."

"I don't understand why you want to go in the first place."

"Because Bethany was in the cricket team. I might learn something useful." Rose was sure she'd been missing something, and every piece of the puzzle seemed to come back to the girls' cricket team. "Please, Maggie. You know I can't go to the match without you."

"All right, but those drinks had better be really cold."

Maggie was even hotter by the time they got to Taylor Park school, after a blisteringly hot bus ride. There was no shade near the cricket pitch, and uncomfortable wooden benches had been set out for the parents to spectate.

"I've got some sun cream." Rose wished she'd remembered to bring a hat.

"Ice cream might be better." Maggie seemed resigned to being here. She began to explain about the match. "It's the area finals. The top two teams in the league are playing for a spot in the national final. Our girls are up against Clayborne Grammar school."

"Clayborne Grammar? That's where Grant Wyvern used to teach."

"That's right." Maggie nodded. "Bill Gizzard, our headteacher, is planning to say a few words about Grant. I hope he waits until the match is over, in case he upsets both teams."

Rose made a mental note to watch the reactions of everyone during the headteacher's speech.

The game was already underway when Rose and Maggie sat down to watch. Clayborne Grammar were batting. Ava was bowling for Taylor Park. She looked tiny compared to the beefy Clayborne girl who was about to bat.

"Go on, Ava," someone behind her shouted.

"I thought cricket was a quiet sport," Maggie said.

Rose laughed. "It is normally." Secretly, she welcomed anyone who livened up the game.

Ava started to run, putting on a spurt of acceleration in the last few strides before sending the ball flying through the air.

Whack. The beefy girl hit the ball square on, belting it into the distance. Rose tried to follow its trajectory, but the sun got in her eyes and she lost it.

"Six." The man sitting in front of her exhibited too much excitement, considering he was supposed to be supporting Taylor Park.

Rose leant forward. "Are you sure?" That wasn't a good start for the home team.

"The umpire's put both hands up. It's definitely a six."

Rose hoped such a stunning performance by the Clayborne Grammar girl wouldn't psyche out the Taylor Park team for the rest of the match. "Did you notice where the ball went?"

The man sitting in front of her pointed. "It sailed right over the hedge. It was magnificent."

"Yes, it was good." How had he even seen the ball? Rose lost sight of it before it got halfway across the pitch.

"Yep. That girl's got talent."

"You're meant to be supporting Taylor Park," Rose reminded him. The Clayborne parents were sitting on the other side of the ground.

"Sorry." He looked sheepish. "But it really was brilliant. I bet she'll be in the England team in a few years."

Rose agreed. She glanced up at the scoreboard. Clayborne Grammar had already clocked up a big score. She hoped the other girls on the Clayborne Grammar team weren't as good. Otherwise, Taylor Park would be crushed.

"This heat's killing me already." Maggie's face had already become a bright shade of pink, and perspiration dripped from her forehead.

Since Clayborne Grammar hit a six, the action stalled while someone went to find a new ball. Rose was bored stiff already. "Why don't we go for a gentle stroll in the woods," she suggested. "It will be cool in there, and we might even find that lost ball."

"That sounds much better than sitting here frying." Maggie got up before Rose could change her mind. "I don't know how those girls will manage to play in this heat."

Rose was surprised the school hadn't opted to cancel the match, given the extreme heat, but health and safety considerations obviously got swept aside with a place in the national finals at stake.

"Did you find out which Shakespeare play year eight are studying?" Rose asked as Maggie led the way to the boundary hedge.

"Yes, it's *MacBeth*."

"Not *Romeo and Juliet*?" Rose knew Debbie wouldn't have got it wrong. So, why had Helen lied?

"No, that's year nine," Maggie said.

They squeezed through a gap in the hedge into Brackford woods. "Lots of the kids use it to sneak into Brackford at lunchtimes," Maggie explained. "They're not supposed to go out, but you can see how well-worn the path is towards the town centre."

The woods felt beautifully cool, with the high canopy of trees blotting out most of the sun. "Where do you think the ball went?" Rose looked back towards the cricket pitch, trying to remember roughly which direction the ball came from.

Maggie pointed to a cluster of trees, surrounded by bracken and brambles, several metres off of the path. "I reckon it landed somewhere in there, but we'll never find it. I only came here to cool off."

Rose ignored her, stepping through the bracken, glad she'd opted to wear trousers instead of a dress. "There's a flattened bit over there." She pointed as she headed towards the spot. Something much bigger than a cricket ball had trampled the undergrowth. Keeping her eyes peeled, she moved slowly forward.

"Have you found the ball yet?" Maggie shouted from the path.

Rose twisted towards Maggie. "Not yet." She took another step forwards, catching her foot in a bramble. For a second, she flailed her arms, hoping to keep her balance before lurching into the bracken. Quickly, she stuck out an elbow to help break her fall. As she hit the ground, her scream echoed through the trees.

"Are you all right?" Maggie sounded worried.

Rose pushed herself up onto her knees, taking stock of the damage. She had some scratches on her bare arms, and her knee hit something hard, but she'd survive. "I'm fine," she shouted back, noting that Maggie hadn't bothered to follow her into the undergrowth. "I think I've found the ball." She started to pull back the bracken, careful to avoid the brambles growing amongst it.

She hadn't landed on the cricket ball. The hard, round object she'd hit turned out to be the toe of a shoe. She picked up the trainer, which appeared almost new. Surely someone was missing the shoe. It certainly didn't look old or tatty enough to be discarded in the woods. She gently pulled more of the bracken away. Perhaps the other half of the pair was nearby. Someone may have dropped them accidentally and not noticed.

Rose stood up and rubbed her knee. She'd have a corking bruise by tomorrow. She looked around for a stick to help her poke through the undergrowth, finding a sturdy specimen nearby.

Progress speeded up now that she no longer needed to worry about scratching herself on the brambles. Maggie said something to her, but Rose couldn't hear, so she concentrated on her search. The stick caught on something in the undergrowth, making a rustling noise. Rose used the stick to push aside the bracken and brambles before fishing out a plastic bag full of clothes. Who knew what other rubbish might be hidden in the undergrowth? The Taylor Park pupils probably used it as a dumping ground, which Rose found shocking. She always thought the youth of today were environmentally conscientious, but obviously, at least one of them couldn't care less. If the bag didn't contain the missing shoe, she'd give up and go back to watch the cricket. She'd come here to talk to people, not to hide away in the woods. She wouldn't learn anything that would help Bethany if she stayed here for too long.

She picked up the dirt-encrusted bag, wishing she were wearing gloves. As soon as she got back, she'd scrub her hands clean. It couldn't have been here for long or the plastic supermarket bag would have started to degrade. Tentatively, she opened it up, half expecting a worm to slither from its contents or a big spider to crawl out onto her hand. She'd drop it if she discovered anything alive inside.

Rose stared with shock into the bag. There was nothing living in it. The blood on the once white T-shirt had dried to a rusty brown colour. A similar colour spotted the missing trainer, which would otherwise have been a perfect match to its other half. Other garments were packed beneath the shirt and the shoe, but Rose didn't dare touch anything. The hidden sports kit might be perfectly innocent, except for the blood stains. She tried to stay calm. The blood might belong to anyone. There may be a perfectly reasonable explanation for it.

Rose closed the bag, trying to decide what to do. She wished she could leave the bag where she found it, but it was too late for that. If there was any chance it might be Grant Wyvern's blood, she'd have to hand it over to the police.

"What have you got there?" Maggie asked when Rose got back to the path.

"Nothing." Rose couldn't tell her it might be Madison's missing PE kit and decided not to mention the blood. Maggie found it difficult to keep secrets, and she didn't want to alert the wrong people. "I'm just picking up litter." She mustn't jump to conclusions. Madison said her PE kit was stolen. Someone else may have worn it. Would the police be able to test for that? Or it may not even be blood.

"Let's go back." Maggie appeared to accept Rose's explanation. "I need something to drink, and you need to clean yourself up."

Chapter 49

The first person Rose noticed as they walked across the sports field was DI Waterford. She left Maggie to go straight over to him. "What are you doing here?"

"I could ask you the same question." Waterford regarded her quizzically.

Rose ignored him. "You need to take this." She held the bag towards him.

"What is it?" He pulled a pair of latex gloves from his pocket. "Have you touched it?"

"Only the bag. I haven't touched anything inside. It's a sports kit. The T-shirt's covered in blood. I think the blood might be Grant Wyvern's."

Waterford raised an eyebrow. "Where did you get it?"

"I found it hidden in the woods." Rose pointed in the direction she'd just come from.

"Can you show me where? And I'll need a statement from you."

"Can I do it later? I really need to get cleaned up and deal with these scratches." She held out her arm towards Waterford. Cleaning up was an excuse. If she took DI Waterford into the woods now, it might put the guilty party on their guard.

"I'm glad I've seen you. I came to tell you we arrested Danny Wyvern. We're sure he fire-bombed Irina King's house the other night, but we don't have enough proof. We'll have to let him go. Are you sure you don't remember anything else about the person you saw running away from the fire?"

"It was dark, and I really didn't get close enough to them." Rose had spent many hours since then, lying in bed, unable to sleep as she turned the events over and over in her head, but she couldn't recall anything more.

Paul sighed. "Well, if you think of anything... We've got a few hours yet. He was limping badly when we brought him in, so we got the doctor to check him over. The doctor insisted we took him to hospital to get it X-rayed. Turns out he's broken his leg."

"Broken his leg?" Rose stared at Paul.

"Yep. The hospital consultant said he must have been walking around on it for a few days. He's in surgery now, having it pinned."

"It's him," Rose said. "He's the person I saw." Rose had no choice now but to tell the truth. "I have a confession to make."

Paul looked worried. "What have you done?"

"I hit him in Irina's car."

"You hit him? Why didn't you say anything before?"

Rose ignored Paul and carried on. "He was dressed in black and there's no street lighting there. He ran across the road right in front of me. I didn't see him until the very last moment."

"Are you sure you hit him?"

"Yes." Rose remembered feeling a bump when the car made contact. "I knocked him over. I got out of the car to help him, but before I reached him, he got up and ran off. He was limping badly then. Is it his right leg that's broken?"

"Yes." A huge smile lit up Paul's face. "We've got him."

Rose washed her hands quickly, dabbing at the scratches with a wet paper towel. She'd clean them up properly later, when she got home. She went back out to watch the cricket, sitting with some parents from Clayborne Grammar and carefully avoiding bumping into DI Waterford again.

The game had moved on since Rose and Maggie were in the woods. Rose didn't realise they had taken so long. Taylor Park was batting now with Clayborne Grammar fielding. A few of the Clayborne team had been caught out, and Taylor Park were on their way to evening up the score, so Rose guessed there couldn't be many more girls left to bat in the Taylor Park team.

"Look at the scoreboard," Rose said to Maggie. "We might actually win this." That was a big surprise after Clayborne Grammar's fabulous start.

Most of the Taylor Park team stood together watching or waiting to bat. Rose gazed at each one of them in turn. Had one of them killed Grant Wyvern? Of the eleven girls, only two of them were the same size as Madison, her best friends, Ava and Shaz. The other girls were all larger and none of them would have fitted into Madison's PE kit, assuming it did belong to Madison. She glanced around for Helen Trenton, who she'd spotted earlier, but there was no sign of her now. It would be useful to see her and Madison together. From memory, Rose recalled Helen was petite. She'd never seen her and Madison together, but it was possible they were a similar size, even though Helen was taller.

A scream from the pitch interrupted Rose's thoughts. Ava Browning lay sprawled out on the grass, clutching at her leg.

"What happened? I didn't see."

One of the Clayborne parents answered her. "The ball hit her. That was unlucky."

"Are you sure she didn't aim it at her deliberately?" one of the dads asked. "Taylor Park only need one more run to win, with two wickets in hand."

Ava got up, helped by two of her teammates and a teacher, who had rushed onto the pitch as soon as Ava screamed.

"She can't carry on like that. Look at the poor girl. She's limping," a shrill voice behind Rose said.

Rose glanced behind her but couldn't tell who had spoken. When she turned around again, Madison was getting ready to bat. Even from this distance, she looked nervous.

"Keep your fingers crossed," the shrill woman said. "Someone needs to catch her out first time. Otherwise, Clayborne's going to lose."

"Taylor Park's coach did a good job." Rose crossed her fingers. The only difference being that she was crossing them for Taylor Park. After recent events, they needed some good luck. She focused on Madison, who now sported a look of steely determination. For the first time, Rose noticed Madison wore gloves. It seemed crazy in this heat, but maybe they helped her to grip the bat.

"I don't like to speak ill of the dead." The shrill-voiced woman didn't sound too sorry about it. "But Grant Wyvern was trouble. I'm glad he left Clayborne."

"Really? What happened?" Rose hoped for confirmation of the story she'd already partially heard.

"Shush, that's my daughter bowling."

The bowler started to run.

"Go on, Madison," Rose whispered under her breath.

Madison held the bat ready, her face a picture of concentration.

Thwack. The sound of leather on willow echoed towards the spectators' benches. Then Madison was running, flying across the pitch towards the wicket at the other end, arms and legs pumping as if her life depended on it.

Rose kept her eye on the ball this time. One of the Clayborne team ran towards it, leaping in the air to try to catch it. She thought the girl had got it, but the ball slipped from her fingers and landed on the grass with a dull bounce.

Immediately, the girl swooped on the ball and began to sprint towards the wicket. Her long legs powered her along and, for a moment, Rose held her breath, unsure whether the Clayborne girl or Madison would get there first.

A huge cheer erupted from the Taylor Park benches as Madison reached the wicket, beating the Clayborne fielder by a whisker. Taylor Park had won the match and qualified for the National Championships.

Chapter 50

Rose hurried over to the Taylor Park spectator benches. The atmosphere was jubilant. Families crowded around the team members, congratulating them on their win.

"Well done, Madison," Rose said, noting that Madison eyed her suspiciously. Madison had treated her warily since Rose questioned her for a second time recently.

"Ladies and gentlemen." A booming voice came from the edge of the cricket pitch.

Bill Gizzard stood on an upturned wooden box facing the small crowd. He waited until he gained everyone's attention.

"For those of you who don't know me, I'm Mr Gizzard, headteacher at Taylor Park school."

A half-hearted round of applause punctuated his speech.

Gizzard smiled. "Firstly, I'd like to extend a warm welcome to everyone from Clayborne Grammar school."

Rose wondered if he would have been so magnanimous if Taylor Park had lost the match.

"Congratulations to all the players for a wonderful game. I'm delighted to announce that Taylor Park's win will take them to the National Schools Championships."

A couple of parents whooped. Rose leaned towards Maggie. "Is he always this smug?"

"He's toned it down," Maggie said.

Gizzard carried on talking. "I can't let today pass without mentioning a much-valued colleague who tragically lost his life recently. Grant Wyvern trained our amazing cricket team, and it's a testament to his skill and dedication that they all performed so well today. Please put your hands together for Mr Wyvern, PE teacher extraordinaire."

The enthusiastic applause for Mr Wyvern, mostly from the Taylor Park benches, put the earlier trickle of claps for Gizzard to shame. People began to drift towards the pavilion before Gizzard even finished speaking.

"There are refreshments for sale in the pavilion. Thank you all for coming." Gizzard wrapped up his speech.

A couple of minutes later, only five people remained outside in the blazing sun.

Rose felt mean as she approached the little party. They were celebrating the team's win and Madison's winning run. Ava, Shaz, Jenny, and Helen all crowded around Madison, making an enormous fuss of her.

Rose's gaze fixed on her prime suspect as she stopped in front of the group. The smile dropped from her face and all five of them grew quiet.

"I found a sports kit in the woods," Rose said.

Nobody answered.

"Why did you kill Grant Wyvern?"

"What are you talking about?" Jenny looked as if she wanted to slap Rose. "We're trying to celebrate here. The team's qualified for the national finals, and all thanks to my brilliant daughter."

Rose ignored her. "Well?" Her gaze didn't waver.

Tears started to fall down Madison's cheeks. "He grabbed my wrist." She spoke so quietly her words were barely audible. "He wouldn't let go. I tried to pull away, but he wouldn't let go."

"It's ok, Madison, just tell me what happened. You must have been scared."

"I was. Helen always told me never to be alone with him, but I needed him to help me with my batting."

At least Wyvern had done a great job with that. "What happened after that?" Rose prompted.

"He took me to the equipment store. He said he had something it there that would help me even more with my game. I shouldn't have gone with him." Madison's cheeks were streaked with tears now.

"Oh, Madison." Helen hugged her tightly.

Jenny, who up until now had been looking puzzled, finally spoke up. "What's going on? What are you saying, darling?"

"Then what happened, Madison?" Rose wanted her to finish before Jenny interfered and made her shut up.

"I struggled, but he was too strong. I had to stop him." Madison began to tremble. All the emotion she'd bottled up for the last few days was about to explode out of her. "He'd been mending the cricket practice nets when I got there. He left his knife on the table next to me. I grabbed it and stuck it in his side. I didn't know what else to do. He was hurting me." She paused, taking some deep breaths as the emotion boiled up inside her.

"What happened then, Madison?" Rose asked softly.

"He didn't let go. It didn't make any difference at all, so I pulled the knife out and tried again. I did it until he let go of me."

Jenny had gone pale and looked as if she might be about to throw up. She stared at Madison with her mouth open.

"Were you wearing gloves that day?" Rose had noticed Madison wore gloves earlier when she batted, despite the thirty-degree heat.

"My hands get really sore when I grip the bat."

That explained why the police only found Bethany's prints on the knife. "Where did Bethany come into it? Was it you who texted Ava to send Bethany to find Mr Wyvern?" That was the only thing Rose hadn't pieced together.

Madison took a deep breath and wiped her eyes with the back of her hand. Rose found a clean tissue in her bag and handed it to her.

"I thought he was still alive. I figured if someone else found him, they'd call an ambulance and I wouldn't get in trouble. Bethany's really good at that sort of thing. She's not scared of the sight of blood or anything."

"Don't be stupid," Ava butted in. "He would have told the police it was you."

"He wouldn't, cos he knew I would have told on him if he did," Madison said defiantly.

"Where did you go after you sent the text?" Rose asked.

"I ran back to the changing room. It's behind the gym, so you can't even see it from the equipment store. I had blood on me. It was disgusting." Madison shuddered, making a face to show her repulsion. "I had a shower. It felt like I was covered in bits of him. I couldn't scrub it off."

"What did you do with your sports kit? Did it have blood on it?"

Madison nodded. "They were disgusting. I didn't want anyone to find them, so I put them in a bag and hid them in the woods."

"This is a load of rubbish." Jenny moved to stand between her daughter and Rose. "You surely can't believe any of this. She's making it up to get attention."

"I think it's true," Helen said. "Grant has abused girls in the past." She turned to Madison. "That's why I told you not to be alone with him. He didn't do anything to you, did he?" She stared at Madison with concern.

"He wouldn't let go of me. I was really scared."

"You mean you knew what Grant was like and you never told me." Jenny shot the accusation at Helen.

"I was ashamed." Helen coughed as if her words might choke her. "When we both taught at Clayborne Grammar, I walked in on him kissing a girl. She was fourteen. It wasn't Grant who broke things off. It was me who dumped him. He made out that he ended things so he'd look like the bad guy, not me, and I wouldn't have to make up an excuse to explain to my family. My father had paid for the wedding. I couldn't tell him I'd broken it off and wasted all that money. Besides, he really liked Grant."

"You should have reported Grant to the police," Jenny said. She pulled Madison away from Helen and hugged her tightly.

"I wanted to, but Grant begged me not to. You don't just stop loving someone because they do something bad. There wasn't a switch I could flick off."

"How did you both end up working at Taylor Park?" Rose asked.

"Grant had to leave Clayborne after a girl made an accusation against him. That was when I knew he had a real problem, even though that accusation was never proven. I couldn't report him then. I'd left it too late. It would have made me look guilty. But when he got a job at Taylor Park, and a vacancy came up in the English department here, I applied. I was terrified he'd do the same thing again, and Madison was here. I couldn't bear anything like that to happen to her. She's like a daughter to me."

"Well, she's not your daughter, she's mine," Jenny snapped, holding Madison tighter.

"Where did you go after you hid the sports kit in the woods, Madison?" Rose was keen to get back on track.

Madison blew her nose. "I went to a shop. I'd left my hairband in the changing room, and I didn't want anyone thinking it was mine if they found it. Then I came back to school."

"And that's where you come in." Rose looked at Helen. "Did you know about this? Is that why you gave Madison an alibi?"

"Madison was with me," Helen insisted.

"I don't think she was." Rose focused on Helen, but the teacher turned away. "When people lie in police interviews, sometimes they get a bit flustered and get simple things wrong. Is that why you told DI Waterford that year eight were studying *Romeo and Juliet*?"

"I didn't say that. That's the year nine one."

"Yes, you meant to say *MacBeth*, but you didn't, because the whole story about handing in homework was a lie. Why did you give Madison an alibi?" Rose repeated the question.

Helen shook her head. "I wasn't giving Madison an alibi. I was giving myself one."

Rose hadn't expected to hear that. "Why?"

"Because I'd had a blazing row with Grant that morning. Someone would be sure to tell the police, and they'd think I had every reason to kill him as it was common knowledge that he'd jilted me at the altar, even though it didn't happen like that at all. I didn't know about Bethany at that point. All I knew was that Grant was dead. If I'd known the whole truth then..."

Rose glanced at Helen, and for a brief moment, their eyes met. They both knew Helen would never have given up Madison, the daughter she'd never had. "What was the argument with Grant about?"

Helen gave a deep sigh. "I found him alone with Sharon. I was worried about what he may have done or planned to do." She turned to Shaz. "He didn't touch you, did he?" Her voice conveyed her uncertainty.

"No," Shaz said adamantly. "He wouldn't dare."

"I didn't know that." Helen went on. "I accused him of all sorts of awful things. When I heard about his death, I felt dreadful that those were the last words I said to him."

"You should have said something when Bethany was arrested." Rose couldn't forgive her for letting Bethany and her parents go through hell for nothing.

"I'm sorry. I should have done. I thought she must have done it and, if there was a good reason for it, she'd tell the police. I was sure he must have tried something with her. But I couldn't say anything. I couldn't betray Grant."

"You still love him, don't you?" Rose didn't fully understand the hold Grant Wyvern continued to have over his ex-fiancée despite everything he had done.

Helen nodded. "I still haven't found the off switch."

Chapter 51

Alfie topped up his wineglass. "I'd like to propose a toast to Rose for saving the day, yet again." He raised his glass and clinked it with Rose, Billie, and Jack. "To Rose."

Rose blushed, partly from embarrassment and partly because she'd just eaten a rather hot Thai green curry.

They were celebrating in The Tiny Elephant, a Thai restaurant situated in Brackford's marketplace. They were also sadly saying goodbye to Billie, who was returning home to New Zealand, and Jack, who was going travelling in a few days with some friends from uni.

"And to Billie and Jack," Rose added.

"Where are you going on your travels, Jack?" Alfie asked.

"Australia and New Zealand. We're starting in Sydney, then Melbourne, Bondi Beach, then we're visiting Billie in Wellington."

"I'm looking forward to it already," Billie said.

"Billie's promised to take me on the *Lord of the Rings* tour."

Rose smiled. Jack always loved those books and had watched the film several times.

"I can't wait," Billie said. "I've never done it myself."

Rose turned to Alfie. "Are you looking forward to getting back to work when Jack goes?" she asked, trying to take his mind off the prospect of losing Billie. He hadn't seen his daughter for twenty years until recently. But she'd been staying with him for the last few weeks. Billie would leave a big hole in Alfie's world, but she had her own life on the other side of the world, and she needed to get back to it.

Alfie laughed. "The sooner the better. There's only so much daytime TV I can cope with. If it weren't for Billie, I'd be bored stiff."

Rose was certainly looking forward to getting back to normal, although she was considering advertising for another part-time employee to help run the shop, and had broached the subject with Sarah Marek, the shop's owner, earlier that day. The long opening hours were a lot for two people to cope with.

"Anyway, you still haven't explained exactly what happened. What made Madison murder Grant Wyvern?" Alfie asked.

"Yes, why did she? She was such a sweet girl," Jack said.

"Not that sweet." Rose pushed her empty plate away. "She bullied Bethany relentlessly."

"Did she set up Bethany?" Billie asked.

"I don't think anything was planned. Bethany was just unlucky to be in the wrong place at the wrong time, and Madison took advantage." Rose was relieved that Bethany had been cleared and was now living in a rented house a few miles away with Irina and Richard until their own house was rebuilt after the fire. "Wyvern gave Madison a private cricket coaching session. That in itself rings all sorts of alarm bells, given his previous history."

"We've done a lot of child protection stuff on my course." Jack was thinking of training as a PE teacher when he graduated from his sports science course. "It's a minefield. He should never have got into a position where he was alone with a young girl."

"Anyway, he took Madison to the equipment store and grabbed her. Both the police and the legal team agree that it was self-defence, so the consequences won't be too bad for Madison. The first wound was fairly superficial. If he'd got medical help then, he'd probably have survived, but Madison plunged the knife right into some vital organs. Madison still tried to get him help by telling Ava Browning to send Bethany to find him. She didn't count on Bethany pulling the knife out. He stood no chance after that."

"Doesn't everyone know you should never do that?" Billie asked.

"Bethany's a child. She panicked. But then she was convinced that it was her pulling the knife out that killed him. She was frightened, and she felt as guilty as if she'd plunged the knife in."

"Poor girl. But it sounds like she did everyone a favour, if Wyvern was a paedophile," Alfie said. "How is Bethany now?"

"She's getting counselling." Rose sighed. It would take Bethany a long time to get over her ordeal. Richard King was talking about leaving the area. Perhaps that would be the best thing for them all.

"Cheer up," Alfie said. "You've got one big thing to be happy about. Your new car."

Rose smiled. "Yes, it's so lovely to have some transport. I was getting fed up with catching buses or walking everywhere."

"I'm dying to see this new motor. In fact, I think you should take me for a spin in it."

"Of course I will, if I ever get the time."

"No time like the present." Alfie beamed at her. "You can drive me home. Billie can take Jack in my car. I don't know why we came in two cars in the first place."

Rose knew. She'd been to visit Irina and Bethany on her way here. She'd wanted to make sure that Bethany was going to be all right, so she'd made an excuse to meet the others at the restaurant.

Alfie got the bill. "My treat," he insisted. "I don't know what I would have done without the three of you while I was injured."

"Thank you. I'd better drive extra carefully, now, and get you home in one piece."

It was raining lightly when they left the restaurant.

"I hope your car's got a good heater to dry us off." Alfie hadn't brought a coat with him. Nor had Rose as she wasn't expecting rain.

"We won't get very wet. The car's parked just around the corner."

They walked quickly, neither of them wanting to get any wetter than necessary.

"Are we nearly there?" Alfie asked.

Rose was scanning the rows of cars parked along the side of the road. She was certain she'd parked the car in Sycamore Road, as close as she could get to the restaurant at this time of day without having to pay for parking. "It's somewhere around here." She thought she left the car under this tree, but there were several similar trees in the road. Perhaps she parked it further down than she remembered. She held up the remote control key and pressed it, to see if any cars flashed their lights as the doors unlocked.

"What model of car are we looking for?"

"It's blue."

"Blue?" Alfie laughed.

Rose thought that was a very useful description, given that most of the cars in this road were white. She ignored him. "It must be further along. Wait here. I'll run up the road and find it."

She set off at a jog, glad she'd worn flat shoes instead of heels. She didn't want to admit to Alfie, but she may have parked it in the next road along. She'd been upset at how worried and depressed Bethany had been, so she wasn't concentrating on mundane details, like where she'd left her car.

The rain began to lash down. Rose ran faster, hoping Alfie would find somewhere to take shelter while he waited. She didn't want him to get a soaking because of her.

Sycamore Road turned into Oak Tree Road. It was the only other place she could have parked. Part of the way down the road, she spotted a flash of blue paintwork further along. Relieved, she ran towards it.

The blue paintwork belonged to a Mini Cooper. Rose cursed. She racked her brain, trying to remember where she parked her car. She was certain she left it behind a red car. That shouldn't be too difficult to find among the plethora of white vehicles. And she'd nearly dropped her keys down a drain as she got out. She recalled that clearly now. Annoyed but reassured, she walked back towards Sycamore Road.

As soon as Rose turned the corner, she saw the front wing of a red car sticking out slightly into the road. She started to run again. As she neared the spot, she saw no sign of her own car. The adjacent parking space was empty. She looked down. The drainage grid grinned back at her. She stood in the empty space, turning every which way, realisation dawning on her rapidly. It was definitely here. They'd walked past this empty space a few minutes ago and not noticed anything, but now she was certain.

The front wing of the red car sported a small scrape where it had been carelessly parked and stuck out. Rose peered at it more closely. There were touches of blue paint embedded in the red paintwork and the damage seemed fresh. She barely noticed the pouring rain had soaked through her clothes. How could this have happened? How could she be this unlucky? She'd only owned the car for a day.

She saw Alfie walking towards her. He was also soaked through.

"It's gone," Rose wailed at him. "Somebody's stolen my car."

"Are you sure?"

Alfie looked as if he doubted her, as if she were a ditzy woman who'd forgotten where she'd parked. Maybe she almost had, but she was absolutely certain now. This was where she left it.

"Of course I'm sure."

"Then you'd better phone the police," Alfie said.

ROCK BOTTOM

Discover the shocking truth of how Rose ends up living in her mother's flat. Rock Bottom is the prequel to The Murder Mile series. It's **FREE** to download when you sign up to my author newsletter.

The locals call it the Murder Mile because of the rising number of murders, but she didn't expect her own mother to be one of the victims.

When Rose Marsden receives the devastating news of her mother's death, she rushes to London to find out what's going on. At first, it looks like a burglary gone wrong.

As she struggles to come to terms with her tragic loss, the shocking revelation that her mother died of a drug overdose rocks her world still further. The police have labelled her mother as a junkie and closed the case, but Rose is certain her mother would never touch drugs. She is desperate to find out the truth and get justice for her mum.

Despite her efforts, Rose is frustrated by lack of proof, and her own safety is put at risk during a frightening encounter with a local gang member. Now, fear of reprisal means the only way to survive is to find evidence to convict the murderer.

The Hale Hill estate is a dangerous place. Will Rose's stubborn persistence turn her into the next victim?

Be the first to find out about new releases, special offers, and other interesting stuff. Download the free book and sign up using this link: https://dl.bookfunnel.com/6vtvzlvamf

Other Books by Christine Pattle

The Murder Mile Series
    Book 1 INTO THE RED
    Book 2 STONE COLD
    Book 3 DARK SHADOW
    Book 4 KNIFE EDGE
    Book 5 WHEEL SPIN (to be released later in 2024)
    And more to come

The Clarke Pettis Series
    Book 1 THE FRAUD
    Book 2 THE COVER-UP
    Book 3 THE PAYBACK

All books are available on Amazon.

About The Author

Christine Pattle writes thrillers with a bit of mystery. Her trademarks are interesting characters who have issues, and lots of suspense, building to an action-packed climax. Her aim is always to write a good page-turning story that readers will love.

When she's not writing, she's busy scaring herself silly, riding big, feisty horses, or walking round the countryside dreaming up exciting new plots. As if that wasn't enough, she also has a day job, trying to make small budgets do great things in the fight against homelessness.

You can contact Christine by email at christine@christinepattleauthor
 Or visit her Facebook page https://www.facebook.com/ChristinePattleAuthor

Acknowledgments

A HUGE thank you:

To you, the reader. Readers are by far the most important people in an author's world. Of all the millions of books you could have chosen to read, a massive THANK YOU for giving my book a chance. I really hope you enjoyed it. If you can spare a few minutes to leave a review for the book on Amazon, or even a couple of seconds to give it a star rating, I would be very grateful. It helps other readers to discover my books and inspires me to keep on writing.

To my brilliant editor, Emily at Laurence Editing.

To my cover artist, Get Covers.

And, lastly, to all the authors who have ever inspired me. I love reading.

Printed in Great Britain
by Amazon